THE HOODOO OF PECK FINCH

A NOVEL

Jerome Mark Antil

Copyright © Jerome Mark Antil 2021

ISBN-13: 978-1-7353076-7-1
(Paperback Edition)

Library of Congress Control Number:2018911244

*All characters appearing in this
work are fictitious. Any resemblance
to real persons, living or dead, is purely coincidental.*

No part of this publication may be reproduced, stored in a retrieval system, or transmitted in any form or by any means electronic, mechanical, photocopying, recording, or otherwise, without the written permission of the author or publisher.

To Leah Chase
January 6 – 1923 – June 1, 2019

A Southern Louisiana Bayou

Chapter 1

GABE AND PECK SHARED A SMALL SHOTGUN HOUSE in the Garden District. Peck now drove to his work cleaning offices and to a private tutor. One morning Gabe decided to take a walk, for a stretch of the legs to Walmart to get housekeys made. It had been sixty years since the retired veteran had been in a Penny Arcade and played with the pinball machines long before there were video games. Penny Arcades near army bases were nostalgic for homesick soldiers when he was young. When his Army friends had day passes from Korean battlefields and only had time to kill in the 1950s, they'd belly up to a pinball machine.

Needing keys, Gabe remembered hearing of the vending machine that could make duplicate keys while you watched and waited and he heard of other vending machines lining the front hall of Walmart that could virtually do anything else.

Gabe's buddy, a retired sergeant at the VA hospital in Pineville was first to stir his imagination by telling him about the machine.

"Just put a card in and a key you want copied and hit a few buttons and tell it how many you want and if you want it plain or with a favorite NFL team logo on the bow for fifty cents more," his friend would say.

Gabe's imagination did the rest.

He set his mind on the Saturday morning errand to witness this gadget and to get house keys made.

The store's front hall lined with machines was everything his veteran friend had told him. So fascinating was the machine Gabe bought a pair of reading glasses for $9.95, just to catch all the action behind the window.

"Hey, mister," the young man at the next machine said.

Gabe glanced over at the boy. Twenty, twenty-two was his guess. Clean cut, clothes neat, a book bag on his back. Gabe nodded but didn't answer, busy reading the directions on the key-making machine.

"Mister, can you let me use your card for a second, please? I'll give it right back," the young man said.

"No," Gabe said without looking up.

The young man turned and asked a passerby and was turned down. He turned to Gabe again.

"Mister, this machine won't charge anything to your card, but it'll give me ten dollars and I'll give you two dollars just for letting me use your card. It'll only take ten seconds, and I'll give it back."

"Nope," Gabe said.

"Not even for two dollars, you won't let me use your card?"

"I can't son, sorry," Gabe said.

"You can't? You can't? A grown man telling me you can't? You lying old motherfucker, mister, telling me you can't."

Gabe looked over at the boy.

"Old man you're a dead man the second you walk out of this store—you're a dead motherfucker. You hear me, old man?"

With cold, gray eyes, the boy stared at Gabe and backed down the hall, pointing a finger at him and cursing his threat.

Visibly shaken, Gabe turned to his left and went looking for the store manager.

CHAPTER 2

GABE'S FRONT DOOR PUSHED OPEN and Lily Cup stepped in. "I just spoke with the coroner, the kid's dead," Lily Cup said.

The aging army captain, veteran of Korea and Vietnam, lowered his newspaper just enough to see over the entertainment page.

"Was it murder, Gabe?" Lily Cup asked.

"Close the door, honey, AC's on," Gabe said.

In a black skirt with a matching waistcoat and white Nike walking shoes, she leaned and propped a black leather briefcase against the wall by the door. She stood like an exasperated tomboy, adjusting and refastening her grandmother's diamond brooch on her lapel.

"I heard you've been walking with a cane, dancing man. What's that all about?"

"So?"

"You don't carry a cane."

"I've owned canes for years."

"You jazz dance for hours on end a couple of nights a week and all of a sudden, out of the blue, Sasha tells me you started carrying one everywhere? I know you don't need a cane."

"I just prefer wearing a cane now."

"Wearing a cane?"

"A gentleman wears a cane—a color befitting his ensemble."

"Well excuse me."

"A gentleman carries an umbrella or walking stick."

"Wearing or carrying, it smells premeditated to me, Gabe. What's up with the cane thing?"

"Does Sasha know about it?"

"I've been putting out fires all over town. I haven't had time to tell her anything. She'd have a canary."

Gabe lifted the paper again to read.

"I need to know if it was premeditated," Lily Cup said.

"I don't want to talk about it," Gabe said.

He closed the paper, folded it in half, and in half again. Dropping it on the arm of the chair, he stood and left the room.

"Define premeditated murder," he said from the kitchen.

She tossed a handbag and white driving gloves onto the other chair, lifted Chanel sunglasses to the top of her head.

"Gee, I'll have to think on this one. Hmmm…Oh, I know. How about there's a dead man with no weapon and the police have a cane with blood on it?"

"It's a walking stick. My cane is over by the door."

"Well now it's a goddamned murder weapon, Gabe. They checked for prints, and yours are the only prints on it, and their guess is the lab will say the blood has his DNA."

Gabe came out with a coffee urn in one hand and his finger and thumb through handles of two empty cups. He held the cups out for her to take one.

"No more," Gabe said.

"You're nonchalant for the spot you're in. Why'd you clam up on me like that at the precinct? It didn't set well with any of them. The DA entered a charge of second-degree murder. With pressure from New Orleans tourism folks the police chief put out a warrant for you from his lunch at Brennan's."

He held the empty cups closer to her.

"Just made it. Chicory and cinnamon."

"If you had a damn television here, you'd have seen it—'Daylight killing on St. Charles Avenue.' It's all over the news, freaking out the DA and the Visitors Bureau. No telling how many videos from streetcars going by will wind up on You Tube."

"That's enough," Gabe said.

"People can live with violence after dark. That's expected in any city, but when it's in broad daylight, forget about it. The DA pushed for an early docket and it's Tulane and Broad for you at nine a.m. tomorrow."

"What's Tulane and Broad?"

"Why don't you have a television?"
"What's Tulane and Broad?"
"Magistrate Court."
Gabe was silent.
"You're being arraigned in the morning."
Gabe glanced at the coffee mugs in his hand.
"Congratulations, Gabe, you made the big time. You have to appear before a magistrate to hear the second-degree murder charge against you."
"What then?" Gabe asked.
"We enter a plea. Guilty, not guilty, or nolo contendere."
She took an empty cup in one hand, pinched his arm with the other.
"Gabe, look me in the eye and swear it wasn't premeditated."
"Is this some technique they teach at Harvard Law, Miss Tarleton?"
Gabe poured her coffee.
"Now is not the time to fuck with me, Gabe. You're a big boy—you know the difference— premeditated and self-defense."
Gabe returned the coffee pot to the kitchen, came back out and sat down.
With his silence she rolled her eyes and turned to the other chair.
"The only reason they haven't busted down your door and you're not behind bars is they trust me, Gabe. I know the system and how to get around in it."
"If they come, they come."
"You're a decorated veteran, and I'm your attorney, and I promised you'll show up in the morning."
"Tell me where and when, I'll be there."
"Sasha warned me about you."
"Oh, I'm sure she has."
"You're an ornery, stubborn old coot when you have a mind to."
She sat down.
"I'm never ornery," Gabe said. "But that's enough."
"I should have listened to Sasha."

"You're a damned good attorney, Lily Cup."
"Yeah?—if I'm that good why are half my clients in Angola."
"I know you're good."
"Now that we're on it, there's something I need to tell you."
"I appreciate you."
"You may want to get somebody else."
"You were third in your class at Harvard—"
"Gabe, I was bottom of my class at Harvard—I had to take my bar exam three times."
Gabe sipped his coffee, looking into her eyes.
"Sasha tells everybody I was third in my class—"
"Drink your coffee while it's hot."
"—but I'm smart."
"I know you are, little sister—that I do know."
"I wasn't good with books, even in high school. I'm what they call an observational learner—a hands-on learner. I learned more after I got out of school than I ever did in. It was painful just going to class—but I never missed a class and that alone got me through."
"You're dogged," Gabe said. "That makes you good."
"You still want me after tomorrow, Gabe?"
"It's you and me, little sister—it's you and me all the way."
Lily Cup clenched her coffee mug with both hands and a grin like a school girl with a cup of hot chocolate.
"We're lucky we have Judge Fontenot."
"Why is that?"
"I heard her dad was killed in Vietnam."
"I wonder if I knew him."
"She's always been fair to me in the past. A new school gal, tough on the letter of the law, but she'll listen to reason if it solves a case. She hates red tape with a passion, and seldom lets the DA or the defense use the system for delays. If things can get resolved out of court she doesn't get hung up on tradition."
"Have you heard?" Gabe asked.
"Heard what?"
"Sasha asked me to give her away."
"Like she's been my best friend since kindergarten, she tells me everything," Lily Cup said.

"How about them apples?"

"It's sweet."

"I'm thinking Peck and I throw her a party," Gabe said. "Something she'll remember."

"Costumes, she'll remember costumes."

"So, we commemorate their engagement Mardi Gras style. Lots of pictures; close friends."

"Will you print invitations, like a formal do?" Lily Cup asked.

"But of course," Gabe said.

"It's party time! She would flip over a costume party, all our friends would," Lily Cup said.

"We have to come up with some music," Gabe said.

"You and Peck celebrating her engagement will mean a lot to her."

"Should we do it here or over at Charlie's Blue Note with live jazz?"

"Gabe, you've got one picture on your mantle, two chairs, and a cardboard box in the living room."

"More space for people," Gabe said.

"This isn't exactly what I'd call a Commander's Palace party room, Gabe."

"I was thinking a streetcar *day pass* in the invite if we do it here."

"That's a great idea—parking sucks on this street."

"I have to make a list," Gabe said.

"When are you going to buy some furniture?"

"I'm too old to impose furniture on Peck."

"You need furniture for you."

"Peck would only feel obligated to keep it after I'm gone. I'll let him and Millie pick out the furniture doodads, curtains, and the dishes when they play house. There's time."

"How's your stomach?"

"What stomach? They removed it."

"I don't mean since the operation. Were you hurt today?" Lily Cup asked.

"He missed me with his knife."

"The DA is having a problem with that, Gabe."

"What problem?"

"They found no knife anywhere at the scene."

Gabe watched the bubble floating on his coffee and took a sip.

"I'm a hospice survivor with some time left in me, hopefully. At least enough time to plan a party."

"You might be partying in Angola if the DA decides to push this to a grand jury," Lily Cup said.

Gabe stood, got the coffee urn from the kitchen and brought it into the living room.

"Let me warm your coffee?"

"Do you two have beds?"

"Of course, we have beds, little sister. Peck thinks he's a prince—a mattress and sheets after sleeping on a canvas cot most of his life with a saddle blanket that wouldn't cover his legs."

"This all must be a new world for him," Lily Cup said.

"For fifteen years he slept in a shed with no heat at a boat maker's wood mill," Gabe said.

"No heat?"

"He had a hotplate for his coffee pot. Saw blades hanging over him like Macy's parade balloons. It took him weeks getting used to sleeping on a bed."

Lily Cup stared in wonder.

"I'll find him curled on the floor, no blanket, with his window wide open," Gabe said.

"Peck and Millie," Lily Cup said.

"Peck and Millie," Gabe repeated.

"They do seem like a good fit," Lily Cup said. "At least they did when I saw them together. That seems forever ago—last Thanksgiving."

"She's loved that boy with a passion from the day he made the Greyhound pull over so he could jump off just to give her a doll she left on the bus," Gabe said.

"That's right—now I remember—her baby doll—Charlie, wasn't it? Sasha told me about the doll."

"Her Charlie."

"Hell, I had my Teddy bear all through Harvard. I still have it," Lily Cup said.

"Millie does love her Charlie," Gabe said.

"Does she like the house?"

"The girl loves New Orleans."

"What's not to love about New Orleans?" Lily Cup said sarcastically. "Killings in the streets before brunch."

"It's a different world for her from the strict Southern Baptist home life in Tennessee and Baylor University," Gabe said.

"Millie is Baptist?"

"She is."

"Oh, my Lord."

"A Southern Baptist."

"Gabe, I had an old maid great aunt one time who used to lecture me. She'd sit next to me at the dinner table and say, "Honey, a person can't help being black, but they sure can help being Baptist.""

"I would have loved your great auntie," Gabe said.

"Does Millie know about the ambiance, the dancing, drinking, and debauchery that goes on at Charlie's Blue Note?"

"Little sister, that girl would love Milwaukee if Peck were there."

"Good fit then, I guess."

"Her folks love Peck like a son, and he's a Baptist preacher and she's a missionary."

"As for her liking Charlie's Blue Note," Gabe added, "I'm not certain Millie's even had a good look at this house the few times she's come on her school breaks at Baylor. I know she hasn't been to Charlie's."

"They don't waste time dancing, I'm guessing," Lily Cup said.

"She hits that door, pauses just long enough to hug ole Gabe here a genuine hello and kiss on the cheek, then she'll grab Peck's arm like it's an empty egg basket, pull his bedroom door behind them and climb his bones."

"Damn—" Lily Cup said.

"That pretty much sums up her visits here."

"Sounds like an Erskine Caldwell?"

"What's an Erskine Caldwell?"

"*God's Little Acre.* Caldwell wrote *God's Little Acre.*"

"I thought you didn't like books?"

"I like the dirty parts. This one's a hottie about religion and sex."

"I don't know about any praying going on in that bedroom, but our Peck will come out looking peaked, step on the porch for air and go back in for another round."

"Whoa," Lily Cup said.

"The lad has the stamina of a young bull."

"Now that takes me back," Lily Cup said.

"I can only imagine."

"I remember my younger days of wild, reckless abandon," Lily Cup said.

She sipped her coffee, smiling.

"Innocent times," Gabe said.

"They weren't so innocent," Lily Cup said.

"Oh?"

"I remember after school sometimes—Sasha and I'd be feeling randy and we'd corner us a couple of momma's boys we thought showed promise. We'd sneak into one of those backyard storage rooms on Magazine Street and wear them out."

"Lord help 'em," Gabe said.

"The Lord stays off Magazine Street, Gabe. Sinners only."

"Impetuous youth."

"We had perfect lures."

"A pint of rye?"

"Nope."

"A joint?"

"Oh, nothing that prosaic."

"I'm afraid to ask."

"Sasha was the first in our grade to wear a D cup bra," Lily Cup said.

"Her girls," Gabe said.

"They were magnets for high school bad boys dying for a peek," Lily Cup said. "The bigger her girls, the 'badder' the boys."

"Youth," Gabe said.

"We developed our fancies. Hers was arousing a dude with his stares and putting his condom on him. She'd ride it like a sailor on a rowboat—the boy gawking up at her girls in her

Victoria's Secret bra she saved her allowance for. She wouldn't take it off. She'd say a boy appreciates a cleavage—why spoil the fantasy?"

"And you?"

"Let's just say I developed a liking for the feel of a firm cigar."

"Ha!" Gabe guffawed. "Is that why you smoke the short Panatelas?"

"Over the years I've learned to keep my expectations low."

"Youth is uncouth," Gabe said. "At least you're sophisticated and couth now, little sister."

"Too couth. I like to get mussed up on occasion."

"You're an attractive woman. It'll happen."

"She's talking about the wedding reception maybe being at Charlie's Blue Note," Lily Cup said.

"If that's true, I'm surprised James hasn't put up a scuff," Gabe said.

"Why?"

"A jazz joint in an alley off Frenchmen Street isn't what I'd call his cup of tea."

"I think the house would be best for the engagement party, fixed up a little. I'll help," Lily Cup said.

"It would be more personal here," Gabe said.

"I think so," Lily Cup said. "This is like home to her."

"This little shotgun? Our Sasha lives in a Garden District mansion."

"But you two are family."

"I'll have Peck paint the porch ceiling," Gabe said.

Lily Cup stood, coffee cup in hand. She walked to the door looking out at the porch ceiling.

"Why?" she asked.

"I'm changing the sky-blue to another color, maybe a white."

"It looks freshly painted."

"It's a tradition thing," Gabe said.

"What tradition?"

"A lady at the library told me a sky-blue ceiling on a front porch signals an available woman-of-age living in the house."

"That's phooey," Lily Cup said.

"You've never heard that?" Gabe asked.

"I heard that one and three others like it. Like sky-blue wards off spiders and attracts bees away from people sitting on porch swings. I wouldn't bother painting it."

"I'm a Chicago boy—what would I know from superstitions?"

"It's an old wives' tale," Lily Cup said.

"I thought maybe it was voodoo superstition," Gabe said.

"Blacks weren't allowed to practice voodoo back then, Gabe. It was considered savage, and the French made voodoo illegal for blacks. The practitioners were criminalized and arrested."

"That doesn't make sense—during Korea and our docking in the port of New Orleans, I saw plenty of it. Black voodoo—how'd they get away with it without getting caught then?"

"They added a statue of the virgin Mary and some rosary beads and passed it off as a Catholic ceremony. That kept the law away."

"The things I'm learning, little sister—and me an old man."

"Sasha and I still sit on a roof in the Quarter under a full moon if it's not lightning—bad *Gris-Gris* if there're thunderstorms under a full moon. We light candles and talk through the night about the mystical, mumbo jumbo, and voodoo. It's fun. It's how we play when we're not dancing."

"And I thought most girls play with dolls," Gabe said.

"Only voodoo thing I've heard about front porches in Acadiana is some still clean them with red brick dust to ward off bad spirits," Lily Cup said.

"Can these séances tell my future?" Gabe asked.

"I saw no alligator under the house when I got here. It's life, not death in this house today. I can't speak for Lee Circle, where you did the kid in this morning."

"I still can't quite wrap myself around it," Gabe said.

"Around killing him?" Lily Cup asked.

"A tired old black man like me owning in the Garden District."

"And why not?"

"Fifty years ago, all I could have done here would be scrub floors or wash dishes for *massah*."

"We're sinful and excessive, Gabe, but the survivors grow character, usually in our twenties."

"Talk to me."

"New Orleans is an anomaly of prejudiced behavior," Lily Cup said.

"I see it every day. It's not like any other city," Gabe said.

"We're a melting pot of French, Spanish, African and English—Native American. My daddy made me study it—family cultures—before I took my Louisiana bar exam the third time. Family law was always stumping me. Daddy told me if I didn't study people and cultures along with the law books on family and I failed again it would be my own fault, and I might ought to think of working in a hardware store."

"Your dad sounds like a smart man," Gabe said.

"Throughout and after the Civil War, the French-speaking Creoles of color had racial alignment that was like no other place in the south. That's a big reason we love to cook and eat well, and we live, work, and play together. We respect each other. It was the Jim Crow laws at the start of the twentieth century that fucked it up. Even the streetcars were segregated in 1902. We've had our problems since, but after the Martin Luther King times, prejudice hasn't been that much of an issue here. Oh, don't get me wrong, Gabe. When a black man offs a white kid on St. Charles in broad daylight, all bets are off."

"So how is it we've gone full circle?" Gabe asked.

"Did Sasha think twice about dancing with you that first night you came into Charlie's Blue Note?"

"She asked me to dance," Gabe said.

Lily Cup pulled a cord, lifting a venetian blind and pointed across the street.

"The Garden District you live in Gabe, is just a Monopoly box with play money, houses, and hotels in it."

She pointed.

"Huge houses like that one that nobody lives in, but the maid and gardener still come to once a week. Mansions in the heart of a pauper-poor, diversity-rich city. The wealthy from the corners of the earth buy here just to show off owning a piece of New Orleans—a city like no other place. They don't need reservations to party with locals during Mardi Gras week.

You're special, Gabe. You own and live here. Streetcars work for you just as they have for Anne Rice and for Tennessee Williams and Truman Capote."

"It's still something," Gabe said. "Fifty—sixty years ago, Louis Armstrong couldn't have lived in the Garden District."

"If he had the cash and could afford it, I wouldn't bet he couldn't."

She lowered the blind and turned toward him.

"I don't want you scrubbing floors for 'massah' in Angola. I know you, Gabe, and I know Angola."

Gabe looked at his coffee mug.

"My guess is you had a reason for killing him, but that's not good enough in a court room. I have to hear from your lips that it wasn't premeditated. I'll defend you in any case, but I have to hear it. There's a lot of fucking prep work to do."

"It's not much to look at—Lily Cup—we're missing furniture, draperies and trappings—but it's more than a house. This is our loving, blessed home. As long as we're here, it is Peck's and my private sanctuary away from those parts of our lives that have haunted their full share of pain and suffering. This is our safe haven—our resting place. It's always welcome to good friends like you and Sasha—"

"Gabe, I can't help you if you won't—"

"Our home is not the place for these words and for conversation of this nature. I'm asking you as a friend to kindly respect our space."

"I'll pick you up in the morning. We'll talk then," Lily Cup said.

"I'll have Peck drive me in the morning. He likes sporting me about in his new pickup."

"Peck drives?" Lily Cup asked. "Since when?"

"He does."

"In this short a time? What's it been—a couple of months since he's been here?"

"Nine months—" Gabe started.

"Has it been nine months? He's been cleaning our offices all that long? I never see him."

"And he can read every word in the driving manual."

"He reads?"

"He only missed two questions on the written test. He didn't know what 'yield' meant. I forget the other. Now he's trying to read a John Steinbeck novel, can you imagine?"

"Which one? Like it matters."

"*Cannery Row*. He got it with his library card."

"He's like one of those big fat cans," Lily Cup said. "You know, the restaurant ones, I think they call them number-ten cans. They fill them with beans, but he's filled with brains waiting for someone to come along with a can opener," Lily Cup said.

"That's Peck," Gabe said.

"Amazing."

"Listen to this one," Gabe said. "He's reading out loud, one word at a time, after telling me it was harder for him to read out loud than it was reading to himself."

"Huh?" Lily Cup asked.

"It makes no sense, right? So I ask him why he doesn't just read to himself with no talking it out."

"What'd he say?"

"He said, 'Gabe if'n I don't say 'ever' word out loud so I can hear 'em good, how am I supposed to know what they sound like so I can say 'em good when time comes to use 'em proper?' Can you imagine?"

"Know what's scary?"

"What?"

"He has a point," Lily Cup said.

"How can you not love the boy?" Gabe asked.

"When will he get his GED?"

"This month. Illiterate to a high school diploma in months."

"Jesus."

"Sasha's tutor friend is a miracle worker," Gabe said.

"Polly Lou, she was the smartest one in our school."

"She actually taught him conjugations in a French he understood—and had him translate them into English. He was reading in weeks."

"She's damn good."

"When Millie comes in for the ceremony, we'll celebrate at Dooky Chase's—you too."

"Does Peck know about today?"

"No, he was gone when I got home from the police station."
"Where's he now?"
"Probably on his way."
"Should I not be here so you can tell him?"
"Stay. He went over to Tulane, talking with a guidance counselor. After that he may be talking with Xavier. Depends on how it goes at Tulane."
"You must be proud of him."
"We knew he had it in him," Gabe said.
"We did," Lily Cup said.
"Do you think James is right?" Gabe asked.
"What?"
"James."
"You mean right for Sasha?"
"Yes. Think he's right?"
"Where in the hell did that come from?"
"You're her best friend."
"What does that have to do with it?"
"Think James is the man?"
"Why are you asking now?"
"No reason."
"What's on your mind, Gabe?"
"She's full of life, she's giving—she's successful, intelligent—a great dancer," Gabe said.
"But?" Lily Cup asked. "I know there's a *but* coming…"
"But—and girlfriend, this goes no further than these walls…"
"I swear," Lily Cup said.
"The woman has much more to offer the world and James is a…well, James is a…"
"Yeah, I know," Lily Cup said.
"James is a self-indulgent dilettante, full of himself," Gabe said.
"He's all that all right."
"I mean is he just a bad habit or does the woman love him?"
"She says she does."
"Sombitch doesn't even like to dance," Gabe said.
"James is an asshole," Lily Cup said.
"You took the words right out of my mouth."

"Maybe he's hung like a polo pony and knows how to use it," Lily Cup said. "Ever think of that?"

"You mean like our Peckerwood, little sister?"

Lily Cup swung her head around, eyes in a wide-open glare.

"Hush," she declared, grinning through clenched teeth as if someone might hear. "I was drinking rye. Murder case on my mind."

"I heard, little sister. Sasha shared."

"No one is to know about that night. You're a friend— keep it between us that Peck and I ever...you know."

"I saw the smile on your face when I put you in a cab," Gabe said. "I think they call that smile an afterglow."

"I can't remember it that well."

"I think you remember, lawyer lady, and you weren't drunk when the two of you had coffee and disappeared. You skipped from the bar to the lady's room to knock one off. You remember."

"I always get drunk before a murder trial."

"Your only regret is people gossip."

"Drunk and horny—I can't help it—before every murder case, ever since I finally passed the bar."

"Murder makes you horny?"

"Drunk makes me horny—murder makes me drink. Rye."

"You choose to mask a tryst the night you met Peck behind rye? Your secret is safe with me."

"Thank you."

"Does Sasha smile like that after James stays over?"

"Like what?"

"Like you did that night?" Gabe asked.

"Not even," Lily Cup said.

"I've wondered."

"She says it's good sex, but I never catch her looking into space."

"What do you mean?"

"Women know these things."

"Do tell."

"We'll play good nights over in our minds. There're girl signs only girls know how to read about a morning after. Her and James? Not even close."

"Sex isn't all there is, I suppose," Gabe said.
"It isn't?" Lily Cup asked.
"There's more to life than a roll in the sheets."
"Damn."

Lily Cup's eyes brightened in a mischievous smile while interrupted by the front door opening and Peck walking in.

"Hey, cher, how you are?" Peck asked.

He gave her a hug and a kiss on each cheek. He picked up her cup from the cardboard box, slurped a mouthful and set it back down.

"Hey, Captain," Peck said.
"How'd Tulane go?" Gabe asked.
"I'm goin' to night school—I start in June," Peck said.
"My man!" Gabe snorted.
"I can work the days and school and study the nights. I liked him a lot. Nice man."
"Didn't laugh at you, did he?" Gabe asked.
"Nah, nah," Peck said. "Not ever."
"No one worth a salt will ever laugh at a person trying to get ahead, trying to improve themselves," Gabe said. "I told you."

Peck turned to Lily Cup.

"Lily Cup, can I clean the law offices daytime instead of night when I start night school?"

"Sure—but it'll have to be on Sundays or early mornings and be out of there before nine."

"I can did that. Sorry, cher— I mean I can do that."
"I knew what you meant," Lily Cup said.
"I'll clean before you open up," Peck said.
"Congratulations, Peck—"
"Hanh?"
"—on getting into Tulane," Lily Cup said.
"T'anks, cher."

She paused a reach for her coffee, copping a reminiscent glance at his package, then up at his eyes.

"How come I don't ever see you come and go?"
"I always come after dark."
"When are you coming this week?"
"Midnight tonight."

Peck's cellphone beeped. He opened the text and with a wrinkled brow studied the words. Gabe flicked his finger at Lily Cup so she could watch Peck reading.

"It's Millie," Peck said.

He reread the text.

"Gabe, it say here she'll be in New Or-lee-anh in May, she coming for all summer," Peck said.

"Your lady is always welcome in this house, Peck," Gabe said.

Peck read another text.

"Millie say here can she meet my mamma," Peck said.

Peck lifted his head and looked over at Gabe.

Gabe looked at him, turned his head catching Lily Cup's eye, winked as he leaned on the chair arm to bolster getting up and standing.

"Peck, my brother—we've been blessed with Sasha's and James's engagement and now with you— a bonafide Tulane man, and we're blessed with our Millie. I'm going for a walk and when I come back I'll take my nap. What say you and I grab shrimp and grits and a couple of drinks at the Columns tonight? The streetcar will give us some quality time to talk and catch up."

"Hokay."

"We have a deal, son?"

"We got a deal, Captain," Peck said.

They shook hands.

Peck kissed Lily Cup on both cheeks and exited to go read in his room. Seeing the bedroom door pulled closed, Gabe leaned toward Lily Cup, lowering his voice.

"Has Sasha ever told you anything about Peck's childhood—about his foster mother or nanna or whatever and her old man—gator man?" Gabe asked.

Lily Cup stood, paced nervously as if she was hoping to avoid any subject only Sasha knew she was far too familiar with. Lily Cup knew gator man had "disappeared" and how. She believed if it got out it could get her disbarred, or worse. She walked to the coffee maker, filled her cup and returned. Seated again, she placed her cup on the cardboard box and played with her driving gloves as a distraction. She looked up at Gabe.

"Not much. Oh, I heard some things, but not much."

"Apparently they're a couple of mean bastards—vicious drunks," Gabe said. "I'm surprised Sasha hasn't told you."

"Does Peck ever talk about it?" Lily Cup asked.

"Not to me."

"He's blocking it. Nothing wrong with that," Lily Cup said.

"Oh, he called himself a boney white French Cajun boy one time but not much else."

"I'm surprised he hasn't told you more, Gabe, as close as you are."

"I don't think he likes to talk about it. I know he told Sasha some things that time we were all up in Providence," Gabe said.

"Do you think Millie knows anything?" Lily Cup asked.

"Anything?" Gabe asked.

"He ran away from home when he was ten or something, didn't he?"

"Eight or nine," Gabe said.

"Jesus."

"I hear you, little sister. And since the age of eight or nine, whichever it was, the boy hasn't taken a handout or one penny of welfare."

"Where'd he get the name *Peck*?" Lily Cup asked.

"Around these parts they'll call a poor white, usually a no-account from the swamps and bayous a *Peckerwood*."

"Meaning white trash?"

"Yeah. Like calling me nigger. Same thing."

"Lucky he wound up in Carencro," Lily Cup said, "and not here."

"How so?"

"Beggary and the handout are a way of life in New Orleans."

"A city's poverty wouldn't have changed him, I don't think," Gabe said.

"You don't think it would have swallowed him up?"

"The boy has character in his blood."

"I can see that, look at the year," Lily Cup said. "And now Tulane."

"I think he would have assimilated with blacks, the French, and the Spanish—but still he would have mowed lawns and sharpened knives to get by, just as he did in Carencro. I could see him throwing his trotline somewhere each morning and selling his catches to restaurants or trading at the market for his eggs and chicory."

"His character had to come from someone," Lily Cup said.

"My thought exactly," Gabe said.

"It'd be interesting to know from whom."

"Knowing would be the Holy Grail," Gabe said. "Maybe one day we'll know the story and can give him a past he can be proud of."

"I heard some of it..." Lily Cup started as she prepared to leave.

Gabe lifted his walking stick from the corner it leaned against and stepped out of the house alongside her as she headed to her car. He pulled the door closed and adjusted his honey-cream, linen newsboy cap.

"Charges for second degree murder are no easy thing," Lily Cup said. "We have to declare a plea to murder—guilty or not guilty—no in-between—there's no getting out of it."

Gabe nodded his head, with an understanding of the situation.

"It's not smart to be cavalier, Gabe. They know you killed the kid. They didn't see a weapon on or around the body. I need to know if it was premeditated."

Gabe stood there motionless.

"The DA can really hurt you. Why won't you tell me? I can help. I'm good—I know my way around."

He paused on the step above the sidewalk.

"If I knew myself, darlin', I'd tell you in a heartbeat, and that's the truth," Gabe said. "I'm not holding anything back. I'm not being cavalier."

"Then why won't—?" Lily Cup started.

"I'm just not sure, yet. I need time to think it through."

"We have no time, Gabe."

"It's the way I am. Sorry."

"Whatever you do, don't talk tomorrow. Don't say a word unless I tell you it's okay to speak. Putting your foot in your mouth can wind you up in prison."

"Fair enough."

"And if I say you can speak and you don't know something tell them you don't know. Don't be caught in a lie."

"Let me work it out in my mind, "Gabe said. "I'm an old man. I need to make it right in my head and with God."

"It'll take more than the Almighty in the morning, Gabe."

"There's a young man lying naked on a cold, stainless-steel table in the city morgue because of me," Gabe said.

"I think I need a drink," Lily Cup said.

"God gave me a longer life to live. He didn't give me a longer life just so I could take another life. I have to work it out in my head."

"What are you going to tell Peck?"

"About what?"

"You know about what, Gabe."

"Millie meeting his mother?"

"Well that too, dancing man," Lily Cup said, "and about the trouble you're in?"

Gabe didn't answer.

She stepped down to the sidewalk and started walking toward her car. She turned and looked at him standing on the step as a gentleman would, waiting for her to reach her car.

"Sasha isn't sure that lady is his mother, right? You knew that much, didn't you?" she asked.

"I knew."

"I'm going over and light a vigil candle at St. Patrick's for you, Gabe, and the Almighty."

"You mean that, little sister?"

"I'll see you at the courthouse in the morning. Don't be late."

"Light two," Gabe said stepping down to the sidewalk and turning away for his walk. "Better light two."

Lily Cup turned again.

"Gabe?"

Gabe paused and looked around.

"Yes?"

"In there you said I was smart—did you mean that?"

"I meant every word, my little sister. Every damn word."

"I'm not all that book smart, Gabe, in case you want to get somebody else."

"You're street smart, Lily Cup."
"I am that."
"Plenty street smart, little sister."
"I know my way around pretty good."
"Lily Cup, you're Peck in a skirt."
"Peck is plenty smart. You really think I'm—?"
"Street smart is better than book smart any day," Gabe said.
"I'm lighting three candles," Lily Cup said.

Chapter 3

THEY STEPPED FROM THE SEVEN-FIFTY STREETCAR, and it rolled on behind them, whining off into the night.

Soon they were at the front gate of the Columns Hotel, brightly aglow with floodlights washing historic columns and walls of a porcelain white majesty.

"Stand a minute, my brother—let's take it in."

"Take what in, Gabe?"

"This place—the Columns—one of the few things that still belongs to New Orleans and isn't for rent like some cheap, painted-up whore that sells her soul once a year so the rich world can come for pre-Lenten entertainment, throw money for plastic beads and gloat at their lot in life. They have an arrogance about them. It's like they can leave when they want and leave us to pick up. This one is ours, Peck. Isn't it magnificent?"

"*Tres grand*," Peck said.

"It looks big—I'm not sure how many rooms they have for hotel guests. Not many, I suppose—but I don't know. It was a private home in its day. They shot a movie here once."

They climbed the steps, paused on a landing surrounded by various size tables with linen cloths, couples silhouetted by a moonless night, drinks in hand, chatting and listening to their partners, as in a Toulouse Lautrec print.

"Look around, Peck. Locals enjoying the night away from toils of a long day, the streetcar sounds, the smells of New Orleans."

Peck understood Gabe's sense of living every single moment of what life he had left in him.

"My brother, would you prefer sitting here on the patio in the night air or inside?"

Peck didn't answer.

"We might talk better inside," Gabe said. "Night folks congregate in the bar or out here. Let's take our chances in the front room."

A server carrying a tray of drinks told them to find a table—she would be back to take their order. The smaller parlor room that Gabe preferred had a front window with dark-stained indoor shutters that dated back a century. Bay and framed, the window looked on St. Charles Avenue and its glass pane height rose from the floor to a twelve or fourteen-foot ceiling. Romantics like Gabe could imagine children of the 1800s who were supposed to be taking their naps sitting on the floor in the bay, watching the parade of horses, carriages, and streetcars going by. The table was for four, but he and Peck sat on both sides of a corner V with an avenue view, their backs to the next room with its round red leather settee and an ornate, wood-carved barroom behind that.

Peck reached out and rested his hand on Gabe's.

"*Quel problème avez-vous, mon ami?*" Peck asked. ("What trouble are you in, my frien'?")

"My brother," Gabe said, "I know when you speak with the French, you have something important on your mind. I only made out the word *problem*—and I'm here for you. What problem do you have—let it out, my brother."

"Nah, nah...not me. What trouble you in, frien'?" Peck asked.

Gabe reeled his torso, eyes wide, mouth open, caught off-guard. He pointed to the seat across from him.

"Sit over there, son, so I can look into your eyes."

Peck got up, moved, and sat again.

"Just what do you know about so-called trouble you speak of, my brother?" Gabe asked.

"Gabe, I dunno—"

"What exactly have you heard, son?"

"I heard nothing, Gabe."

"I'll be damned."

"I see plenty though."

Peck stared into Gabe's eyes.

"You in trouble, old frien'—tell Peck about it.

"I swear—" Gabe started.

"Hanh?"

"I spend a lifetime in the army learning to be aware of things around me, and in all those years—not one time—have I seen anyone even come close to having your sense of observation. My brother."

The waitress came to the table, about to interrupt. Gabe interrupted her first.

"Honey, how about bringing us two shrimp and grits and maybe bring one crawfish *etoufee* that we'll share. Bring a couple of spoons, if you will, and two small plates and start us with a Chivas on the rocks for me and a long neck for my brother here and keep them coming."

"Yes, sir," the waitress said.

"Young lady, the streetcar is our driver tonight."

"Thank you, sir."

Gabe waited for her to step away, turned his head and looked Peck in the eye, while leaning in over the table.

"Okay, sure," he said.

"Sure what, Gabe?" Peck asked.

"I'll tell you my story, my brother—"

"Hokay."

"But only after you tell me how you found out."

"Hanh?"

"Who told you about this morning?"

"Lily Cup," Peck said.

"Hogwash," Gabe said. "She's a total professional. She wouldn't say a word."

"Lily Cup at the house," Peck said.

"Not buying it."

Peck just looked at Gabe, lifted his beer.

"What gave you the idea there's trouble?" Gabe asked.

"Her satchel by the door," Peck said.

"Her briefcase tipped you!?"

"If no trouble, satchel would be in her car. She took it into the house. Only could mean trouble for my frien'."

Gabe sat back.

"The eyes of a fucking bald eagle," Gabe said.

He inhaled and exhaled, as if in defeat. He sat rubbing his chin and shaking his head, as if he was letting the moment sink in. Peck's keen observation had picked up the scent of trouble just as if the boy were on his pirogue in a bayou swamp tracking a gator for bounty or turtles for soup. Gabe leaned in and lowered his voice.

"I killed a lad today, I surely did."

Peck rested his beer on the table.

"He couldn't have been twenty, maybe twenty–two."

Peck was motionless.

"Killed him deader than a cold mackerel." He put the flat of his palms to his eyes and rubbed as if he wanted to wake from a bad dream.

"Old Gabe here is in big trouble with the law, my brother, and bigger trouble with the Almighty."

He looked around for prying ears, leaned in further.

"That's the mess I'm in, son."

Peck reached across the table and held his hand again.

"Tell Peck, Gabe. When?" Peck asked.

"Happened this morning, after you left for your meeting at Tulane."

"Where you was, Gabe?"

"Thought I'd stretch my legs on Andrew Higgins Boulevard."

"You walk all that way?"

"Not all the way. I thought I'd take the streetcar to Lee Circle for a look at the World War II museum; thought maybe I'd sit with a coffee on the park bench and have a chat with President Roosevelt."

"You been there before, Gabe."

"I stepped from the streetcar and was crossing St. Charles. There was no traffic, and I remember looking up at the tree branches and phone wires still draped with strings of beaded necklaces from Mardi Gras hanging from them. I remember thinking it must be they get caught in trees when they're thrown from the tall parade floats. That's about when he came up."

"Who?"

"The kid."

"From behind you?" Peck asked.

"No—from straight on in front of me."

"On the sidewalk?"

"Well, it was when I was stepping onto the sidewalk, he was there."

"He was standing there or walking?"

"I don't remember but I do remember when I caught his eye he was smiling a big, cold smile."

"He smiled, Gabe?"

"He pulled a knife from under his shirt—I'd say six, eight-inch blade. He walked toward me grinning and smiling, pointing and poking the knife at me and he kept saying, "Wallet, mister...give me your fucking wallet, old man...wallet...your fucking wallet..."

A woman at the next table turned in her chair.

"Sir, do you mind? The language."

Gabe looked at her—lifted his scotch and nodded his head.

"What'd you do?" Peck asked.

"I grabbed my stick with both hands and turned sideways—taking a stance. I poked the tip at his eye. I missed his eye, but I know I hurt him. Then I reeled and slammed the back of his upper calf full force with my stick, just like it was a baseball bat and took him down."

"He go down, Gabe?"

"He buckled and went down hard, but he didn't drop the knife."

"What'd you do?"

"He grabbed my shirttail with his fist and swiped up at me, cut my shirt—took a button off, and that's when I did it. God'll judge me, I could only see red. I turned the stick around and struck his head. I remember bashing it down—hearing it—feeling it hit his skull. I don't remember anything after that, but that someone grabbed me and held me until I came to."

"Bonk him dead, frien'?"

"I didn't look—but he was dead."

"People see?"

"For damn sure, at least I think."

"Did you stay there?"

"I didn't run. A cop cuffed me, put my stick in his trunk and drove me to the station. He was a vet, a brother. He called Lily Cup for me while he drove. She was at the station waiting when we got there. They booked me and let me go home because of her. I have to go before the judge in the morning."

"*Mais vous essayiez seulement de vous defender*," Peck said. ("But you were only trying to defend yourself.")

"Are you saying self–defense?"

"*Oui.*"

"Lily Cup said the DA can build a case proving the boy was defending himself from me."

"She say that, for true?"

"She did."

"Hmm."

"It's a pickle."

"And why you not in jail, Gabe?"

"Lily Cup. They trust her that I'll show up. Tomorrow I have to hear the murder charges against me and plead something."

"Oh, hokay."

"It's a big dill pickle."

The waitress served them. Both men paddled forks through the fragrances and tastes of the town. Family secret ambrosias of red sauce warming the shrimp and grits made things all right.

"All right" in the Big Easy is when the tastes of the food to the palate can make you forget all else, at least for the moment.

"Peck, can I ask you something personal?"

"Ax."

"You don't have to answer if it makes you uncomfortable."

"Ax."

"I was thinking about Millie—you know, her text to you today."

"Ah *oui*."

"Her wanting to meet your mamma."

"*Oui.*"

"What can you tell me about your youth, son? We never talk about it."

Peck looked up from his shrimp and grits.

"How far back do you remember, Peck?"

Peck placed his fork in the bowl and sat back.

"If it's uncomfortable, we'll drop it," Gabe said.

"I grow'd somewhere at Bayou Chene, I t'ink—there and Petit Anse Bayou, 'tween Bayou Sorrel and Choctaw. Foster nanna is most all I remember good. There was gator man. Gator man belt-strapped me if I dropped the bait shrimp buckets. I had to scoop shrimp and carry the buckets until his pirogue was full. He'd sell bait to tourists at the fishing docks."

"How old were you?"

"I couldn't swim is what I remember."

"Did he pay you?"

"Nah, nah...he'd dog collar me around my neck and chain me under the porch back of his house. I worked, is all."

Gabe sat silently.

"My foster nanna would tell me gator man was lar'ning me and to see I mind him good. He'd tow me for gator bait."

"That bastard," Gabe said.

"When the moon come out, I'd look up near all night pretending the moon was my mamma looking down, and I'd talk to her and I'd promise her I was a good boy now and no trouble, and I'd be quiet and behave if she ever come back. I talked to the moon."

"She heard you, son."

"For true, Gabe?"

"Your mother heard every word, I'm certain of it."

"I don't even knowed my mamma, Gabe— what do I tell Millie?"

Gabe lifted his scotch for a sip, waiting for Peck to speak again.

"Peck is scared, Gabe. Scared she'll run away when she knows I don't know my own mamma."

"Listen to me, my brother. Listen good. Millie may still hug her baby doll, but she's stronger than you think, son."

"Dass for true, ain't it, Gabe?"

"Spoon some *etoufee* and let me think a minute. I need to think."

The lobby of the hotel and both party rooms to its left were empty. The front desk was an ornate wooden antique table with carved legs—a man sitting behind, chin in hand, dozing off. Some guest was at the piano in the bar among laughter and an occasional cheer of a celebrated moment.

"Peck, you owe it to your Millie," Gabe said.
"Owe her?"
"Tell her the truth."
"Hanh?" Peck grunted.
"You have a problem, Peck. You don't know the truth."
"Ain't dat for true."
"This all took place a long time ago in your life. You've been gone from that world like fifteen or more years. It's impossible for you to remember the truth, my brother—the whole story."
"What you sayin', Gabe?"
"I'm saying you have to go back to that Bayou Chene—or Choctaw or wherever—and find out for yourself."
"Go back?"
"When you know the truth, that's when you can tell Millie the story."
"Tell her the truth?"
"She's strong. She'd never be afraid of the truth coming from you."
"Ya t'ink?"
"That woman loves you so much—."
"I know."
"—but it's up to you to learn the truth—if not for her, then for your children."
"I love her too, frien', just as you say—so much."
"It's settled, then."
"It is?"
"You'll go search it out, my brother."
"Good idea, Gabe, after I help you."
"I love you, Peck, but old Gabe here needs to get out of my fix on my own. I got into it—I must get out of it on my own one way or another. You don't have a minute to waste. I'll handle my mess. You want to make me happy, son—go find your answers for you and Millie. Promise you will, my brother."
"I'll go, I surely will."
"You'll leave in the morning, son."
"I'll go in the morning, Gabe."
"Now remember this, Peck. You're a strong man. Look them straight in the eye. Don't let anybody frighten or intimidate you."

"I'm not scared no more, Gabe."

"Take your time. You have some weeks before night school starts," Gabe said. "Take all the time you need to get the answers you're looking for."

"Gabe, can I ax you something?"

"Anything, my brother."

"Why did that boy with a knife smile?"

"What?"

"You say he kept smiling at you? Why did he smile at you like that?"

Gabe picked up his scotch with an eye as if the military in him was wondering where Peck might be coming from.

"Where you know the boy from?" Peck asked. "A body with a knife pointed for business don't smile at a stranger. He only smiles when he knows him. Where you know him from?"

Gabe set his drink down.

"Remember that day I went to have keys made for the house?" Gabe asked.

"I remember. You wanted to walk then too."

"I was in Walmart. I was at their key-making machine and it was next to another tall vending machine. The same kid was at that machine next to me, working it." Gabe described how the kid pressured him for the use of his credit card and threatened to kill him when he refused to provide it.

"What'd you do?" Peck asked.

"I've never been so street-scared. I'm not agile or strong like I once was. I found the manager and told him. He said he'd walk me to the streetcar. Outside he asked me if I could recognize the kid and I told him yes, if I saw him again. We stopped for a light, and when I turned around, there he was—the kid was waving a knife. He was leaning on a bicycle looking me in the eye with a smile and waving his knife. 'That's him,' I told the manager. 'That's him.' The manager told me to stay put and he turned and ran toward the guy, yelling and waving his arms until the kid pedaled away in a scoot. The manager walked me to the streetcar and waited until I boarded."

"So that's when you started with a cane, Gabe?"

"Learned self-defense with one in the army."

"You're innocent," Peck said.

"Peck, I know I— "

"Tell Lily Cup the story, cher."

"What story?"

"Walmart."

"What about Walmart? It's only my word."

"Tell her to find the manager and get the video. They'll have it."

"I'll be damned," Gabe said.

"It's all the proof you need, frien'," Peck said.

"I'll be damned."

"Video—it's how we catch'd the Kentucky motorcycle knife man, remember, Gabe?"

"How can I forget that night?"

"Innocent, my frien'. Tell the story to Lily Cup."

"When are you going back to learn the truth, my brother?"

"To see my foster nanna?"

"To learn the truth," Gabe said.

"Tomorrow."

"Promise me you will, son."

"I already promised, Gabe."

"Good."

"I clean offices tonight. I'll go tomorrow."

"Let's get some pecan pie and call it an evening," Gabe said.

"You sure you be okay tomorrow, without Peck?"

"I promise you I will— I have Lily Cup."

"Lily Cup is plenty smart, dass for true."

"What a night."

"Good we talk like this, Gabe."

"A guardian angel brought you to me, my brother."

Gabe caught the waitress's eye and indicated dessert and coffee for both. He looked at the ceiling and into the heavens.

"Thank you, Butterfly—thank you, my darling."

"Butterfly?" Peck asked.

"Butterfly, my brother. Butterfly was my girlfriend, my lover, my wife, and the mother of my son...longer than I can ever remember. Now she's my guardian angel—my Butterfly."

CHAPTER 4

THE LAW OFFICES ON CARROLLTON AVENUE where Peck had cleaned every week for nine months were in a nineteenth-century, French-styled, mansard-roofed, three-story building. A florist on the ground floor looked orchid expensive and a tall, narrow, dark, forest-green wainscoted stairwell next to an elevator in the adjoining side hall rose to the second and third floors. Walking from his truck parked a block away, he could see lights in one window on the second floor. The elevator was locked after hours, so he made his usual climb and let himself in, shouting "Peck" as he pushed the door open, not wanting to alarm anyone after midnight.

As routinely as he once prepared, baited and would cast his trotline every morning in Carencro to catch turtles or mashwarohn he'd barter for eggs and coffee, he dusted the floor moldings, the conference table, and desktops. He vacuumed carpet; he sponge-mopped restrooms and kitchenettes of both upper floors. He was leaning down into the trash container inserting and fastening a new liner when a hand came up under his crotch from behind with a grab, causing a startled jump and a turn so off-guarded he fell back into the container, folding the side in.

"What?" he snarled.
"Oops," Lily Cup said.
Peck stood motionless.
"Sorry."
"You thinkin' I was someone else?"
"I knew it was you."
"Scared me—"
"Just thought I'd say hello to William."

"Hanh?"
Lily Cup offered a wry smile.
"Who?"
"William."
"Who told you about—?" Peck asked.
"About William?" Lily Cup interrupted.
"Who told you?"
"How William got his name?"
"You're drunk?"
"I know."
"How long you been drinking, cher."
"I always get drunk before a murder case."
"Who told you?"
"Sasha's my best friend since we were six. Who do you think?"
"What'd she told you?"
"We have no secrets…she told me she named him William seeing it through a crack in the door when you stepped out of a bathtub in Memphis."

Lily Cup moved toward Peck, drink-tumbler in one hand, gazing into his eyes in a daze as she moved closer.

"You need to close bathroom doors, Peck. But no worries. William is a secret safe with me."

She touched her flat hand on the front of his jeans, moving slowly in search of William.

"You remember that night?" Lily Cup asked.

Peck watched her hand.

"What night, cher?"
"At Charlie's Blue Note, when we met?"
"I remember."
"I had a murder case that next morning too."
"Last year. I remember. Do you remember, cher?"

Her hand found William, who was visibly not annoyed with the warmth of her touch.

"Things happened pretty fast that night," Lily Cup said.

"Gabe and me went to Memphis with Sasha," Peck said, not taking his eyes off her hand.

"Oh, a lot more than that happened that night. You remember?"

"I remember."

"I won the murder case the next morning, Mr. Boudreaux Clemont Finch. William brought me luck. Well, I sort of won it. How about some luck for my murder case tomorrow?"

Peck stood tall and motionless, thinking—weighing options as the hunter he was—while her palm and fingers took turns gripping William playfully through his jeans, as if it were a fine cigar.

"You're a plenty smart lawyer, Lily Cup."

"You think I'm smart, baby?"

"You don't need luck."

"Oh, I do."

"You letting the wine talk."

"Rye—" Lily Cup said.

"Rye," Peck repeated.

"—and I'm not all that smart."

"You're smart, cher."

"I was having a cigar, sipping my rye, scared to death, thinking about my murder case tomorrow."

Peck looked through the dark front offices to Lily Cup's office in the back.

"Don't worry, my window was open to let the smoke out."

"I'll be waggled," Peck said.

"It bothers you, doesn't it?"

"Hanh?"

"Bothers you, women smoking cigars."

"Ain't seen it until you."

Her hand clenched his throb.

"I like the way one feels in my hand—"

She pinched the zipper toggle to his jeans and began to pull down.

"—the way one feels in my mouth."

He gently lifted her hand and pulled it away.

"Gabe your murder case, tomorrow, cher?"

Lily Cup bolted in a sobering stupor, stepping back.

"Huh?"

"I know, cher."

"Know?"

"I know."

"You know what?"
"I know about Gabe, cher."
"What do you know?"
"Can you help him?"
"I have no idea what you're talking about—"

Peck lifted his brow as if to ask her to admit Gabe was her case. He lightly kissed her hand.

"Even if I did, I can't talk about it. It's the law. It's called attorney-client privilege."

"*Peut–etre que vous pouvez ecouter?*" Peck asked. ("Maybe you can listen?")

"I can listen?" Lily Cup asked.

"You speak the French?" Peck asked.

"I understand sometimes when Sasha speaks it...but I won't discuss Gabe in any way."

Lily Cup turned to walk away and then turned back.

"What did you mean, I can listen?"

"Just listen, is all."

"Listen to what?"

"Listen to a story, cher."

"What kind of a story?"

"A story that will make you a most happy lady."

Remembering she was buzzed, Lily Cup slurred another awkward invitation.

"Can we play after?"

Peck stood there.

"Just a little...a quickie, like that night?"

"Nah, nah."

"Millie is so lucky."

"Millie?"

"You're such a fucking prince."

Peck placed his hands on her shoulders, turned her, pointing her toward her back office.

"You won't have to do anything, Peck. I'd do it all."

"*Non, désolé.*" ("Sorry, no.")

"Can I smoke my cigar?"

"*Oui.*"

She took him by the hand and led him to her office in the back. She pointed at where he could sit and stepped to the side of her large walnut desk and pulled the window up a foot. From a neighboring saloon, sounds of a trumpet softly flowed up and into the room, as if a songbird of a New Orleans evening was flying by, making its rounds.

She plopped down into her desk chair and leaned back. The big leather wingback once was her father's and it seemed to swallow her. She kicked her heels off one at a time, lifted and rested her feet on the desktop, crossing bare legs at the ankles, concealing the black satin panties that had just seconds before made their first curtain call under her short tight skirt during her shoe removal and leg lift. She snipped the end of a cigar as though it was in the way, held a platinum lighter, rolled the Panatela with her fingers and puffed until the end was a burning coal glow. She caught his eye and winked.

"Tell me a story, big boy," she said, taking a puff.

"Once upon a time…" Peck started with a guffaw.

She snickered as best she could—sobering up and cigar smoking at the same time took thought and coordination. She didn't change her expression. She waited.

"It was after Valentine's Day, cher—I remember sure. I watched 'em dance late that night at Charlie's. You were there that night."

Lily Cup nodded.

"Gabe had to get house keys made next day. I didn't have my license, so he said he'd streetcar and walk or maybe, how you say, Uber."

"Taxi," Lily Cup said. "Gabe doesn't have a phone."

"Can I open the window bigger?" Peck asked.

"I'll do it," Lily Cup said.

She stood and pulled the window another foot higher. The trumpet sound was the same tone—a sad blues sound. She sat down and lifted her legs, Peck looking away so he wouldn't be obvious seeing her personal nature wrapped in smooth satin.

"Go on with the story."

"Gabe was using the machine that made keys, and a kid was at the next machine. Kid ax him for a credit card to use in his machine…and Gabe say no."

"Well of course he'd tell the little snot, no," Lily Cup said.

"The kid say he was going to kill him, so the manager walks Gabe to the streetcar— "

"The kid was a creep. This kind of thing happens every day."

"But he sees the kid outside the store waving a knife."

Lily Cup sat up and folded her legs Indian style in the chair, oblivious to the view from Peck's side of the desk.

"Knife?" Lily Cup asked.

"Knife," Peck said.

"The same kid who asked Gabe for his card had a knife? Pointing it?"

"Dass for true, cher. Kid had a knife."

"Were you with him, Peck?"

"Nah, nah, Gabe was alone."

"Did Gabe tell you this when it happened?"

"Tonight, cher—at the Columns. You know the Columns."

"The kid was a bully. But what's all this got to do with Gabe now?"

"The kid is dead now, cher," Peck said.

"The same kid is dead? The bully?"

"*Oui.*"

"What's that got to do—?"

"Same kid Gabe killed today."

"How did you know?"

Peck sat there.

"Why are you telling me this, Peck?"

"Maybe there's a video?"

"What store?"

"Walmart," Peck said.

She stood, pushed her skirt down on her thighs and stepped into her shoes.

"Did Gabe tell you all this in secret, Peck? Did he ask you not to talk about it?"

"Nah, nah, cher. We were eating shrimp when he told me."

"Did you drive tonight, Peck?"

"*Oui.*"

"Where's your truck?"

"Around the corner."

"You okay to drive?"

"*Oui.*"

She reached in her purse, pulled two fifties and tossed them to Peck.

"Here."

"Hanh?" Peck asked while stretching to catch the bills.

"You're now my investigator, Peck. That's a retainer. If anyone asks, you were paid to do research for one of my cases."

"Coo coo," Peck said.

"You can't tell what we talk about, got it?"

"Peck keeps his word and secrets, cher."

"Drive me to Walmart. I've been drinking and don't want a cab or Uber this late."

"Let's go," Peck said.

He sat in the pickup waiting in front of the Walmart for Lily Cup to come out. He was patient, as he took pride in her confidence in him, and that he understood the seriousness of her helping Gabe in the morning.

Eventually she walked out with a paper sack. She opened the door, set the sack on the seat and reached her hand for him to pull her up and in.

"Holy shit," Lily Cup said. "It doesn't get any better than this."

"How'd it go, cher?"

"You were right on the money, Peck. They have two tapes— and they're perfect," Lily Cup said.

"Two tapes?"

"One from inside the store and the manager says he can see things so clearly he could read his lips."

"That's good, then?" Peck asked.

"There's one taken outside with him waving the knife, just like you said. They'll be perfect."

"Did the manager remember?"

"The manager from that day wasn't working tonight, but this one— Larry Albright— called him at home. He remembered it all happening, he remembered Gabe, and he will be at the court whenever I need him."

"*Que Dieu vous benisse, Lily Cup.*" ("God bless you, Lily Cup.")

"Back at ya, Mr. Boudreaux Clemont Finch. None of this could have happened without your help, Mr. Investigator."

"That mean it's over now, cher?"

"Oh no, it's only started—but it's a hell of a start!"

"Does it mean Gabe innocent?"

"It means Gabe can maybe plead not guilty and get out on bond."

"That's good then, right?"

Peck reached in the bag to look at the DVD cases. There were none, only two pints of rye.

"Where they are, cher? The tapes?"

"Oh, they have to download them and copy them—I'll get the copies in the morning when the manager comes in."

"Ahhh."

"I have to figure a way to use this information."

"What you mean, cher?"

"I've got to get the DA to see them without opening a legal can of worms."

"Tell Peck."

"If Gabe goes to trial before I get the right people to see the videos, having them at all will be a gamble. The court may not allow them in—it happened in the past and now the kid is dead and can't defend himself. They can trump up legal bullshit like that."

"So, the more you give the DA man that proves Gabe is innocent before court, the better your chances?"

"Something like that."

"It's like baiting three snoods, cher."

"I have no idea what a snood is, Peck."

"If Peck need to catch a *bait* snake real bad, there's a special way to do it."

"Who's the *bait* snake, Peck, the DA?"

"Nah, nah, he the snapper, cher—he the prize."

"What do snakes have to do with snappers and what's a bait snake?"

"Bait snakes are for bait. They're crawfish snakes?"

"Snakes for bait?"

"*Oui*. Need bait snake to catch snapping turtles."

"So what are you sayin?"

"You in control, cher. Think like you the fisher."
"You're saying I need a snake for bait?"
"*Oui.*"
"And how do you propose—?"
"Jess catch one, cher."
"Are you saying you can catch a crawfish snake for bait anytime you want?"
"Pretty much, cher."
"Anytime you damn well please—guaranteed?"
"*Oui.*"
"Okay, I give—tell me."
"If you want a snake right now, quick-like, use you a live frog and hide the hook good."
"You use a frog that's still alive?"
"*Oui.*"
"How?"
"You hide the hook somewhere on it."
"And a live frog will guarantee you catch a crawfish snake?"
"*Oui.*"
"I'm not getting it, Peck. I thought crawfish snakes liked crawfish."
"They like frogs better."
"Crawfish snakes like frogs better than eating crawfish?"
"Cher, I seen a crawfish snake climb on the back of a gator sleepin' on a big ole log just to catch a frog settin' in the sun. They sure do like frogs good, dass for true."
"So what's your point? What's any of this got to do with a kid who's lying dead in the morgue and the DA?"
"You say you can't talk about nothin' without Gabe being there."
"It's the law."
"Maybe you should stop t'inkin' what you can't do, cher and start t'inkin' what you can do."
"We're back to the frog, I suppose."
"*Oui.*"
"You're saying I need a frog?"
"*Oui.*"
"So, you're saying if I could figure out what my live frog is, and I hide the hook on it and then find a way to get the DA and

some others to see these videos and hear what the store manager has to say—"

"That would end it, maybe?" Peck asked.

"Not sure."

"Why?"

"I haven't seen the dead body yet."

"What's that mean, cher?"

"Are you sure it's the same dude I saw on the video?"

"Same one. Gabe told me he crossed over St. Charles Street and on the sidewalk the same kid came up, pointing a knife at him and this time ax'n for his wallet and money."

"They didn't find a knife."

"He had a knife, cher."

"You know for sure the kid had a knife today and was pointing it?"

"Dass for true, cher."

"But they didn't find a weapon, Peck. That's pretty serious for Gabe."

"Gabe don't ever lie to Peck."

"If Gabe tells me it was self-defense when he saw the guy he killed today, I'll believe him. He's just not saying anything," Lily Cup said.

"He told me it was," Peck said.

"He hasn't told me anything, yet."

"He's sad, cher."

Out of the blue Peck bolts.

"That's it!" he barks.

"What's it?" Lily Cup said.

Peck sat up tall and with inspired confidence. He clicked his thumb and finger.

"Cher?"

"What!?"

"You say dat you can't talk what Gabe say—how you say—?"

"What?"

"Cher, in the breakroom you say there was a law you can't talk about anything what Gabe say."

"Attorney-client privilege?"

"Dass it, cher— attorney-client privilege."

"That's the law, Peck."

Peck started the truck and slowly pulled out of the parking lot.

"And you say Gabe won't talk?"

"He clammed up on me at the station—he won't talk."

"Then from now on maybe don't talk to Gabe about nothin' cher."

"What in the name of Blaze Starr are you talking about?"

"Dass your frog, cher."

"My frog?"

"To catch our bait snake."

"I need a drink, Peck. Take me home."

"Say tomorrow Gabe say it, say—self-defense—would the DA go away then, cher?"

"If not guilty is his plea tomorrow, the DA won't go away. It would go to preliminary hearing and then most likely the grand jury and then go to trial."

"Trial?"

"Not right away. The DA has to decide. He can take it to a grand jury or drop it."

"What's he t'inking, cher?"

"You mean with what he's got?"

"*Oui.*"

"A kid is dead—he knows Gabe killed him and he knows there's no weapon on the kid."

"Hokay."

"Gabe is screwed."

"What you need, cher?"

"If the defendant doesn't tell his attorney what happened—"

"You mean Gabe."

"—I can't build a defense if he won't talk. Take me home. I'll sleep a few hours."

Peck made his way through the nightlife like a gator in a murky swamp, avoiding traffic that might have been drinking and partying. He pulled in front of her house and brought the pickup to an idle.

"Can I ax you something, cher?"

"Park, I feel like talking."

"Hokay."

He pulled into her driveway.

She kicked off her heels and grabbed the paper sack. She hiked her skirt to mid-thigh while turning on the seat facing him, her back now leaning against the door. She folded her knees, her bare feet on the seat steadying her like a bookend. She pulled a pint of rye from the sack, opened it and took a swig.

"Turn it off," Lily Cup said.

He obliged.

"What did you want to ask?"

"Let me understand something, cher—"

"Okay."

"You say if Gabe tells you a whole lot of t'ings about what happened and how it happened and where and when, you know all that stuff—"

"I get it, I got it—what's your point?"

"If he tells you everything you can fight his case, right?"

"That's the way it works. At least I can try."

"But you can't tell what Gabe tell you to nobody who could help you before trial, right?"

"Right, not without Gabe's permission."

"What if Gabe don't never tell you anything?"

"Nothing?"

"Nothing, cher."

"Where're you going with this, Peck? What are you thinking?"

"Gabe don't say a word—what is it when all you know you hear the truth from what Peck here tole you—remember Gabe never tole you nothing?"

"Fuck."

"Is that how you say—?"

"Attorney-client privilege?"

"—attorney client privilege, cher?"

"You sure he didn't tell you about what happened in confidence, Peck?"

"What that mean, cher, confidence?"

"Did he tell you to keep it secret when he told you?"

"No way."

"Are you sure?"

"Like I say, he tole me while we was eating shrimp and grits. People at next table could hear. The lady even told him to watch his language."

"Then it would be hearsay."

"What's that, hearsay?"

"Somebody telling me what happened, not Gabe—that's hearsay."

"Dass your frog, cher—"

"You're saying?"

"—you can talk about what I tole you and maybe show the video too. I give'd you that too."

Lily Cup lifted the bottle for a belt, her eyes glazed over at how naturally instinctive it was for a boy who grew up in the swamps to put food on the table.

"That'd be all hearsay," Peck said.

She took another swig.

"Peck here is your frog, cher. Don't let Gabe talk—I'll tell you what I know."

"I wonder why he didn't tell me about the tapes?" Lily Cup asked.

"It's cuz I figured it out for him," Peck said.

"What do you mean?"

"He didn't remember. I think old man was sad from killing the kid."

Lily Cup gazed at Peck as if she were in awe of his insight. She had listened to stories of his accomplishments from Gabe and Sasha. He went from illiterate to earning his GED in nine months.

Peck was waiting for a reaction.

"Can you talk about what I say, cher, you know, that hearsay stuff if Gabe never say nothing to you?"

"Yes, I can."

"Then you need to bait some snoods with it, cher."

"I'll read up and figure approaches that won't land me in hot water."

"Read then, cher. Promise you'll read good."

"Do you believe him, Peck?"

"Ever' word, cher, Gabe don' lie."

She had a gaze of trust as if Peck was the brightest, most perceptive mind she'd seen, even at Harvard. He reminded her of a young her, a street-smart survivor.

"Are you really reading *Cannery Row*?" Lily Cup asked.

"Yes'm."

"Why *Cannery Row*?"

"I ax the lady for a book about oceans, fish, and frogs," Peck said. "She tell me, *Cannery Row*."

"Talk to me about why you ran away from home, Peck."

She reached between her bare knees and handed the opened pint to him. He sniffed the piquant, took a swig and handed it back, swallowing with wrenched lips.

"What you mean, cher?"

"When you were a little boy. You ran away from home."

"*Oui*."

"Sasha told me."

"Ah *oui*."

"How old were you?"

Peck started.

"I want to know what it was like."

He didn't appear offended with the question. To him his new friends like Lily Cup were genuine, loving, and honest to the core. He just wasn't certain how to answer.

"Scared."

"I can't imagine what it must have been like."

"I didn't have no shoes."

"You ran away barefoot?"

"I remember, dass for true."

"Didn't anyone try to help you?"

"Nah, nah."

"Didn't anyone see you running?"

"I hided from cars passing me, I saw a truck and hid in the back."

"How long were you running?"

"I run a long way but the truck took me to Carencro."

"No, not miles—how many hours?"

"It was night two times before I got to Carencro."

"Why Carencro? Did you know someone there?"

"Nah, nah—the truck stopped there and my leg was bleeding bad. I had to get off and sleep. Slept in a container at the slaughter house."

"Did you know it was a slaughter house? You couldn't read, could you?"

"I know'd the smell. I couldn't hardly breathe and I can tell the sounds. When I waked up I see a man and ax him what they was killin'. He say veal calves. I told the man can I bonk 'em full day for some rubber boots and sandwiches."

"Jesus, how old were you?"

"I could swim."

"You mean you just learned to swim?"

"*Oui.*"

"So, you were maybe eight or nine?"

"*Oui.*"

"Were you big for your age?"

"Big maybe. I just look old, I t'ink."

"Did the man give you boots?"

"*Oui.* They had a rip on the side.

"And?"

"He gived me sandwiches and a pickle."

"What did you have to do for them?"

"That time shovel out the back of his cattle truck. He let me bonk some calves that come through the opening. One bonk after the first couple times."

"What do you mean, bonk?"

"A steel pipe." He held his hands out. "About so long, filled with lead. I'd hold it tall and bring it down like a sledge between their eyes. I'd bonk 'em dead, one bonk."

Lily Cup lifted the bottle, took a glassy-eyed swig, slowly shaking her head.

"Other days I go back and work then come a lady she ax me how old I was. I told her I didn't know, and she fired me."

Lily Cup stretched her arm, held the pint between her spread bare knees. He took it and raised it for another swig.

"Did she let you keep the boots?"

"I walked away in 'em."

She shook her head as though she was waking from a bad dream.

"It's good it was so long ago. You probably don't remember a lot, and now you have Gabe and Millie."

"I'm going in the morning to find the truth," Peck said.

Lily Cup sat up, away from the door, looking startled, confused, and tipsy.

"What?"

"In the morning, I'm going. You can pick Gabe up maybe?"

"Where are you going?"

"Gabe say I need to find the truth about where I grow'd, so I can tell Millie the truth."

Lily Cup took a swig, corked the bottle and set it on the floor.

"Can you even remember where to go after all this time?" she asked, as she repositioned herself. Hoping to change the subject, she managed to lay on her stomach, putting a palm on his thigh, and resting her chin on the back of her hand.

"S'okay if I rest here?"

"Hokay."

"It's been a long time, Peck. Can you remember names and what any of them look like?"

"Foster nanna, gator man, Elizabeth—'tween Bayou Sorrel an' Choctaw. I remember."

"Who are they to you?"

"My foster nanna; gator man her boo—least he was then...Elizabeth, a special frien' in Anse La Butte."

Hearing 'gator man' Lily Cup perked her head up, reached and lifted the bottle from the sack on the floor of the truck.

"So, this gator man— "

"*Oui?*"

"Like is he, this gator man guy your father?"

"Nah, nah."

Lily Cup took a long thankful swig, put the bottle back in the bag and leaned her chin on his thigh again.

"And the special friend? What kind of special friend was she?" Lily Cup asked, looking up.

Peck grinned.

Her eyes devilishly smiling, she moved her hand to the bulge on his inner thigh pant leg and clenched William.

"Would you say Elizabeth is this kind of a special friend?"

"A frien', cher. She ain't no boo."
"Boo? You mean girlfriend?"
"*Oui*. Lover."
"Did you fuck?"
Peck's grinned silence spoke for him.
"Wait! When you were nine?" Lily Cup started.
"Nah, nah." Peck laughed. "Elizabeth in Anse La Butte long time after Peck run away."

Without moving her right hand from his thigh, she rose to her knees and unzipped his jeans with her left. Peck sat frozen, wondering his next move. Her warm hand slithered into the unzipped cavern, retrieving a throbbing William. She grasped and held it.

"This kind of special friend?" she repeated.

He pondered. It wasn't as if they weren't sexually familiar, but Millie was now in the equation—the girl he'd promised his heart and hand to. Lily Cup fondled William, stroking it with her forefinger and thumb watching it impatiently, like she was stopped and waiting for a red light to turn green. He glanced down at her hand touching William as though he was considering surrender. He looked out his side window to see if the coast was clear. He turned his head to look out the passenger side when he first saw a possible compromise. He prolonged his watch of the reflection from the passenger window of her on her knees, her butt up as she leaned down on him, her sensual black satin crotch and the seductive curves of her butt cheeks, her linen–white bare inner thighs. He pulled her hand away, lifted and kissed it and put William back in the barn and zipped up.

"It's the rye, cher," Peck said.

Lily Cup looked up in defeat and pouted. She pushed on his thigh for leverage, rising tall on her knees. Turning completely around on her knees, she bent over in the opposite direction, this time looking again for the bag and her bottle. He reached between her thighs up under her skirt from behind, gently cupping her love island with a soft hello just as she had earlier grabbed him.

"Oh?" She churned, jerking her head up like a kitten in heat with opportunity. She braced one arm on the front dash, the other on the door, arching her buttocks as a sign of welcome. Peck maneuvered his thumb gently in and under her panty crotch elastic and in between a moist warmth of love lips. With the feel, he started, opened his eyes, finding his outstretched arm reaching his hand under her panties his curled knuckles masking her pearl.

"Yes," she whispered, this time lowering her head.

His welcomed thumb moved inside her wet warmth and in slow, steady, never–ending circles it massaged the velvet wall of her inner G nerve endings until the streetlamp spotlighted her milky white silken–thighs flex and grip on his arm, again and again, her butt cheeks lifting and squeezing in aggressive, quick thrusts as in a hope the moment would become a day. The clenching of her crotch and the short, crisp gasps were signal of climax in perfect rhythm with her heaving stomach contractions. At the end a tight quiver and she went limp and rested.

She exhaled a "whew!" as if she were perfectly satisfied, followed by a deep breath and "Hot damn!" as if it was 'back to business.' He slowly removed his hand, patting her love island tenderly.

Her head fell, she looked under herself down between her legs and then reached and adjusted her panties.

A newsboy bicycling by threw that day's edition of an *Advocate* on her porch and caught Peck's eye.

"Don't worry, he's gay," Lily Cup panted.

Climbing from the pickup, she stood with the passenger door open and pushed her skirt down her thighs. She gathered herself and finger-brushed hair strands from her face. She reached in for the pints of rye in its paper sack. All in hand and leaning on the passenger seat, she looked over into Peck's eyes and smiled.

"You okay?" she whispered.

"Make it good for my frien', cher."

"The frog idea is genius, Peck."

"Pirogues are slow, cher, but they find gators."

"Don't worry about Gabe, honey. I'll take care of him."

He nodded.

"Peck, hint to Gabe to let me do the talking tomorrow."

"He'll be asleep."

"Wake him and tell him to catch a cab in the morning and that I may be late getting to court, but don't tell him why. I have to pick up the tapes. I'll text you the address and court he has to be in. But don't say any more to him."

"Hokay."

She straightened upright and stepped back.

"You sure we're okay, Peck?"

"We good, cher."

"What time are you heading out?"

"When I get up," Peck said.

"Take a phone charger."

"Yes'm."

"This Elizabeth, does she live in the area you're going?"

"Oui. Anse La Butte—near t'ings."

"Does she know about what happened to you there?"

"*Oui.*"

"Does she speak French?"

"Cajun French, *oui.*"

"Is she a good friend?"

"*Oui.*"

"Is she smart?"

"Ah *oui.*"

"Why don't you go see her first?"

"For true?"

"She maybe can help you. Go see her first."

"Hokay," Peck said.

"Be careful, Peck. It can be dangerous in those swamps."

"I know."

"You'll need a base so you won't have to sleep in the truck. Maybe Elizabeth will let you stay with her while you're looking around."

"Ah, *oui.*"

"Be careful."

Lily Cup lipped a smooch at Peck and stepped into her house.

CHAPTER 5

IT WAS A SMALL CAJUN RESTAURANT in a strip mall, just big enough to keep secrets in a corner with its blue and white checked tablecloths and curtains. A touting of Creole chicken and home-battered fish was on a hand-painted sign over the door. To the right of the restaurant was a locksmith; to the left an empty space that once sold lawn mowers and sparkplugs, with a *for rent* sign taped to the window.

Pulling in front of the restaurant, Peck stepped on the brake, paused in an idle as if he was thinking back, before he met Millie, how he and Elizabeth once passed lonely nights away from his fishing and mowing and away from her man on some oil rig weeks at a time. They were unintentional lovers; they chose to be friends. Their bond was in the holding and the talking and the laughter. Peck had grown up learning to be there for Elizabeth since their eyes first met. He had just turned nineteen, a lawn mower and fisherman. She was twenty-four, a sous chef.

Nearly five years before, he had walked the dozen miles from Carencro that 103-degree day in search of fishing holes and stopped to quench his thirst. Something brought them both to that store in nearby Anse La Butte at the same moment of the same day. At first sight, it was as if they were already together as he caught his own reflection in a glass door of the refrigerated water cabinet behind her. His hair was sun-bleached and trim; hers, long, brunette and brushed, framing a quiet beauty in her face and blocking her view of impressions her nipples made through the yellow T-shirt. His face and arms were a ruddy tan, while her face was ashen and her eyes an emerald green, and she seemed open for smiles over quiet delicate pastries or for sitting for an artist's canvas.

It was generally not in her nature to stare, so there must have been a reason they could not take their eyes from each other as Peck reached behind her for a bottle of water. Destiny nudged him to buy two bottles and the strangers refreshed with cold swallows on the hot summer sidewalk like pollywogs at play, and he walked backward in front of her and made things up to talk about in French, and she laughed and pulled a lock of hair away from her eyes and rolled it in her fingers and studied his eyes until they didn't seem like strangers and found themselves in front of her house. She liked him and invited him in.

"*J'ai plus d'eau dans la maison*, Peck," Elizabeth said. ("I have more water in the house, Peck.")

Only they knew the roads they'd traveled in secret moments of second lives. With or without a moon, they could sense when the loneliness of an empty bed would fill their night, and Peck would walk the eleven miles to be with her after his mowing in Carencro and Elizabeth would have a candle lit on the mantle if it was safe.

They'd sit in the tub, her legs wrapped around his waist and she'd wash his back and they would talk of where he could buy a spark plug for his mower and if she should frost her hair and would he like crepes and jam?

Peck climbed from his pickup, stepped over to the restaurant and pushed the door, ringing the same bell he remembered, sat on a stool at the red Formica counter and asked the waitress if she knew Elizabeth and if she might be coming in.

The girl disappeared behind the curtain of beads into the kitchen to inquire. A man in a white T-shirt, red bandana around his neck, and sporting a Saints' cap, came out, wiping his hands with a white towel.

"Elizabeth don't cook here no more, mon," he said.

"Did she move? I went by her house. It has a rent sign on front," Peck said.

"Elizabeth, she know you, *mon ami*?" he asked.

"*Oui, ça fait un moment que je l'ai vue,*" Peck said. ("Yes, it's been some time since I've seen her.")

"Let me call d' wife. She know, sure. Have you some creole chicken, *mon ami.* It's so good."

"Shicken, red beans, and coffee," Peck said.

"You like d' white or dark meat, *mon ami?*"

"I like shicken," Peck said.

"Comin' up. I call d' wife."

The man disappeared through the beads.

Peck turned and glanced out the front window at his khaki-colored pickup. His road trip to the Anse La Butte suburb of Breaux Bridge had taken the better part of three hours, but he was refreshed. He'd been to Anse La Butte many times to see Elizabeth, but he had walked before, from Carencro after his Thursday lawn-mowing duties at the hospice, and this was the first time he felt he wasn't an outsider. It was as though he belonged, having driven alone on an Interstate and parked in front of a Cajun restaurant in Breaux Bridge, just like other customers.

The girl came from the kitchen and placed a plate of chicken and a bowl of red beans in front of Peck, then a paper napkin, fork, and spoon. She set a coffee cup in front of him and filled it.

"It's fresh," she said. "Need cream?"

"Nah, nah," Peck said. "Sugar. T'ank you."

He spooned into the beans.

A firm, stocky, lady of medium height wearing cargo shorts and a white cotton shirt, a denim apron tied in the back, and a straw gardening hat, opened the door, ringing its bell. She walked over, removing gloves and stuffing them into her apron pockets.

"You the one asking about Elizabeth, hon?"

"Yes'm," Peck said.

"Can I sit with you?"

"Sure, yes ma'am."

She sat down.

"I'm Flora. What's your name, hon?"

"Peck is what they call me." He extended his hand. "I'm Boudreaux Clemont Finch."

"Carol," Flora said. "Get me a cup of green tea, will ya, sweetie?"

"She's told me about you," Flora said, shaking his hand. "Pleased to make your acquaintance."

"You know where Elizabeth is, Miss Flora?"

"Baton Rouge."

"Baton Rouge?"

"Moved over a month ago."

"Ahh."

"She didn't tell you?"

"Nah, nah," Peck said. "Peck's not seen her for a long time."

"Baton Rouge. She has a nice apartment in Baton Rouge. It's right downtown, close to her school," Flora said.

"She hokay? Elizabeth hokay?" Peck asked.

"She's fine, hon. Woman just got bored waiting on him every few weeks out here. She's a young girl. She told me she felt strangled, couldn't breathe. She wanted a city where she could meet people, go to restaurants, take some classes—you know, live a little."

"I know," Peck said. "She still his boo?"

"She's still with him, but I think it's getting a little thin, if you know my meaning—him gone a month at a time out on the rig."

"*Oui.*"

"She's getting into a cooking school, hon. Our Elizabeth will make quite a chef," Flora said.

"She like cooking, dass for true," Peck said.

"I'm thinking it was fine when you were coming by, but when you stopped coming around, things changed," Flora said.

"Changed, cher?"

"She seemed anxious, impatient about the little things."

"*Je comprends,*" Peck said. ("I understand.")

"She told me you might be by," Flora said. "She wanted me to tell you to come see her. She misses seeing you. I have her number. You want it?"

"Yes'm, please," Peck said.

"Where'd you drive in from? Carencro?"

"Nah, nah. New Or–lee–anh," Peck said.

"Honey, you must have already come through Baton Rouge to get here," Flora said.

She sipped her tea, staring off into the limbo of a wall as though she were thinking of Elizabeth feeling vibrations of Peck driving past her earlier.

"Imagine," Flora said. "Did you come through Baton Rouge or the other way, hon?"

"Baton Rouge, *oui*," Peck said.

"Imagine that."

"I know."

"Maybe it's a sign."

"*Oui*."

"Such a shame you didn't know."

"*Oui*."

"Baton Rouge isn't far, though. Finish the chicken. You can make it by early afternoon."

She penned Elizabeth's phone number on a slip of paper and handed it to him.

"What'd she say about Peck?"

Flora held her teacup with the palm of both hands and looked him in the eye.

"It was all good, hon. She said nice things about you."

"She did?"

"I know she misses you."

"We were just..." Peck started.

"Ain't none of my business what you two are," Flora said. "You're grown adults; life has its twists and turns. Good friends are not that easy to come by."

"Dass for true, Miss Flora."

"Ain't nobody's business how some steer through the turns, Peck."

"I'm tracking for truth now," Peck said.

"Truth?"

"About my real mamma. I'm going to go find my foster nanna and ax," Peck said. "I'm trying to know the truth about my real mamma."

"You from around here, honey?"

"Well—"

"Acadiana?"

"Yes'm, but Elizabeth's French is better. I'm thinking she maybe could help me good."

"Where exactly are you from?"

"Raised up in Bayou Chene," Peck said.

"Bayou Chene, you say?"

"Yes'm, and Bayou Sorrell, I think—over near Choctaw."

"Are you sure it was Bayou Chene?"

"Ah *oui*, I runned two whole nights. Bayou Chene."

Flora placed her palm on the back of his hand.

"Honey, just how long has it been since you've been back home?"

"Sixteen, fifteen years about, I reckon," Peck said.

"In all that time have you been in touch with your foster nanna?"

"Nah, nah, no ma'am," Peck said. "I runned away when—"

"That ain't none of my business why you left, hon—when you left—none of my business."

"*Pardon*," Peck said. ("Sorry.")

"And you say you haven't spoken with your foster nanna for a time?"

"Not since I runned."

"And you think she's in Bayou Chene?"

"Yes'm."

Flora looked over at waitress Carol.

"Carol, honey, get me a fresh tea."

She placed her palm on his hand again.

"Honey, there ain't no Bayou Chene."

"Hanh?"

"I hate to be the one to tell you, but Bayou Chene was flooded. Word was if it wasn't the water, it was the silt that buried people and animals alive. There ain't no Bayou Chene, hon."

"No Bayou Chene?"

"The whole town is under ten, twelve feet of silt."

He turned the spoon in his half-empty cup, staring out, as if he were trying to get his mind around what Flora had said.

"Dass for true, cher?"

"The whole town sunk, it's only a memory now—it's not even a ghost town, hon."

She nodded at Carol. "Get him some coffee, sweetie."

"Are you going to be all right, Peck?" Flora asked.

"Nah, nah, I'm hokay."

"I'm sorry to be the one that had to tell you, hon."

"T'anks for tellin' me, though."

"Your foster nanna must be up there in years."

"Been a long time since I seed her."

"How old would you say she'd be today?"

Peck held both hands out, counting on his fingers.

"I don't know, maybe sixty—maybe fifty."

"Oh no, hon," Flora said.

"Ah *oui*, I t'ink of her now as her bein' maybe fifty maybe back then."

"That couldn't be."

"I t'ink so, *oui*. I remember she didn't look old when I runned off," Peck said. "She was young."

"How old are you, Peck?"

"Twenty-five."

"You're twenty-five?"

"*Oui.*"

"Then you sure didn't run from Bayou Chene," Flora said. "I don't know what I was thinking."

"Hanh?" Peck asked.

"You couldn't have, hon."

"I couldn't?"

"Bayou Chene sunk in the sixties. Your foster nanna would have to be in her eighties, maybe in her nineties, if she was ever in Bayou Chene. The Atchafalaya Spillway levees kept flooding until it busted and the whole town and every living thing in it disappeared."

He stirred his coffee.

"I'm t'inking sixty, maybe fifty maybe."

"Maybe you just don't remember things right," Flora said.

Peck watched his spoon stir.

"You've been gone a long time, hon. Maybe it was another place and maybe your foster nanna could still be alive."

Peck lifted his phone from his pocket and began keying in a number.

"What're you doing?" Flora asked.

"Text Elizabeth."

Flora placed her palm on his hand, stopping his movement.

"Wait, hon."

"Hanh?"

"Why don't you let me text her for you?" Flora asked.

"I can text her good," Peck said.

"Carol," Flora said, "Get him a slice of key lime. On me, hon."

She leaned into his ear. "Ain't none of my business, but if a certain someone out on a rig sees a number showing up on his phone bill, there could be questions. Get my meaning?"

"*Oui*," Peck said.

"Let me text her for 'ya, hon. You use my phone to call her if she says okay."

"Good idea," Peck said. "I forgot…"

"Not to worry."

"T'anks, Miss Flora."

"Ain't none of it my business; nobody's business."

Her thumbs danced on the keys. There was an instant response. She read it first and held it up for Peck to read.

"Good," Peck said. "I'll go there."

"Finish your pie, hon. I'll run to the house and get her address. I'll send you with some fresh okra and tomatoes."

"Thank you, Miss Flora," Peck said.

"If you need to get her a message, text me, and I'll get her answer for you."

"You're a nice person, cher," Peck said.

"I try to be a good Christian like I was raised, praise Jesus," Flora said. "I'm a child of God doing His work. The paths we take are our own chosen journeys and the self-righteous can butt out. Ain't none of it anybody's business but your own."

As Flora was stepping from Breaux Bridge's only Cajun chicken and fish restaurant to go to her house behind, exactly 126 miles away, at the corners of Tulane and Broad avenues in New Orleans, the bailiff was opening the morning like a rooster crowing.

"Order in the court. All rise. Section M of the Criminal District Court is now in session. The Honorable Judge Lindsay

Fontenot presiding. Silence is commanded under penalty of fine or imprisonment. God save this state and this honorable court. Please be seated. There is no talking in the audience. Good morning, Judge."

The bailiff stood in this magistrate court and spoke with loud, officious resonance.

"The State of Louisiana calls Gabriel Jordan. The defendant will rise," the bailiff said.

Gabe looked about for Lily Cup, who was not in the court room. He stood. The bailiff swore him in.

"Remain standing," the bailiff said as he turned and walked to a waiting chair by the court reporter, busily typing away.

The judge adjusted her microphone.

"District Attorney Holbrook?" the judge asked.

"Your Honor, the defendant is being charged with second-degree murder."

"Mr. Jordan, do you have an attorney? If you can't afford one, I will appoint a public defender for you."

"I have one, Your Honor. I'm sure she'll be along."

"Who's your attorney?" Judge Fontenot asked.

"Lily Cup Lorelei Tarleton, Your Honor."

"Be seated, Mr. Jordan, "Judge Fontenot said. "Bailiff do you have Ms. Tarleton's cell number?"

The bailiff scribbled on a piece of paper and handed it to the judge. The judge handed it to her assistant who lifted a cellphone, tapped the number and put it to her ear.

"She's not answering her phone, Your Honor," the assistant said.

"District Attorney Holbrook, as this is an arraignment, we can either move it to another day or have a public defender stand in for Ms. Tarleton during her absence."

"The state wishes to move forward, Your Honor," District Attorney Holbrook said.

"Will the defendant rise," Judge Fontenot said.

Gabe stood.

"Defendant Gabriel Jordan, at the time you were arrested were you read your Miranda Rights?"

"Yes, Your Honor, they read them to me."

"Murder is a serious crime," Judge Fontenot said. "The court has options of temporarily appointing—"

Lily Cup interrupted by pushing the court room doors open wide, announcing her attendance as she rushed down the aisle.

"I'm sorry, Your Honor—I had to pick something up and it wasn't ready—I had to wait, the traffic—the whole morning."

"We have a busy docket, counselor."

"Your Honor, I didn't know about this until one a.m. this morning. I'm sorry and ask the court's indulgence. I'm here now."

Lily Cup set her leather satchel on the table and sat next to Gabe, who was still standing.

"Counselor Tarleton is your attorney, Mr. Jordan?"

"She is, Your Honor," Gabe said. He pointed to Lily Cup seated beside him. The judge spoke to the court reporter.

"Let the record show that counsel for the defendant is Ms. Tarleton."

The judge looked at Lily Cup, then at Gabe.

"Gabriel Jordan, you are being charged with the violation of a criminal code written and enforced by the Louisiana State Legislature. The code is RS 14:30.1. I must inform you that statute 30.1 is second-degree murder—the killing of a human being. Under the definition of the charges—the offender, that would be you—had a specific intent to kill or inflict great bodily harm."

The judge lowered her head and peered over the tops of her reading glasses.

"Do you understand the charges as read by me?"

"I understand them, Your Honor," Gabe said.

"By this statute, whoever commits the crime of second-degree murder shall be punished by life imprisonment at hard labor without benefit of parole, probation, or suspension of sentence. Do you understand the penalties as I have read them?"

"I understand, Your Honor."

"How do you plead to these charges?" Judge Fontenot asked.

Lily Cup stood.

"Captain Jordan pleads not guilty, Your Honor."

Lily Cup leaned and whispered into Gabe's ear, "I have a plan." She straightens and addresses the judge.

"The court will now consider bail and—" the judge started.

"Your Honor," the district attorney said. "This was a most heinous crime. A young man in the prime of life—of college age—bludgeoned repeatedly by a hardened military officer. I pray the court refuse bond. The man is capable of doing it again, Judge Fontenot."

"District Attorney Holbrook—"

"I'm not speaking without cause, Your Honor. The man has scurrilously rearmed himself and sits here defiantly in your courtroom, a weapon at his side."

"Weapon?" Judge Fontenot asked.

"He has a cane, Your Honor."

"Counselor Tarleton, just how did the defendant get that cane past security?" the judge asked.

Lily Cup leaned toward Gabe and whispered.

"They didn't stop you?"

"I showed them my military ID, they ran my cane through the x-ray conveyor and handed it back to me. Nobody said a word."

"Your Honor, the defendant did not slip through security—security permitted him through."

"How did the defendant get through security with a cane?" Judge Fontenot asked.

"Your Honor, the District Court's security inspected the cane and let the defendant pass," Lily Cup said. "By law's definition a cane is not considered a weapon, no more than a wheelchair is. There is nothing hidden in his cane. My client walks with a cane."

Judge Fontenot penned a note and handed it to her assistant for follow-through.

"Your Honor, the defendant has served honorably in the Korean and Vietnam conflicts," Lily Cup said. "He has been decorated numerous times. He does not run from his responsibilities. He walks with a cane. There is no law prohibiting the use of a cane. They are allowed on commercial airplanes."

The judge's assistant returned to the bench and handed the judge a slip of paper.

The judge read it and looked at the court reporter.

"Let the record show the defendant's cane had been examined and approved by security."

"I would like my concern noted—" the DA started.

"So noted," Judge Fontenot said.

"—and the state will fight bond, Judge Fontenot."

"Your request is noted. Will the defendant stand?" Judge Fontenot asked.

Gabe stood, and Lily Cup stood as quickly.

"Your Honor," Lily Cup said. "May I approach the bench?"

"So soon?" the judge asked.

"Your Honor?"

"Approach."

Lily Cup stepped to the aisle and walked to the right of the bench, the DA by her side. Judge Fontenot put a hand over the microphone and leaned in.

"Your Honor, I have good reason to ask—"

"You're here Counselor Tarleton, ask."

"I'm asking the court to consider a pretrial conference."

"You mean a preliminary hearing. I plan to schedule it—after bail is determined," the judge asked.

"No, Your Honor, I mean a pretrial conference."

"Now?"

"Yes, Judge."

"Counselor Tarleton, this case hasn't even been to the Grand Jury. We're nowhere close to a trial."

"There are extenuating circumstances in this case, Judge, I think—"

"Your Honor," the DA barked in a whisper. "The facts are clear."

"Let me understand. You're asking for a pretrial conference before we even know there'll be a trial?" Judge Fontenot asked.

"You have the power to request one, Your Honor."

"Counselor, you'll have opportunities to negotiate a disposition."

"I don't wish to negotiate a disposition, Your Honor."

"You're asking me to interrupt proceedings and have it here, now?"

"Your Honor, there are times when legal issues must be resolved before a trial."

"That's what Preliminary Hearings are for, Counselor Tarleton," District Attorney Holbrook whispered.

"Counselor, we're not—" Judge Fontenot started.

"Perhaps if we discussed it in your chamber, off the record, Judge, that would be best," Lily Cup said.

"I could clear the courtroom," Judge Fontenot said.

"This is a stall, Your Honor," the DA said.

"Please, Judge Fontenot," Lily Cup said.

"Give me a good reason," Judge Fontenot said.

"Your Honor, television documentaries have named New Orleans the most violent city in the western hemisphere."

"I'm well aware, Counselor."

"Murder capital, they called us."

"Do you have a point to make, Counselor?"

"We have an audience of hungry press people sitting in this courtroom waiting to be fed so they can draw conclusions just to make news at our expense."

"A man has been murdered, Counselor."

"Clearing the courtroom so we can meet in here will only raise their ire," Judge—"

"The press is paid to be here, Counselor."

"—if, on the other hand, you call a pretrial conference, which you have the power to do, closed, off the record, and in your chamber. That won't raise suspicion."

"District Attorney Holbrook?" Judge Fontenot asked.

"I think it's a stall, Judge, but I'll oblige the court's decision."

"If we're all together—the district attorney, the assistant district attorney, you and me, Judge, it can be off the record—" Lily Cup started.

"What you're really saying is with no press," the judge said.

"No press, no court reporter, and no New Orleans Visitor Bureau."

"It's that important to you?" the judge asked.

"It's that important to New Orleans," Lily Cup said.

"Go back to your seats. Let me consider it and look at my schedule," Judge Fontenot said.

After a quiet visit with her clerk of courts Judge Fontenot looked at Gabe, still standing.

"Captain Jordan," the judge said. "The court is ordering a pretrial conference in my chamber. I'm releasing you on a twenty-five-thousand-dollar bond."

"But Your Honor," Lily Cup said.

"No bail, Your Honor, the defendant is a dangerous man," District Attorney Holbrook said.

"Twenty-five-thousand dollars for a man who is a decorated military officer, a veteran who served honorably in two wars?" Lily Cup asked.

"Twenty-five-thousand dollars."

"Your Honor, the ordeal alone has taken a toll on his health."

"Murder often does that," District Attorney Holbrook said.

"Bail is set," Judge Fontenot said.

"Your Honor, my client doesn't pose any threat of skipping out."

"I want to send a clear message of how seriously the people of Louisiana take these matters. Twenty-five-thousand-dollar bond."

The judge slammed her gavel.

"Your Honor," the DA said. "I would like it noted that counselor's request for pretrial conference is a delay tactic of the unprepared—an unnecessary delay."

"Miss Tarleton is respected in our courtroom," Judge Fontenot said. "I am trusting she won't waste the court's time. Captain Jordan, you're excused. Counselor Tarleton, please see the defendant settles with the bailiff. Captain Jordan, your attorney will be apprised of the date and time you will need to be in court."

"I'll be here. You have my word, Your Honor," Gabe said.

"This court is adjourned until further notice," Judge Fontenot said, pounding the gavel.

"Will counsel for the defense, District Attorney and the Assistant District Attorney meet in my chamber?"

Lily Cup whispered to Gabe.

"Go straight home, Gabe. Talk to no one out in the hall or in front of the courthouse. Catch a cab and go home."

"I will."

"When you get there, don't answer the door for anybody. I'll come by later."

Chapter 6

IT WAS A SECOND-FLOOR APARTMENT in a newer building on South Fourteenth Street in Baton Rouge—commutable to the cooking academy and her restaurant job. Elizabeth pulled the door open. She was barefoot in sun-bleached jeans with threaded holes in the knees and a short-sleeve, yellow V-neck sweater and no bra. Elizabeth didn't need a bra. She leaned her head on the door and smiled a lingering "hold me" smile, but it was the city, and there were neighbors.

"Come on in," Elizabeth said.

He stepped in, closed the door behind him and turned into her arms, folding around him tightly, her cheek pressing into the side of his neck with a pout as if she was remembering her nightmares of never seeing him again.

"Hi, cher..." Peck said.

"Shhhhh," Elizabeth whispered.

The hold lingered.

"*Un sandwich aux oeufs?*" Elizabeth asked. ("An egg sandwich?")

"*Bien,*" Peck said. ("Sure.")

"You didn't walk?" Elizabeth asked.

"*Non.*"

"I have to hear about the man who doesn't walk now, *mon ami.*"

He picked a postcard from the kitchen counter.

"See this," he said. He turned the card over and read it slowly, deliberately.

"Special pre-summer carpet cleaning."

She raised her hands to her face. "You read?"

"*Oui.*"

She approached with arms out and hugged him with warm, happy congratulations, a pride in having believed in him.

"*Je suis si fierè. Tellement heureuse,*" Elizabeth said. ("I am so proud. So happy.")

"What does *pre-summer* mean?" Peck asked.

"Before. Pre-summer means before summer," Elizabeth replied.

"Ahh," Peck said. "Maybe it's good help if we speak English?"

She took his face in her hands, leaned in, kissing him sensuously, her tongue darting under his upper lip, nibbling it, pulling on it with her lips.

She leaned back. "We still do some French things maybe, *non*?"

"*Oui*," Peck said.

"*Bonne.*"

She kissed his nose and stepped back.

"Egg sandwiches," she said, turning into the kitchen. "Did you bring a bag?"

"How long before…?" Peck started.

"Before we're not alone again?"

"*Oui.*"

"He left for the rig two days ago. We have a few weeks. Can you stay a few weeks?"

"Nah, nah," Peck said. "But some time, sure. Maybe you can help me with something."

"Do you have a bag?" Elizabeth asked.

"*Oui.*"

"Make sure you're parked legally. They ticket around here. The gate code is seven, three, two, five—can you remember that?"

"Seven, three, two, five. I'll remember."

"Are you still living in Carencro?"

"Nah, nah. I'm in New Or–lee–anhs."

"We are so fancy. I must hear about my big-city boy. Get your bag. You're my cousin, don't forget," Elizabeth said.

"I won't forget, cher."

As Peck pulled the door behind him on South Fourteenth Street in Baton Rouge, it was in the Orleans Parish Criminal District Court in New Orleans, that Judge Fontenot's chamber door was being closed by the judge herself.

"Sorry for the delay, folks," the judge said. "I had some reshuffling with my bailiff. Would anyone like coffee?"

Judge Fontenot sat in her chair. Seated in the room were the district attorney, the assistant district attorney, and Lily Cup.

"Judge Fontenot," the DA said, "this is—"

"I'd like some coffee," Lily Cup said.

"I would too," the judge said. She picked up her phone, buzzed her assistant.

"Pamela, can you arrange coffee and trimmings for two...?"

She looked around the room for other coffee takers. The assistant district attorney raised his finger, much to his senior's scowl. "Three cups. Thank you, Pamela."

"Your Honor..." the DA began.

"I mean what's the pleasure of having a conference in a judge's chamber if the judge can't show off and serve coffee?" Judge Fontenot asked.

The judge noticed the district attorney looking at his wristwatch impatiently. "The city has enough crime," she said. "I'm only trying to lighten the tension."

"With all due respect, Judge—"

"There's blind justice, District Attorney, and there is blind rage. I ask you to join me in respecting our colleague and let's have a listen to what she has to offer."

"—the people of Louisiana are protected under the law and only the law," the DA said.

"How was it, Bob, that you waited nearly forty minutes with a filled courtroom to express concern about a weapon? A wrong party might consider that a bit of grandstanding."

"I didn't see the cane until the defendant stood up, Judge."

The coffee came and was served about.

"Should we have a court reporter, Your Honor?" The DA asked.

"This is a pretrial conference and so long as you, the district attorney, the assistant district attorney and the defendant's council—in short, all sides are present—there can be no surprises. We can be off the record."

"Thank you, Judge," Lily Cup said. "I'm asking for a forty-eight-hour delay in scheduling a preliminary hearing."

"Your Honor, criminal pretrial conferences are for—" the district attorney started.

Lily Cup snapped. "I know what they're for, Bob—if you'll give me a chance."

"Tell us why we're here, counselor," Judge Fontenot said.

"I need some time," Lily Cup said.

"The people will need more than a 'the defense needs time' to delay a preliminary hearing," the DA said. "They're looking for answers."

"Judge, on February fifteenth, a man was inside a Walmart, at the key-making machine, making house keys for his home."

"This is not a trial, Judge," the DA said. "Why is counsel presenting evidence?"

"I'm not presenting evidence, I'm telling you a story that may be of interest to the city of New Orleans and the court," Lily Cup said.

"Counselor Tarleton, are you toying with a defendant's right to attorney-client privilege?"

"Judge, I haven't spoken with my client about the case."

"Excuse me?"

"I've asked, but he's not talking. A police sergeant called me when the defendant was arrested. I bailed him out—"

"This seems to be your problem and not the court's," the judge said.

"Judge, my client is a friend of mine, a hospice survivor. He's not a murderer. I just need a forty-eight-hour delay. Please, Your Honor."

"Forty-eight hours to try to get your client to talk to you?"

"Without a weapon, we're screwed, Judge. I need time."

"District Attorney Holbrook?" the judge asked.

"What's on your mind, Lily Cup? I have a city to answer to," District Attorney Holbrook said.

"You know me well enough, Bob. I wouldn't be asking this if I wasn't right. Give me an hour with you in your office and then give me 24 hours to sniff around."

"It's your call, District Attorney Holbrook," Judge Fontenot said.

"Thank you, Judge," Lily Cup said. "I need your help, Bob."

"My help for what?" the district attorney asked.

"You can pull strings—I've helped you before. You owe me."

"A quid pro quo on a murder?" Judge Fontenot asked.

"One day?" the district attorney asked.

Lily Cup looked at her watch. "I need forty-eight hours."

"We can't meet here," the district attorney said.

"Let's go to your office first and then to Dooky Chase for lunch, my treat," Lily Cup said.

Judge Fontenot picked up her cellphone and pressed a key.

"Commander's Palace, how may we be of service?"

"This is Judge Fontenot. Might I get a table for three at seven, please? No occasion—a night out with my daughter, just home from college."

She stood, gathering her purse and her briefcase.

"Judge Fontenot, if you'll give her the forty-eight hours, I can give her an hour in my office."

"Done," the judge said. "You have forty-eight hours, counselor."

"Thank you, Judge," Lily Cup said.

"Preliminary hearing in two days," the judge said. "Play nice, you two."

In the DA's office a clerk handed Lily Cup and District Attorney Holbrook bottles of water, waited for them to go into the office and pulled the door closed behind them.

"You have the floor," Holbrook said.

"Bob, on February fifteen," Lily Cup said, "a young man was standing at a vending machine at Walmart that was beside a machine a man was making house keys on. The young man turned several times, asking the key man for the use of one of his credit cards for the vending machine he was standing in front of. The key man turned him down each time. The young man turned again and threatened to kill the key man the minute he left the store and got outside."

"Were you there?" the DA asked.

"I wasn't," Lily Cup said.

"I'm to listen to hearsay?" the DA asked.

"I have it on this tape," Lily Cup said, holding it up. "It's the Walmart security video tape showing that incident, just as I said."

"That incident has nothing to do with this docket and security tapes do not record conversations," the DA said.

"I had a lip reader read the man's lips. I have it typed here."

"You know it won't be admissible."

"I know, but I just want you to read it."

"You read it," the DA said.

"Here goes: The young man says—*'You can't? You're telling me you can't? You're a lying old motherfucker. You are dead, you motherfucker, the second you step out of this store. You are a dead man.'*"

"You say this happened weeks ago? What is the relevance?" the DA asked.

Lily Cup placed the DVD into a television monitor. She pressed play and ran it through, reversed it and ran it through again and again.

"This proves nothing," the district attorney said.

"I have another DVD," Lily Cup said. "Same day, same Walmart, nine minutes later. Watch this."

She turned the player on.

"Bob, the kid is brandishing a weapon. A knife. The old man he's threatening is my client."

The DA did not respond. He sat back in his desk chair, he swirled around and looked out the window. Lily Cup sat and waited for his reaction.

"I take it this kid in the video is the corpse we have in the morgue."

"Same one."

"Any idea why the courtroom was full?" the DA asked.

"The NOLA Film Festival this weekend. They're filling hotels with Hollywood and press," Lily Cup said. "Press snooping around, is my guess."

"Without a weapon you don't have much of a case," the DA said.

"Without a weapon, I'm fucked," Lily Cup said.

The DA lifted his bottle of water and took a swig. Lowering it he paused as though he had an inspiration.

"Yes!" the DA said to himself with a snap.

His chair swiveled around.

"Larry Gaines," he said.

"Larry Gaines?" Lily Cup asked.

"Larry Gaines."

"I know the name," Lily Cup said. "Larry Gaines, where do I know it."

"Lieutenant Larry Gaines, he's a detective. He works the Quarter."

"That's where I know him. What about him?"

"He's the best there is, and I trust him," the DA said.

"I think I know—" Lily Cup started.

"Call him up. Ask my clerk for his number. Tell him the spot you're in."

"Can he just drop what he's doing and—?"

"He's on vacation. I had dinner with him Saturday. Call him."

"Thanks, Bob. I owe you."

"You're good for it."

Lily Cup stood and smiled, embracing her valise and video disks.

"You mean that?"

"I know you, Lily Cup. This guy is too close to you somehow."

"I've known him almost a year. He's a friend. This is so not him, premeditated murder."

"You're way too close to him."

"I am, I know."

"Don't let it get so close you can't see straight."

"I'll be careful."

"Call Larry."

"Thanks, Bob."

"Good luck, but know right now, if you don't come up with something more than what you've got, your client's dead meat. I'll nail him."

Lily Cup left the office, found her car and drove to Orleans Avenue and parked around the corner of the Dooky Chase restaurant. She was still burning off a rye hangover, the stress of the arraignment and Leah's gumbo was just the ticket she needed. She made her way up the steps, looked at the picture of President Obama and the inimitable Leah Chase eating together and she stepped into the dining room and up to the hostess podium.

"No reservations, sorry," Lily Cup said.

"Not a problem, Ms. Tarleton, let me take a look," the hostess said.

"Is Ms. Leah here, hon?"

"She is, Ms. Tarleton, how are you today?"

"Hungry and hung over."

"Well you've come to the right place."

"Think I can see Ms. Leah before I leave?"

"I'll tell her you're here. I'm sure she'll want to see you. Let me seat you and I'll come let you know."

Lily Cup chose to do the buffet. Her first order of business was a bowl of New Orleans' world-famous Dooky Chase seafood gumbo. Two pieces of cornbread, of course. At the table Lily Cup spooned her gumbo in a pensive manner, as if her mind was stirring about what a dangerous position Gabe was in. It was as if she was thinking he was giving up on life and wanted to be punished for taking a life, regardless of the reason. She enjoyed a small helping of potato salad when the hostess came to her table.

"Leah would love to see you, Ms. Tarleton."

When she was finished, Lily Cup settled her tab and stepped back into the famous Dooky Chase kitchen. Chef Leah Chase wearing her iconic red chef coat was sitting behind a small table stacked with papers. It was in the heart of the kitchen's activity. Leah caught Lily Cup's eyes walking in and beamed her famous smile. They kissed cheeks with Lily Cup squatting down to talk, resting her arms on the table top.

"Gabe's in trouble, Leah."

Leah started. She rested her hand on Lily Cup's hand and patted it gently.

"Why, how can that beautiful man be in trouble?"

"He's killed somebody?"

Leah started again, sat up, her hands clasped. She lifted her hands to her face and rested fingers on her mouth. It was as if more than seventy years of Jim Crow was coming back. The civil rights movements she had lived through, Martin Luther King eating and meeting in her back rooms—memories of her Dooky Chase serving all colors regardless of the law—it was as if it was all coming back."

"Who did that beautiful man—?"

She couldn't say the word.

"He's a kid, Leah—twenty-two, we think."

"A child," Leah said.

"Pretty much," Lily Cup said.

"Does the young man have a name?"

"He was a John Doe."

Leah knew the buzz words, the slang. She listened.

"Prints came back, identified him as a Kenneth Bauer."

"Why did it take prints to identify that boy?"

"He didn't have any identification on him?"

"Was he a brother?"

"No, Leah, he wasn't."

"Gabe—and a white boy?"

"Yes."

"A local?"

"We don't know."

"An Acadian boy?"

"We don't know yet, Leah."

"There was no identification on his person?"

"No."

"So, his wallet was missing?"

"His wallet was on him, Leah—and it was filled with various things, but no identification, no photographs, no addresses of any kind."

"Officers were on the scene?"

"Immediately."

Leah looked into Lily Cup's eyes for the big answer. Lily Cup knew what she was looking for.

"The officer, was he?"

"The officer was black, Leah."

"How did—?"

"Gabe's cane. He did it with his cane—you know, his walking stick. The young man pulled a knife on him and I'm pretty sure it was self-defense, but Gabe's totally depressed about killing someone. He's not talking."

"Would you tell that beautiful man he has my prayers?"

"I'll tell him, Leah."

"The boy has my prayers, as well."

Leah reached and took Lily Cups hand and held it.

"I've seen it too many times," Leah said. "The spoils our floods and desperate hurricanes cause attract wrong intentions. They come to New Orleans like pirates. After the shop windows are repaired and the evacuated homes are again inhabited, they turn from looting to menacing our citizens and tourists, and in this case a vulnerable senior—a beautiful black man."

"My problem, Leah, is without a knife my hands are tied—the law is the law—and it goes to trial if there is an indictment, which sounds likely."

Leah took and squeezed Lily Cup's hand.

"Lily Cup, you listen to Leah now. I've seen it all. There's some good in everybody. Sometimes they have trouble finding it. New Orleans is like no other place. There are times—times in the shadows and devastation of our hurricanes and our floods—when to the world we—under sea level and where the Mississippi empties into the world—we must resemble the old untamed west."

"Leah, that's beautiful—and saying it politely."

"We must be strong and streetwise for everyone's survival and sanity and for our community's benefit.

"The judge has given me forty-eight hours."

"That's a lifetime, my friend. Anything you need from Leah, you come by. You've got my prayers."

"Thank you, Leah."

Minutes later Peck's phone beeped, waking him. It was a text from Lily Cup. He also had an unread one from Millie.

"Pray," Lily Cup's text said. "We'll know in a couple of days. I'm at Dooky Chase for chicken."

He looked at the next text, from Millie:

"I love you, hunk—baby Charlie says hello."

He closed his eyes and rolled over, returning to his nap. Elizabeth was in the kitchen, wooden spoon in hand, a fresh French loaf on the counter and her butter sauce carefully being stirred in a copper pot; a dark Bordeaux stood by, waiting to be opened and decanted.

Elizabeth was smiling.

CHAPTER 7

LONELY DRONES OF THE SAX floated from Charlie's Blue Note as Gabe stepped from Frenchmen Street into the alley. It was as if another night was celebrating the old man's life and welcoming him with a grace.

Vaaaa vaaaa da veeeeeee...Vaaaa ve voooo vaa vaa vava ve voooooon.

Familiar velvet sounds were reaching out, as they had the night he and Peck first walked into the city a year before. The sax seemed to offer promise and calm for the old man, jazz aficionado, dancer, and troubled soul. He pushed the door open, stopping its return with his cane. Holding the jamb with a grip, he stepped up and in. On the small stage in the far-left corner, his favorite quartet was playing blues. The tall, broad-shouldered sax man, a blue–black faced brother with gentle eyes, caught his friend's eye and winked welcome during a rambling ride down to a long and low B flat.

Sasha's perfect form perched on her preferred stool at the end of the bar. She was in one of her dance-night ensembles—a red satin strapless Chanel designer gown so haute it was insured. Her elbow posed on the bar, a lipstick–smudged martini glass delicately balanced in her fingertips. Eyeing Gabe through a wall mirror, she begged Charlie's pardon for the interruption and for a Chivas on the rocks for their friend. Turning on the stool, she lowered a Cyd Charisse–like long leg to the floor, baring a slender, snowy white thigh above a sheer stocking carefully puckered to a black satin garter strap button. She stood and organized the dress as if it were a first dance at the prom, lifted her martini in one hand, a tumbler of scotch in the other, and ambled with a sway to the music, elbows out, balancing the drinks, her celebrated cleavage leading the way toward his usual table by the band. Gabe rose, pulling out a chair.

"You look ravishing, darling," Gabe said. "Make an old man happy. Do sit."

"Give a hug, baby," Sasha said. "Been worried sick all day."

She set the drinks down and they embraced, her cheek buried into his neck. She lifted her head, kissing his neck.

"Buy a damn phone so I can find you," Sasha said.

"Never," Gabe said.

"Did he hurt you?"

"Who told you?"

"Peck. He texted me some of it and said that Lily Cup would explain but she hasn't answered her phone all day."

"It's been a day," Gabe said. "No telling where she is."

"You okay, Gabe?"

"Okay is not a word that comes to mind, darlin'. A boy is dead," Gabe said.

"What happened in court must have been good, you're here?" Sasha asked.

"Can we dance?" Gabe asked.

The band was midway into a sax rift of "Louisiana Blues." He took her by the hand, wrapped an arm around her waist and pulled her to him. He tapped his toe three times slow—a fourth time—a fifth time, then pulled her hips in syncopation, and they swayed, turned, and started it again. They moved about their corner of the room like they were instruments in the band—as if they'd spent a lifetime together on dance floors just off Frenchmen Street. In one turn Gabe caught the eye of the sax man and winked as the song's sound was fading to close. The sax man looked over at his drummer, caught his eye, then at the bass, then the trumpet man.

"Our brother wants it easy, just one more time, gentlemen," sax man said. "And one, two, three," he said, clicking his finger and thumb.

The band ripped into "Louisiana Blues" again. Gabe was now in the zone, moving in perfect sync with her, the lady who saw to it he was able to dance one more time. She had saved his life the year before. As the sounds of the second playing faded, he turned her slowly, carefully dipping her, smiling into her eyes.

"If I was half my age, your James would be out the door, my darling," Gabe said.

"Now you tell me," Sasha said.

"I would wrap you in my arms and blanket your body with roses," Gabe said.

"I love it when you talk dirty," Sasha said.

He righted them and they embraced. Arm-in-arm they made their way back to the table. Seated, she reached both hands across and held his.

"How are you?"

Gabe looked at her.

"Tell me true."

"Much better now that I've danced with my best girl," Gabe said.

"Lily Cup's phone is still turned off. All her office says is she's in meetings," Sasha said. "How'd it go in court?"

He looked at his watch. "I guess they're still at it. The judge said they'd let me know when I had to be back."

"That bastard," Sasha said.

"The judge?"

"No, the prick that tried to kill you."

Gabe lifted his hand, softly touching her lips with two fingers. "Not tonight, baby," he said.

She knew what he was saying. Ever since they met, Charlie's Blue Note was off limits for business talk. It was their escape. Dance was their escape, away from the real world. Several nights a month Sasha would leave the real estate world behind her and *slut-up,* as she and Lily Cup still called it, just to dance to jazz and blues. In priceless strapless Chanels that presented her "girls" to best advantage, the finest Prada heels, and Cartier ornaments Sasha dressed to the nines with the sole intention of coming to Charlie's Blue Note to dance.

"They're playing Joe Williams, baby," Gabe said.

He stood, his hand extended. The two intertwined like fine Christmas ribbon wrapping each other in sway and turn with the sounds, the vibrations of the sax, a skitter scattering of brushes on a snare, a heart-thumping, stringed bass.

With the twisting and turning he mumbled into song, his own Joe Williams in her ear.

"Git out my life, woman. You don't love me no more... no, no," Gabe sang.

They would jerk into a turn, then back and forth as one.

"Git out my eyes, teardrops...I got to see my way around," Gabe sang.

She pulled her left hand from his, reached up and placed fingers over his mouth.

"Dance, Joe Williams, just dance," Sasha said.

She took his hand again.

He lowered his right hand from her waist and patted her buttocks a sensual scold, and then held her waist again. She grinned and kissed his neck. The sax player quietly clapped his hands, celebrating Gabe's vocal rendition. It was five more dances before they sat and ordered red beans and rice, and more drinks.

"My darlin', can old Gabe here broach a subject—something that's been preying on my mind?"

"Broach?" Sasha asked. "Sounds like bad jewelry."

"It's about James," Gabe said.

"Where's Peck?" Sasha asked.

"Did he mention in his texts? He got accepted into Tulane," Gabe said.

"What a guy," Sasha said. "His tutor told me he was ready."

"He starts night school in a few weeks. Isn't that something?"

"Where is he tonight? You shouldn't be out alone this late."

"Peck's gone," Gabe said.

"A trip."

"What sort of trip? To see Millie?"

"He wanted to check out his past," Gabe said.

"You mean he's gone to mow the old bird's lawn at the hospice in Carencro?" Sasha asked. "That's a long drive just to mow a lawn."

"Not exactly."

"Where, exactly?"

"Millie's been asking about his momma."

"And?"

"Asking if she could meet her," Gabe said.

"We knew it was a matter of time," Sasha said.

"You think? I always thought she knew—thought maybe he'd have told her."

"I actually figured she'd know better than to bring it up. I haven't held anything from Millie or her family," Sasha said.

"I told him to go, for his own good."

"Go?"

"And it might be best if he finds the answers for himself, so he could know."

"Go? Go where?"

"The man deserves at least that—answers."

"He went alone?"

"Why not?"

"Please tell me you're not serious?"

"He left this morning."

"Jesus," Sasha said.

She turned in her seat and stared at the wall.

"So, I'm getting your back? Now it's all on me?"

"Do you know how dangerous it can be traveling into those swamps and bayous?" Sasha asked.

"He knows the swamps."

"You've heard the stories, the serial killers."

"I've heard the stories."

"How could you let him go?"

"Peck knows the swamps better than most. He'll be fine," Gabe said.

"He hasn't been back there since he was ten," Sasha said.

"He was eight or nine, and now he has maps," Gabe replied.

The band took a break and walked by the table.

"I can't imagine you're letting him go alone," Sasha said.

"He's a grown man."

"You, of all people."

Gabe tightened both fists, raised them and brought them down on the table with a dull thud.

"It's that black thing, right?" Gabe muttered.

Sasha didn't respond.

"God damn it to hell. I'm just about fed up with the bullshit of being talked down to like I'm a delinquent schoolboy or a recalcitrant child that's not sitting in the room. All day I've been pulled on and prodded and poked—even threatened with a knife—and all day not one, 'are you all right?' All I hear is what I've done wrong, or where I've made a bad decision. I'm tired of it."

She sat, staring at him.

"Peck is a grown adult," Gabe said. "He's mature. He knows bayous and swamps better than any alligator—he has an affinity for people we can't even begin to imagine, and he's considerate of them, and how dare anybody tell me he's not person enough or man enough or mature enough."

"You mean me."

"What?"

"You said anybody. You meant me."

"The band's back, baby," Gabe said. "Dance with me."

They stood and held each other without speaking, waiting for any sound. The sax wailed into their favorite, the daydream-soft sounds of "When Sunny Gets Blue," and they moved with it, her cheek nestled into his neck.

"I'm sorry," Gabe whispered.

"It's not you, darlin'," Sasha said.

"Maybe I didn't think it through."

"I'm sorry, Gabe. This has been a day of hell for you."

"I've been too long black," Gabe said.

"Shut up," Sasha whispered.

"It's true, baby. An American black doesn't think about potholes on the road ahead. We count on them. It's been our culture for four hundred years. Trouble has a way of hovering over us like a high-noon sun. I wasn't thinking when I sent him off alone."

The song lingered. They turned, sliding feet slowly with a sadness, a melancholy in motion, Gabe humming the song.

"Do you think we're in love?" Sasha asked.

He turned her and stepped in tune.

"Do you?" Sasha asked.

"I've loved you from our first dance last year the night we met," Gabe said.

"Me too," Sasha said.

He put his arm around her with a loving squeeze, not missing a motion, a step in the dance.

"If James is right for you, it'll be good," Gabe said. "You'll have a long, happy life."

"I guess," Sasha said.

The song ended. They stood, holding each other, waiting. The next piece was upbeat jazz—not appropriate for their mood. They walked to their table and sat down, looking at each other with different eyes for the first time.

"You have me worried about the boy," Gabe said. "Maybe I should call and ask him to come home."

She was silent. She reached and held his hands.

"I mean it," Gabe said.

Sasha didn't speak.

"I know he can deal with the swamps and the bayous and the back roads. I'm not worried about that. He may even get some good fishing or crabbing in, but if this gator man has a long memory and he meets up with him, it could be a problem."

"You know about the gator man, Gabe?"

"You told me about *gator man* when we were in Providence. I haven't mentioned it or let on to the boy I knew."

"Peck'll be okay, Gabe."

"This gator man is dangerous," Gabe said.

"Gator man won't be a problem."

Gabe set his drink down, jerking his head to attention. "Excuse me?"

Sasha just looked at him.

"I didn't hear you," Gabe said.

"Gator man is dead," Sasha said.

"Say again?"

"Gator man is dead."

"That for certain?" Gabe asked.

"He's dead."

"How? When?" Gabe asked. "How do you...?"

"Gabe, do you remember when we drove to Memphis last year, and I begged you to tell me what was wrong with you?"

"I remember like it was tonight," Gabe said.

"Do you remember what you told me?"

"Remind me."

"You said, ask me no questions, and I'll tell you no lies...remember?"

"So, he's..." Gabe started.

"Gator man will never hurt Peck again," Sasha said. "That's all you need to know, and Peck sure as hell can't hear it from us. He's wakened from that whole nightmare. Let's leave it be."

Gabe placed his elbows on the table, rested his cheeks in his hands, thinking to himself.

"Gabe, do you know why every woman in love is like a black man?" Sasha asked.

He sat up.

"This ought to be good. Why, baby?"

"They both know when it's time to keep a secret, and they know how to keep one and take it to their graves," Sasha said.

He smiled, accepting the sanctity of the moment.

"You sure you don't have some color in your veins, darlin'?" Gabe asked.

Sasha sipped her martini with an inquisitive smile.

"My momma's water broke while she was standing in line waiting to get some pralines. I was born in a restroom in Treme, so who the hell knows?" Sasha asked.

"From Congo Square to Everywhere, baby," Gabe mused.

"You got that right, dancing man—so who knows?"

"You were thinking all along Peck will be okay?" Gabe asked.

"Yes."

"You were just putting on..."

"He'll be fine," Sasha said.

"Woman, order some beans and rice. I need a Chivas—you need a fresh martini—and go fix your hair. I mussed it with the dip."

"Aye aye, Captain," Sasha said and saluted.

"Let's dance until Charlie throws us out."

"Don't you sound like a hottie," Sasha said, standing to go to the bar.

"It's not every day a man learns a woman's been in love with him for nine months."

"Unrequited love, you softy," Sasha said.

"I want to dance tonight, baby—and I'm a curmudgeon."

Sasha's phone chimed in her purse. She lifted it out.

"It's her," Sasha said. "Hey."

"Have you seen Gabe?" Lily Cup asked.

"He's here—at Charlie's."

"Goddammit, I told him to go home and wait for me."

"He's here."

"Tell him not to move a muscle. I'll be right over."

Sasha put her phone in her purse.

"She's on her way. You're not to move," Sasha said.

"I'm going to do my business. I shall return," Gabe said.

He walked away.

Sasha adjusted her bodice, pulled her dress down to proper and walked toward the bar, swaying her hips to the music.

They were dancing to a Duke Ellington sound when Lily Cup first came through the door. She looked around the room for them.

"Can I have a rye, Charlie?" Lily Cup asked.

"Coming up, LC," Charlie said.

"Better make it a double, straight up—neat."

"You got it," Charlie said. "Go sit, I'll bring it over."

"Thanks, hon," Lily Cup said.

She eyed Sasha's purse on the table by the band, approached, sat and waited. It wasn't long before she had her drink and the dancers were back and seated.

"All things considered, it was a pretty good day today," Lily Cup said.

"It's over?" Sasha asked.

"Far from it," Lily Cup said. "But it was a good day."

Gabe ate his beans and rice, listening passively.

"How can it be good, if it's not over?" Sasha asked.

"Any day a DA doesn't say, 'fuck you, we're going to trial,' is a good day," Lily Cup said.

"The man nearly gets killed, your phone's off all day—I wish someone would tell me what's going on," Sasha barked.

"Nothing to tell, yet," Lily Cup said.

"You mean you don't want to talk about it," Sasha said.

"That too," Lily Cup said.

"Then I'll shut up," Sasha said.

"Gabe, I'm going to finish this drink and drive you home," Lily Cup said.

"How'd it go?" Gabe asked.

"I need you to get a good night's sleep, and I'll pick you up early. We'll have a busy day."

"What's going on?" Gabe asked.

"I'll fill you in in the morning," Lily Cup said.

Gabe looked at Lily Cup as if she was dismissing him.

"I just want you to get a good night's sleep. Big day ahead," she said.

He pushed the bowl away.

"Woman, for six days I crawled on my belly under a barrage of machinegun fire on Pork Chop hill in Korea; in Nam I sat in a foxhole next to a kid from Teaneck and watched a sniper's bullet go through his eye and blow the back of his head out while he was telling me about his new seven-pound baby girl; I can tell you what napalm smells like on burning bodies in rice patties infested with venomous snakes. Woman, don't patronize."

"Let's all calm down," Sasha said. "We're friends here."

"I've been in the DA's office all afternoon," Lily Cup said. "Watching the tapes over and over. We had the store manager on conference call telling his recollection of the day you had the keys made. They had the lip-reader come in to demonstrate how she did it. When she saw them again, she read the lips of a passerby in Walmart lipping, 'asshole,' at the kid while she walked behind him while he was threatening you."

"And?" Gabe asked.

"We looked at the body," Lily Cup said.

Gabe froze.

"The FBI prints came in on him," Lily Cup said.

"Anything?" Gabe asked.

"His name is Kenneth Bauer and he tried to buy a handgun in Tucson and was turned down. He tried again at a gun show in Las Vegas and was turned down. So a hunting knife became his weapon of choice. Probably bought it at a hardware store."

"Kenneth Bauer," Gabe said.

"There's more," Lily Cup said.

Gabe looked up in anticipation.

"It happens our Mr. Kenneth Bauer is wanted in Dallas for five possible robberies where his prints were found—"

"He's a street mugger," Gabe said.

"And for a stabbing murder of a man in a Dallas parking lot," Lily Cup continued. "A camera at the Greyhound depot spotted Mr. Bauer following the guy. They've since found Mr. Bauer's thumbprint on the dead man's eyeglasses."

"What does this mean for Gabe?" Sasha asked.

"It means Gabe and I have our work cut out for us," Lily Cup said.

"The man's wanted for killing a man in Dallas," Sasha said. "Doesn't that prove he's a killer?"

"First of all, he's a suspected killer," Lily Cup said. "But killing a suspected killer is still murder...and Gabe killed the man."

"I don't get it," Sasha said.

"I do," Gabe said.

"All this may give us a break by giving Gabe's story credibility, but we still have a lot of work to do," Lily Cup said.

"He's a suspected killer, that should prove— "Sasha started.

"We can't prove the kid had a knife. Gabe's charged with the murder of Kenneth Bauer, and an hour ago the police commissioner told the police chief to have him followed and bring him in if he made any wrong moves."

"But it's so obvious the guy killed that man in Dallas, they have his prints and the video," Sasha said.

"Will you please listen, Michelle? There's no such thing as a 'vigilante' defense," Lily Cup said. "As far as the DA sees it, Gabe killed a man who had no knife, and Gabe will have to be there through preliminaries the day after tomorrow to see if they're going to indict him."

"So, maybe I'm not getting it," Sasha said. "He pleads innocent, they take all of the evidence into consideration, and they drop their case."

"He's already pled not guilty, Michelle."

"This is Charlies, I'm Sasha," Sasha said.

"Will you calm the fuck down, Sasha? What you're not getting is that this is fucking America," Lily Cup said.

"So?" Sasha asked.

"There are two courts in America."

"Amen to that, little sister," Gabe mumbled.

"We have Judge Fontenot's court, and then we have the court of public opinion."

"The media," Sasha said.

"The media," Lily Cup said. "That one is truly a circus. There's no way in hell the media will allow the DA of a world's most violent city let the killing of a young white 'tourist' by a trained to kill black army officer on St. Charles Avenue in broad daylight just go away. I don't give a good goddamn how many medals Gabe has, the visitor's bureau would hang the DA out to dry if he buried it, and they represent a lot of his votes."

"Jesus," Sasha said.

"They nailed him to a cross too, remember?" Lily Cup asked.

"Little sister is right," Gabe said.

"I have a plan, though," Lily Cup said.

Gabe put his spoon down. "What do you need me to do?"

"The DA liked my Harvard story I told him," she said.

"Harvard story?"

"When I was at Harvard, a second-year law student—I remember he was the son of some governor somewhere. Anyway, the kid was stoned and he wheeled a homeless drunk and all his belongings in a red wagon to the quad after listening to the guy hallucinate on a soapbox in a park about trial law. The homeless guy had wanted to be a lawyer but flunked out, dropped some acid and dropped out and lived on the streets, pulling his red wagon around."

"Where's this going?" Gabe asked. "Sounds like a sick joke."

Lily Cup threw back her rye and set the glass down upside down for emphasis. "We lawyers are sick fucks, Gabe, or haven't you heard? In trade for a fifth of bourbon, the man revealed to us fledgling law students his *National Enquirer* defense theory."

"*National Enquirer* theory?" Gabe asked.

"This guy told us most people would believe any goddamned thing you tell them if the first sentence is a question."

"A question," Gabe said.

"He called it the *National Enquirer* defense."

"I don't see the point," Gabe said.

"It's impossible to lie with a question," Lily Cup said.

"I get that," Gabe said. "I'm good with that little sister."

"Tomorrow we're going to find that needle in the haystack—that one shred of evidence that raises that one or two questions that could write an end to this whole mess."

"Isn't *the National Enquirer* over the top for the 'media' metaphor?" Gabe asked.

"Gabe, you're old enough to remember when they could only swear or show sex on cable television, right?" Lily Cup asked.

"I am and I do," Gabe said. "There was family television and there was cable television."

"It's all cable now," Lily Cup said. "It's streamed—it's You-Tubed. The so-called news can say anything it damn well wants, show anything it damn well wants and without libel—just as long as their first sentence is a question."

"What do you need me to do?" Gabe asked.

"Gabe, the DA pulled some strings and got the police chief to assign a Lieutenant Gaines to be your arresting officer. I know him."

"There's a warrant for me?"

"No, they're watching you."

"I'm being followed?"

"That's what a watch is, Gabe."

"So, what's next?" Gabe asked.

"Lieutenant Gaines told me he would meet us in the morning, and if you're cooperative he'll try to help you, and we would go from there. I want you to go home like a good boy, get a night's sleep. I'll get you in the morning. We'll go through the details of what happened for the millionth time, and if we can find what we need and have the DA where we need him, then maybe we can prevent an indictment."

Gabe stood, dropped three twenties on the table.

Lily Cup picked up her phone, tapped the keys, waited, and tapped the keys again.

Gabe rubbed Sasha's neck and shoulders.

"This has been a special evening. Thank you, darlin'," Gabe said.

Sasha stood and embraced him. "I love you, you old bear," she said. "Listen to her, she's good."

"I'll flag a cab," Gabe said.

"Uber is outside, waiting," Lily Cup said. "If it's not, wait a few. It will be. It's paid."

The ladies walked Gabe to the door. He stepped outside, climbed into the Uber and rode off.

"Let's go talk," Sasha said.

"I can't, hon," Lily Cup said. "I have a full day tomorrow. I'm going to the office."

"Peck's taken off," Sasha said.

"I know," Lily Cup said.

"You knew?"

"I knew last night."

"How does everyone know things but me?"

"I've gotta run," Lily Cup said.

"Will Gabe be okay?" Sasha asked.

"At his age, he's facing life in prison. Having no witnesses makes it tough. Having no knife makes it impossible. I'll do my best."

Knowing she had just told Gabe the secret of gator man disappearing, Sasha put her arms around Lily Cup's neck and whispered. "Remember when we were seven, our pact of never holding secrets from each other ever, ever?"

"No telling secrets and no holding secrets and we were six, but I remember," Lily Cup said.

"I have one now," Sasha said. "Can I hold this one, please?"

"Depends what it is."

"I told Gabe about gator man."

"Fuck."

"I had to. Gabe mentioned him and said he was scared for Peck."

"Pay Charlie for my rye?"

"Of course."

Lily Cup kissed her on both cheeks.

"Love you," Lily Cup said, stepping to the door.

"Love you," Sasha said, turning to the bar.

CHAPTER 8

ELIZABETH SAT ON THE BED gently running fingers through sleeping Peck's hair, scratching his scalp with loving French manicured nails.

"*Il est temps de se lever, la tête endormie. J'ai pris le jour de congé,*" Elizabeth said. ("Time to get up, sleepy head. I took the day off.")

He rolled over, blinked open his eyes and stared as if he was trying to remember where he was.

"You slept like a little baby," Elizabeth said.

"The food was so good."

"I love cooking for you."

"Too much wine for Peck."

"You're in love, Peck?"

"Hanh?"

"I can tell the way you hold me now. Who is she?"

"You would like her, cher. Millie."

"Do you love her?"

"I'm in love, dass for true.

"I'm so jealous, but we'll always be…"

"*Mais oui,*" Peck said. "Always."

"Besides, when I become a chef I may have to move to a city, New York or Paris, and you need water and a pirogue near you."

"*Oui.*"

"So, will you tell your Millie about your Elizabeth?"

Peck smiled. "*Oui.* Cousin."

She crawled onto the bed, straddled him over the covers and leaned down to his face.

"*Embrasser des cousins?*" ("Kissing cousins?")

"I go to university soon, cher. Elizabeth becomes an important chef and Peck learns to be smart, ha."

"You're plenty smart already," Elizabeth said. "The university will make you wise."

She kissed his lips softly and leaned back, first watching his mouth, then soulfully looking into his eyes.

"Will you forget me?" she asked.

"*Jamais.*" ("Never.")

Elizabeth's eyes didn't believe him, but they smiled.

"So, get up Mr. Peck. Take a shower and I'll make breakfast, and we'll talk."

"*Oui.*"

"Then we can go for a long walk."

"*Oui.* Go to the kitchen, cher."

"Are you pushing me out?"

Peck smiled.

"Ah, I know."

Elizabeth reached down between her legs and felt William, morning erect and throbbing.

"You are such a naughty little boy. You are so shy and don't want Elizabeth to see our friend."

Peck rolled, moving her off.

"Crepes, cher?" he asked.

"Boudin or bacon?"

"Boudin."

"Grits?"

"*Oui*, and jam on crepes?"

Elizabeth smiled into his eyes, kissed the tip of his nose and left the room.

Just as Peck was stepping into a shower in Baton Rouge, Gabe and Lily Cup, in New Orleans, were stepping into the Silver Whistle Café for eggs and coffee. A plainclothes detective stood at his table and greeted them with handshakes.

"Gabe, this is Lieutenant Gaines. He's a detective in the city, but he's an acquaintance of mine and a friend of the district attorney. Lieutenant Gaines is going to try to help us. He's on vacation, so be good to him."

"It's good to see a brother wanting to help," Gabe said. "Thank you, Lieutenant."

"Has Ms. Tarleton explained to you that I've been assigned as your arresting officer?"

"She has."

"It's just a formality, but I'm required to read the Miranda Warning."

"I understand."

"You have the right to remain silent. Anything you say can and will be used against you in a court of law. You have the right to an attorney. If you cannot afford one, one will be provided for you. Do you understand what I've read?"

"I do, Lieutenant."

"One more detail—one you might want to talk over with your attorney," Lieutenant Gaines said.

"Which is?" Gabe asked.

"I need to know if you are giving up your attorney-client privileges in what we discuss today?"

"The Miranda Warning pretty much takes care of that, doesn't it, Lieutenant?"

"It pretty much does, but I thought I'd ask."

"I'm fine with it," Gabe said.

"We're fine," Lily Cup confirmed.

"Captain, Miss Tarleton was telling me you lost a son in Iraq."

"I did."

"I'm sorry to hear that. Which conflict, sir?"

"Desert Storm," Gabe said. "Friendly fire."

"That was an historic engagement," Lieutenant Gaines said.

"General Norman Schwarzkopf—truly heroic," Gabe said.

"Your son was a hero. I served in Iraq, but our second time in."

The three ordered breakfast and waited for coffee to be poured.

"Captain," Lieutenant Gaines said, "Miss Tarleton and the district attorney brought me up to speed on the situation you're in. I've read the files. I have some ideas of what we can do this morning that can be productive and might help with the DA's deciding whether or not to take this to the grand jury."

"I'm at your service, Lieutenant. Please call me Gabe."

"If you're not *Captain*, my brother, then I'm *Larry* to you," Larry said.

Gabe stretched his arm, offering his hand.

"Good to meet you, Larry."

"Nice to meet you, Gabe."

"Maybe you two should get a room," Lily Cup mused. "There's a hotel through that door and upstairs."

"Gabe, according to the notes, you say you were attacked. Did you know the man who allegedly attacked you?" Larry asked.

"To say I knew him wouldn't be accurate. I had seen him before, on February fifteen. I knew his face."

"How can you be certain it was that date, February fifteen?"

"I remember it because it was the day after Valentine's Day, and it's also the date on my receipts for my house keys."

"Did you know this person before that time—before the day after Valentine's Day—or was that the first time you saw him?"

"That was the first time."

"Tell me how you met him."

Gabe methodically recounted the details of his morning in the store where he had his keys made.

"You're an experienced veteran—a soldier, Gabe. What was your state of mind when this happened?"

"I went through boot camp in my teens, Larry. I've been two years in Korea under gun and mortar fire. I've fought mosquitoes, rain, and sniper fire, and napalm for two years in Nam. Like the rest of them, I handled it best I could. My brother, in all that time I have never been as scared as I was that day at that Walmart, the day that snipe stood with his eyes watching my eyes in a deadly cold glare and promised to kill me the second I walked out the door. Never have I ever been so fearful."

"With all you've been through, Gabe, why this one particular time were you so frightened?" Larry asked.

"Twenty years ago, I would have grabbed him by the collar and tossed him into a wall. I think it was that all of a sudden I realized what being old is. I'm an old man now. Sometimes I need help just trying to stand up from a chair. I was scared, my brother. I've never been so scared in my life...not of what the little pissant was threatening to do...I was frightened of what I wasn't anymore."

"Your cane offered you no sense of security?" Larry asked.

"I wasn't wearing my cane."

"You left your cane at home?"

"Yes."

"You must not have relied on it as a defense piece."

"I never wore my cane or carried my walking stick before. I learned cane defense from a communications specialist years ago."

Lieutenant, you understand that *wearing* a cane thing?" Lily Cup asked.

"I have a dad, I surely do understand it, counselor. Man steps out, he wears his cane."

"My brother," Gabe said.

Gabe continued.

"He was a private in a VA hospital in Guam. I've kept two canes and one stick since, just in case I was ever in need—one black cane and one brown, to match the suit or shoes I might be wearing at the time. I've owned them thirty years, but I only started wearing one after that day I was making keys."

"Was it by the book SOP army instruction or a casual one-on-one from the private?"

"He had a manual we paged through, but I don't think it was army issue. I remember it. When threatened, grab cane firmly with both hands and never loosen the grip. Second, assume a side posture to prevent getting kicked in the nuts. Third, distract him with quick jabs to the face and eye if he's in my space. Four, hit the back of the leg, upper calf just under the knee joint, as hard as you can until he goes down."

"Interesting," Larry said. "What was number five?"

"What would you suppose it was, Lieutenant. Number five?"

"Was number five to kill him?"

"Number five was to run—unless he had a gun. If he had a gun, hit it away and then run."

"Did your experience that day at Walmart make you want to kill him when you saw him again, Gabe?"

"It made me want to go home and lie down. I had to stop my heart's pumping from busting my chest open. I went straight home."

"And the second time you saw Mr. Bauer—"

"Yes."

"Did you recognize him right away?"

"Yes. It was after I came out of the store. I was waiting for a streetlight with the store manager, and we saw Bauer leaning on his bicycle, waving the knife."

"I meant the next time after that," Lieutenant Gaines said. "Did you think of killing him when you first saw him two days ago?"

"No."

"You said he pulled a knife on you."

"He did."

"After he pulled a knife, did you think of killing him then?"

"No."

"What happened next?"

"He demanded my wallet and money."

"When he demanded your wallet, did you think of killing him?"

"No."

"What went through your mind?"

"I thought of defending myself."

"What'd you do?"

"I took position, poked him near his eye twice and then slammed his upper calf and he went down."

"Was that when you thought of finishing him off?"

"I thought he'd stay on the ground and let me walk away."

"And did he?"

"He started getting on one knee, grabbed my shirttail in his fist and swiped at me with the knife. Pulling, poking, and stabbing. He cut my shirt twice—cut a button off. I felt the blade and that's when I went blind. That's when I clubbed him. You know the rest."

"I don't, Gabe. That's why we're here."

"From all you've heard and read, Lieutenant, don't you think it's a pretty cut-and-dried case of self-defense?" Lily Cup asked.

"It could be, if witnesses came forward," Larry said.

"And with no witnesses?" Gabe asked.

"We have no knife," Larry said.

"Sounds like I'm cooked," Gabe said.

"We first have to satisfy the DA that it was self-defense and not a revenge crime," Larry said. "We have to help with some clue or clues that prove your testimony is true. We have to come up with more than a no-witness, no knife, 'trust me' self-defense."

"Help me understand, Larry," Gabe said.

"Gabe, a prosecutor's job is to put murderers away for life. A district attorney prosecutor will try to do that by convincing the jury you're a heinous murderer. If the judge allows the videos in, he won't hesitate to raise doubts about you wanting revenge. The prosecutor is the first to talk to the jury. He's going to tell the jury that poor Mr. Bauer was walking along, minding his own business and you, an angry man, recognized him and attacked him in broad daylight, and your claim that young Mr. Bauer pulled a knife to protect himself was a lie—and you, an experienced, highly trained, battle-savvy army captain viciously murdered him."

"Why are we even here, Larry? I could have saved a few dollars and eaten at home. It sounds like I'm at the gallows already," Gabe said.

"Miss Tarleton, perhaps you can step in and help Gabe understand the whole picture."

"Gabe, the DA has the local media on his back. They're looking for answers to a daylight killing on one of the most celebrated avenues in the world—St. Charles Avenue, home of the streetcar. The DA believes me. But he needs more than that to drop the case against you. He needs some corroborating evidence in your favor that can be documented. Isn't that about it, Lieutenant?"

"That's it, exactly," Larry replied. "And the knife would help."

"What now?" Gabe asked.

"Let's finish our breakfast. I hear they make a delightful blueberry muffin. I want to do one of those and one more coffee before we start our search," Larry said.

Just as the three were focusing on a Silver Whistle Café breakfast at Josephine Street and St. Charles Avenue, Peck in Baton Rouge had finished shaving and was toweling his face when his phone chimed.

"*Bonjour.*"

"I love you so much, mister. Have I told you lately?" Millie said.

"Who is this?" Peck asked with a grin.

"It's Millie."

"Hi, cher."

"Have you forgotten me already?"

"Nah, nah," Peck said. "I was having the fun."

"Did you get my text?"

"Text?"

"Last night. I texted and I waited all night and you didn't text me."

"I was asleep. Are you still coming?"

"Yes, and I've been thinking."

"Thinking?"

"I was thinking maybe Lily Cup or Sasha could suggest where I might get summer work in New Orleans."

"All summer, cher?"

"Something like research or canvassing maybe. You know, looking for things or talking to people. I don't know. Could you ask them?"

"When I get back, sure."

"Get back?"

"*Oui.*"

"Where are you? Are you in Carencro again?"

"Baton Rouge."

"What's in Baton Rouge?"

"Can I tell you something you will be happy, cher?"

"Yes."

"I start night school. Tulane in June."

"You are amazing."

"Tulane, cher."

"I love you so much. Daddy will be excited to hear that."

"Tell your daddy I'm reading *Cannery Row*. It's a whole book."

"I will. I love you."

"I love you, cher."

"What are you doing in Baton Rouge?"

"Can Peck tell you that when you come? It'd be better then."

"That's fine."

"Peck honey, try to call me tonight, will you? Please? Please?"

"I will."

"Bye, I love you," Millie said.

"*Je t'aime*, cher."

Peck pulled his briefs up, his T-shirt on and stepped into the kitchen for breakfast.

"Smells so good."

"Did you find the shampoo?"

"*Oui.* I finded it."

"Who were you talking to?" Elizabeth asked.

"That was Millie."

"Sit and eat. Did you tell her where you are?"

"I told her Baton Rouge."

"So, she doesn't know about me?"

"I maybe could tell her tonight."

"You are such a naughty boy."

"I'm not naughty. We slept good last night. I was a gentleman."

"I let you sleep, is why," Elizabeth said.

Peck kissed her good morning.

"There's blueberry and there's marmalade for the crepes."

"*Merci*," Peck said.

"What was it you wanted to talk to me about?" Elizabeth asked.

"Hanh?"

"Your Millie?"

"Talk?""

"Flora told me you were looking for your momma."

"Ah *oui*, cher. I need to find people I runned from way back. I need to find who I am, cher. *Tu comprend*?" ("Understand?")

"Are you thinking your foster nanna?"

"*Oui.*"

"Do you even know where to begin to look to find her?"

"I thought I did, but that Flora lady say Bayou Chene is flooded and gone—gone so long it couldn't be where I growed."

"You told me of the gator man, Peck. What can you remember about him? Maybe that will help."

"He maked me carry bait shrimp buckets and would tar me if'n I dropped one before his pirogue was full."

"Bait shrimp?"

"*Oui.*"

"Are you sure it was shrimp and not crawfish or mussels?"

"I remember big, white plastic buckets of bait shrimp," Peck said.

"If it was shrimp it had to be closer to Choctaw, Peck."

"Choctaw, cher, I remember that."

"Long River," Elizabeth said.

"*Quelle?*" ("What?")

"Atchafalaya Swamp, off the river, Peck. That river is the only place he could get shrimp. It must have been around there, somewhere."

"Shrimp is from the gulf, *non?*"

"There's shrimp there, Peck. In fact the only fresh-water shrimp in America is from the Atchafalaya river. I learned that in cooking school."

"Dass a big swamp, must be."

"*Tu as du mal à te souvenir de tout ça, Peck?*" ("You're having a difficult time remembering, Peck?")

"*Oui.*"

"Finish breakfast. I'll get dressed and we'll go for a walk so you can think."

"Hokay." Peck said.

"Butter in the fridge if you want more," Elizabeth said, stepping into the bedroom.

Peck enjoyed three crepes, two with blueberry and one with marmalade jams and melted butter. The boudin reminded him of who he was, and he ate it and his grits with contentment.

Elizabeth was in the bathroom when Peck went into the bedroom to pull his jeans and shirt on. They met in the kitchen, Elizabeth with a backpack.

"Why so much to carry, cher—for a walk?"

"I have an idea," Elizabeth said.

"Hanh?" Peck asked.

She pulled the front door open and took him by the hand.

"Come with me," she said.

CHAPTER 9

AT THE CAFÉ IN NEW ORLEANS, the server held a breakfast check out. Lily Cup handed her a credit card.

"Let's walk through that morning," Larry said.

"I can do that," Gabe said. "It started out…"

"I don't want to hear it, Gabe. I want to actually walk through every step you took. Like if you walked out of the house. I want to do that just as you did. If you caught a streetcar, I want to do that."

"I got it. So, the house is fourteen blocks or so. Care to walk?"

"Wait for the Uber I already ordered," Lily Cup said. "We'll ride it."

They left the café, stepping into a bright, sun-rich midmorning. Arriving at Gabe's home, the lieutenant was given a tour of the small, typically southern styled, shotgun house. Gabe offered to make coffee.

"I'd rather we be about our business at hand," Larry said.

Gabe looked at his watch. "If we're going to be accurate, I didn't leave for eighteen more minutes."

"We can wait," Larry said. "What were some of your army career assignments? After Korea and after Nam?"

"I was in Fort Hood a dozen or so years. I ran a communications group. Hood is the largest base in the country. Lots of battalion field combat drills. I had a pretty big staff."

"Were you ROTC in college?"

"No ROTC—no degree. I just liked to read, thanks to a mother not letting me leave the house to play stickball until I could tell her about the chapter I just read. She'd tell me that people who read had an advantage in life. It seemed Momma was right. The army needed troops who liked to read. Most of what we did was shuffle paper."

"Did you enlist?" Larry asked.

"I was drafted, but I would have joined anyway. I told the draft board I'd go army if they let me be a career soldier. If not, I'd go marine or air force."

"To make captain on a high school diploma, you must have been a special trooper."

"I liked to read." Gabe looked at his watch. "It's time."

He stood, picked up his cane and pulled the door open.

"My walking stick is with the police. I'll have to use my cane today— we can pretend it's my walking stick."

"That's fine," Larry said.

"Shall we?"

"After you," Larry said. "Best you can remember, retrace your steps, exactly as you went on that day. We'll try not to distract you and we'll follow behind."

"Yes sir," Gabe said.

"Just do what you did. Walk the same speed, try to duplicate your trip to Lee Circle."

"Yes sir."

He stepped from the house and to the sidewalk just as Elizabeth's and Peck's bus stopped on South Tenth Street in Baton Rouge.

"There's a small bistro near here if we get hungry," Elizabeth said. "I want to show you something first."

She held his hand and they walked several blocks to France Street.

"*Regarde, mon amour, c'est Paris,*" Elizabeth said. ("Look, my love, it's Paris.")

"Hanh?" Peck asked.

"*Eh bien, c'est comme un tout petit Paris, mais faisons semblant,*" Elizabeth said. ("Oh well, it's a little Paris, but let's pretend.")

Peck pulled on her hand until their bodies and eyes met. She kissed him softly, at first coquettish and then, wrapping her arms around his neck, she opened her warm mouth, devouring his smile, kissing first one lip and then another, sucking on his tongue—open hands now on each of his cheeks. Peck placed his hands on her hips and gently pushed her away from the kiss.

"People can see," Peck said.

"*Nous sommes trop loin de l'appartement. Pas de soucis,*" Elizabeth said. ("We're too far away from the apartment. No worries.")

"*Si'il te plait, on peut parler Anglais, cher? Ça aidera Peck beaucoup si nous parlons en Anglais,*" Peck said. ("Can we speak English, cher? It will help Peck better if we talk in English.")

"Only if you kiss me whenever I please."

"Ah, *oui.*"

Elizabeth pointed at a sign for Government Street.

"Paris is like a big wheel, Peck. The designer of Paris drew a circle and then had the streets and avenues come together. At the center I know there's the Notre Dame Cathedral and the Louvre. But, so sad, I've never been there. I've only heard stories."

"Someday you be a famous chef in Paris."

"Peut-être." ("Maybe.")

"Peck doesn't see a circle, cher. Where is the circle?"

"It's more of a big x, Peck. That's Somerulis Street, and it crosses that one, Penalver Street, and then there is Beauregard Street, which crosses that one over there, Grandpre Street, and they come together like a big x."

Peck looked confused.

"Never mind," Elizabeth said. "Let's keep walking. I want you to meet someone."

"Who?"

"A lady. She's a diviner."

"Hanh?"

"She's a reader too."

"Reader like Peck?"

"She reads tarot cards. She tells the future. People trust her word."

"But Peck want to find the past. Is that the right word—past?"

"It's the right word. The thing is, she can maybe do that too. She's also a hypnotist."

"What's that for?"

"What you've forgotten about from so long ago. She might be able to get you to remember people and places. Maybe she can help you find your foster nanna from what your subconscious remembers."

"Thank you for showing me Paris."

"Are you being sarcastic?"

"When I get home I look *sarcastic* in my dictionary and then I'll tell you, cher."

Short blocks and narrow streets showed the Spanish and French influences on the historic city. Walking downtown was being in another state of mind a world away from the Carencro or the New Orleans Peck knew. Baton Rouge was a quiet-busy place, with government buildings, a state university, bustling restaurants, celebrated public libraries, galleries, and cooking schools. The downtown felt secure and civilized, away from the beggary, the faceless tourism of New Orleans and its transient scavengers, road pirates who fed on the coattails of floods and hurricanes. Baton Rouge might be Louisianans' hidden treasure, the true soul of a gentle people, while New Orleans was the elephant in the room, a wanton mistress where personal pleasure became its own excuse, a folly to the world. They held hands, only stopping to kiss or take a picture.

As Elizabeth and Peck walked, taking in the sights in Baton Rouge, eighty-three miles away in New Orleans, two blocks from his house, Gabe was walking east on St. Charles Avenue with Lily Cup and Larry following.

"Up here is where I caught the streetcar."

"Which stop, Gabe? The one just across the street or that one farther down?"

"The one farther down. I'm a walker."

"Do you remember where you crossed over?"

"Yes. It was up by that fire hydrant. A black Mercedes was parked there. I remember the passenger door was open and they were talking. St. Charles right behind their car. There was space to cross between the Mercedes and the fire hydrant."

"Do the same now, Gabe."

Gabe stepped off the curb and waited for three cars to approach and pass by. He crossed in the middle of the block and onto the other side. He walked along one of the two tracks until he was at the streetcar stop. He stopped and turned.

"Gabe, was there anyone standing here when you got here?"

"No. I think it was after the commuters went to work. I usually try to avoid them. If the car's full, they make you stand the whole trip. I was alone here."

The streetcar rolled to a stop, the front door opening and the stairs edging out. Gabe stepped up and in. Lily Cup and Larry following suit.

"Three 'day passes', how much?" Gabe asked.

"Just buy yours, Gabe," Larry said.

Gabe inserted bills enough for a 'day pass', retrieved it and stepped back to the third seat.

"Want to sit up here on the bench, Gabe?" Lily Cup asked.

"This is where I sat," Gabe said.

He knew the more he could accurately demonstrate remembering, the more his story about how the killing happened would be believed.

"Is St. Josephs the best stop for the World War Two museum, conductor?" Gabe asked.

"It is, yes sir," the conductor said. "I'll shout it out for you."

"Thank you, young lady."

Gabe looked at Larry.

"Just like I did it," Gabe said, "but the conductor was a man."

Lily Cup sat with Gabe. Larry sat in the seat across the aisle.

"Any word whether James will move here after the wedding, or will he still commute in three days a week, like he does now?" Gabe asked.

"Sasha hasn't said. We don't talk that much about it. She knows what I think," Lily Cup said. "I just leave her alone."

"They live different lives," Gabe said. "It makes no sense to me. Sasha is well respected in the community."

"They wanted her to run for mayor."

"She'd be a good Mayor. She's involved and generous with local charities."

"She knows everybody."

"I get a kick out of watching the woman celebrate the city's culture and romance. How you two gussy up just to dance jazz."

"She got me into that scene when we were in our twenties."

"You were just starting out?"

"We love to dance. You know, the dirty dancing scene—but we were into jazz."

"Blues and jazz, it doesn't get any better than that."

"She convinced me old dudes were better jazz dancers, and we knew Charlie was opening a jazz bar in his mother's place, so we picked Charlie's Blue Note for our dancing."

"She's a pistol," Gabe said.

"She told me if we were going to do it right we had to dress the part, always strut our stuff, so we looked nice on the dance floor."

"Sounds like what she would do to present a house for sale."

"I'll be goddamned," Lily Cup said.

"What?"

"That's exactly what I told her. It was like she was prepping for an open house."

"You lost the debate, is my guess," Gabe said.

"Damn straight. She stood in front of the mirror lecturing me on her world-class tits and how they needed a proper stage and how I had a *boy* ass."

"Boy ass?"

"I don't know. She just said men liked cleavages and bubble butts, so we had to accent our positives. Men pick dance partners like peacocks pick mates—she'd say."

"Boy ass?"

"Boy ass, bubble butt, all the same," Lily Cup said.

"To a cracker, maybe. But brothers like their women with a wagon."

"Women with a wagon? A wagon? What the hell is that, some kind of urban ebonics?"

"A cushion," Gabe said.

"Cracker means white, right?" Lily Cup asked.

"Yes."

"Well, we went shopping for our uniforms. I remember I was in third year law school and Sasha was trying to sell condos in the Quarter. We charged over ten thousand bucks in four hours."

"Canal Street must have lit up," Gabe said.

"We did do a number—a big number. Nothing but the best. My sunglasses were four hundred bucks. Just imagine, in those days."

"Well you did good, little sister. The tights you wear at Charlie's does your boy ass proud. I've seen glances you get walking away."

"I'm a cigar smoking tomboy, but I do have a nice ass, don't I?"

"This James guy is only about himself," Gabe said. "It's about how well he can eat or how he can walk into a place and get a table because of who he is."

"That about sums him up," Lily Cup said.

"I don't get it," Gabe said.

"Being held in someone's arms a few nights a week goes a long way in overlooking some things. It could be worth it," Lily Cup said. "It's lonely being a single woman."

"She could do better. There's many good men who would jump at the chance to embrace her," Gabe said. "Peck, half her age, would be better for her than James."

"Sasha's thirteen years older than Peck," Lily Cup said.

"I knew it was something like that, but he'd be better than James for her."

"Aren't you the feisty old matchmaker?"

"I'm not pushing any agenda. We're only talking. I was trying to make a point."

"Do you really think Peck would be good for Sasha?"

"I was using him as an example— an alternative, but actually, I don't. I think he'd be good pajamas for her lonely nights, not so good for everyday wear...let's just say she wouldn't be into crabbing or splashing around for snapping turtles, and he wouldn't be into two martini lunches in the Quarter."

"I'm glad you cleared that up, because I've got dibs."

Gabe turned in the seat with a surprised grin on his face.

"Excuse me? Dibs?"

"You heard right. Between you and me and no one else, I put dibs on Peck, at least in my dreams I have. We already know he loves my boy bubble ass and the fucker is smarter than a *Jeopardy* champ. He actually reminds me of a young me. I think we'd be a perfect set."

"I'll be damned."

"Mum's the word, Gabe. We all have our fantasies, and I'm not into busting him and Millie up. I think they're perfect together."

"I'll be cool, my sister. My lips are sealed."

"Good," Lily Cup said.

"Fascinating."

"Saint Joseph—Lee Circle—Saint Joseph, next stop," the conductor said.

Gabe turned to Lily Cup. "If I get through this mess, let's take Sasha out and have a talk."

"Good idea. We'll do it. Two on one."

While they waited, Gabe glanced at Larry. "This is it," he said.

A statue-less, tall, granite column surrounded by lawn was all that remained of the iconic New Orleans landmark at Lee Circle. City fathers had removed General Robert E. Lee in deference to offending African Americans. As the streetcar came to a full stop, Gabe stood, cane in hand, and stepped to the front and down one step to just behind the conductor's chair, thanking her for calling out the stop.

"Have a blessed day," the conductor said.

"From your lips to God's ears, my sister," Gabe said as he stepped off the streetcar. He stared up at the tall column that once supported General Lee. Larry and Lily Cup stepped off and joined him, a few feet away from other passengers boarding.

"Okay, Gabe," Larry said. "Let's get started."

"Right."

"Where were you standing when you first got off the streetcar? Was it where you are now?"

Gabe walked ten feet to his right and stood.

"It was over here."

"What did you do then?"

Gabe pointed at the tree and the power lines across the eastbound side of St. Charles Avenue. Beaded necklaces hung on tree limbs and on the wires lining the street. Necklaces of all colors.

"When Sasha was showing me houses, she told me that the Mardi Gras parade came up St. Charles. It wasn't until two days ago I noticed those hanging over there."

"What did you do then?" Larry asked.

"I stood here, taking it in, trying to imagine floats going by, beautiful girls tossing the necklaces; the streets lined with parade watchers and revelers. I stood here for fourteen minutes."

"How did you know fourteen minutes?"

"I had looked at my watch and knew the World War II museum wouldn't open for fourteen minutes, so I stalled crossing while enjoying looking up at the necklaces."

"Then what?"

"I crossed over to that sidewalk over there."

"Where did you cross? Did you go down to the corner, or did you cross here?"

"Here, from where I'm standing."

"Okay, let's talk it through," Larry said. "Gabe, did you walk straight across or at an angle?"

"Straight across. I saw a necklace on that fence over there I thought I would get."

"When you were standing here, did you see Mr. Bauer anywhere in sight?"

"No, sir."

"And when you crossed, was there any time while you were in the street when you could see Mr. Bauer?"

"Never. No sir."

"I'm asking you to stay here, Gabe. Miss Tarleton and I are going to walk over to the sidewalk to observe. We need you to wait until I ask you to come across."

"I'll wait."

Lily Cup and Larry stepped onto St. Charles and walked across. There was a chalk outline of a body and blood stains. Both had been washed to a faint image by a power washer. Just before they got to the curb of the sidewalk, Larry touched Lily Cup's arm, asking her not to move. On the street, Larry walked to the left until he reached the corner. He turned and slowly walked back, leaning down and looking at each inch of the sidewalk's gutter. Just beyond where Lily Cup was standing he lowered himself to a knee.

"Bingo," Larry said.

He stood, retrieved a pair of tweezers from his left pocket and a property baggie from his right. He knelt down again and carefully picked up something.

"What?" Lily Cup asked.

"A button with what appears to be blood on it," Larry replied.

He placed the button in the baggie, locked it closed and put it in his vest pocket.

"If we only had the shirt," he said.

"It's in my valise," Lily Cup said. "Want it now?"

"No. Stay there a bit. I want to walk up the sidewalk and take a look."

He looked over at Gabe.

"Gabe, which direction was he coming from?"

Gabe pointed west, away from the corner. Larry stepped up on the sidewalk and walked west slowly, leaning down, studying every inch along the sidewalk. It was a good fifteen feet when he stopped, retrieved his tweezers again and another property baggie. He knelt and carefully placed several objects in the baggie, sealed it, and put it in his vest pocket. He walked back to where Lily Cup was standing.

"Gabe, go ahead and come across, just as you did."

"Yes, sir."

"Before you come across, I want you to take a minute and think. Think about how and where you crossed over."

"I do remember I was blowing my nose," Gabe said.

"Blowing your nose?" Larry asked.

"Yes, sir. I'm a four-time sneezer, and I remember I had sneezed two times, and knew I had two more to go, so I was getting my handkerchief out."

"Captain, I want you to repeat that again right now, just as it happened—and just how you came across, sneezing."

Gabe tucked and braced the cane under his folded right arm. He pulled the handkerchief from his left pocket with his left hand as he stepped onto St. Charles. As he crossed, Gabe pretended two sneezes with both elbows scrunched to his sides, his hands were occupied holding the handkerchief and wiping or blowing his nose. He stepped onto the curb on the other side, glanced quickly at the bloodstains, grimaced and turned his head away.

"Exactly where were you when Mr. Bauer approached?"

"I was right here where I am now. I had just gotten on the sidewalk and didn't have time to turn the way I was going to walk when he came up."

Larry made some notes in his booklet.

"Miss Tarleton, I think I've seen enough. That's all I need from either of you for now. If you'll get me the shirt, I'll take it in and go write my report."

"Do you want me to run get it now, Lieutenant?" Lily Cup asked.

"You all go on. I want to stay here for a while—look around. We can meet in the DA's office at three p.m. Should give me enough time. Will that work for you?"

"I'll be there, Lieutenant. Just me?" Lily Cup asked.

"Just you."

Larry turned to Gabe, extending his hand.

"Thank you for being so patient and professional with me, Gabe. I am honored for the opportunity to try to help a brother in any way I can."

"You're not going to arrest me and take me in?" Gabe asked.

"You've got a good, caring attorney, Captain. She'll have you at the preliminary hearing. That's all I need to know."

"My brother," Gabe said.

They clutched a hug.

"I wish you all the luck, Gabe."

CHAPTER 10

JUST AS GABE WAS CROSSING ST. CHARLES to wait for a streetcar home, Elizabeth and Peck were in Baton Rouge standing at the door of the tarot reader and spiritual diviner on College Street. The door was a glossy black enamel with small brass stars surrounding a street number. A card above the doorbell read, "Ring the doorbell and be patient."

Elizabeth pushed the button.

"Don't be frightened, Peck. I think she can help you," Elizabeth said.

"I'm good," Peck said.

To pass the time, Elizabeth hugged Peck around the waist nuzzling into his neck.

"*Je n'aime pas si longtemps ne pas te voir,*" Elizabeth said. ("I don't like so long not seeing you.")

The interior curtain of a side window was pulled back and released. Finally the door opened and a woman in a satin robe smiled and welcomed both of them in. There was a freshness about her, as if she had just stepped from a tub. While they stood, the woman grouped her hair from the side to the back of her head and attached a band to it. She had an attractive face because of inquisitive, caring eyes. She looked to be in her late thirties.

She hugged Elizabeth welcome. "It's good to see you, *mon amie.*"

"I brought my friend," Elizabeth said.

"Is this the special friend we spoke of?"

"Yes. Peck."

"I am Audrey," she said. "It is my pleasure to meet you."

Peck tipped his head.

"He's everything you said he was."

"I know."

"I told you he would come back."

The diviner looked deep into Peck's eyes. She took his hand and raised it to gently touch her cheek.

"His hand is warm," she said to Elizabeth. "A fire is burning inside him."

Audrey spoke to Peck. "You are searching for answers?"

"Yes'm," Peck said.

"Come into the next room and sit with me. We'll begin there."

"Would you want me to wait here?" Elizabeth asked

"You come too. You are his guide through the journey ahead, yes?"

"*Tres bien*," Elizabeth said.

"I told you he would come to you one day. Please join us at my table."

Peck looked about the room. There were crosses and dolls hung on walls and resting on a mantle. Rosary beads hung on the edge of a picture frame. There were many drapes of velvet and satin in rich, dark colors, and there were scented candles. On the wall was an unpainted wooden shelf with twenty or so unopened decks of tarot cards in several short stacks. Audrey reached back and took a deck in her hand and opened it, removing the cards. She held them for Peck to take.

"Here, Peck. Shuffle these."

Peck looked at the deck and began to spread the cards with his fingers.

"Peck—take them home with you. Feel each one of them carefully. They will listen and absorb your most inner feelings. Take them home with Elizabeth when you leave, keep them safe, and bring them back tomorrow."

"I don't understand," Peck said.

"Your touch will warm some cards, wake them up. They will serve you and tell your story. They will help us find a way," Audrey said.

"*Merci*," Peck said.

Audrey put her hand on Peck's as he touched the cards. He rested them on the table, his hand covering them.

"Tell me who you are, Peck."

"Hanh?"

"Each of us are three people," Audrey said. "We are who we think we are. We are who others think we are, and we are who we actually are. Who are you, Peck?"

"Peck is a fisher, dass for true. I like larn'ing to read and I catch the turtles and mashwaron. I like boiled eggs."

"And you love friends, *non?*" Audrey asked.

"Ah, *oui*," Peck said.

"Are you in love, Peck?"

"Ah, *oui.* I love my Millie so much."

"Do you want to tell me about Millie, Peck? She must be a special person to have your love."

"Millie is so special. She make Peck feel good about myself and she wants to be with me and have children and raise shickens and okra."

"Do you love Elizabeth?"

"*Oui.*"

"Do you love Elizabeth like you love Millie?"

"Different love. Elizabeth and Peck hold each other. It makes loneliness feel better some nights. We are there for each other."

"That's beautiful," Audrey said. "You have a soulfully tender heart."

Peck reached over and rested his hand on Elizabeth's thigh.

"Elizabeth helps Peck find who I am, so I can tell my children who they are."

"A good start is starting in positive thought. Are there any nice things you can remember about your early childhood, Peck?" Audrey asked.

"I remember the moon, cher."

"Do you want to tell us what you remember about the moon?"

"When the moon was full I kneel in the dirt under the porch and pray to it. I talk to the moon and tell it things. Sometimes it tell me things."

"What would you tell the moon?"

"Sometimes, if the moon was my mamma true, I would tell her I be good if she ever come back to me. I work so hard and not make noises to keep her awake."

"Do you think your momma heard you?"

"Gabe say yes, ma'am. He say my mamma heard ever word. I believe him."

"Did you talk with any others in the moon?"

"I wanted a sign. I wanted the moon to tell me what to do, how to get away, where to go."

"And did you get a sign?"

"Yes'm, I surely did."

"Can you tell me?"

"The big ole bald cypress in the swamp was my frien'. The moon say that to me. It say I can trust the ole cypress."

"Can you explain?"

"The moon say gator man was bringing the pirogue back empty the next day, and he would be so mad he got no gators, and Peck should hide, so he don't find me and belt strap me."

"Did you hide?"

"I climbed the dead Cypress frien' on the swamp edge, you know, where the moon say to and sat in its hollow while gator man shouted my name, looking for me, and he drank whiskey and he broke bottles on rocks."

"Did he find you?"

"I stayed there three days. He never seen me."

"Was he there for three days looking for you?"

"Nah, nah. Gator man left for foster nanna's place right off. Peck stayed in the tree two more days, thinking what to do."

"So, the moon was a good friend, and the cypress tree was a good friend. Can you remember any other good things, Peck?"

"The Wood Ducks helped Peck, I say."

"How did the Wood Ducks help you, Peck?"

"Peck ate their eggs. Four eggs in the tree hollow. They were good to Peck, I'll say. I stepped on some and broke them, but four were good. Ants ate the broke ones."

"Peck, have you ever been hypnotized?" Audrey asked.

"What is that, hypnotized, cher?"

"When you get hypnotized you go into a deep sleep, and sometimes the subconscious can remember things that the conscious mind has forgotten."

"Ah," Peck said.

"Our brain is like a big filing cabinet or a tool box filled with tools. We sometime forget what files we have or what tools we have, but with hypnosis, we can see things more clearly."

"So hypnotized is good, maybe?" Peck asked.

"It can be helpful."

"I like that," Peck said.

"First you must take Elizabeth to help you find some things we'll need. Come back when you've found them, and I will have a reading of the cards you have with you. After that we will have a private divination to hear what the spirits have to say."

"What things you need?"

"Go to a library and find some maps of areas you think you have been to in your life, Peck."

"I been to Rhode Island."

"Just maps of your childhood, Peck. Places you remember during early youth. Maps sometime speak to us."

Audrey stood and politely asked them to leave and do their work. She reminded Peck to shuffle the tarot cards and touch each one and to keep them safe on his person. As Elizabeth and Peck moved to the door and stepped out, the phone rang inside with Audrey waving goodbye, while answering it.

Pulling the door closed, Elizabeth wrapped her arms around Peck's neck and kissed him passionately.

"*Je peux etre ta lune a l'avenir, mon amour?*" Elizabeth asked. ("Can I be your moon from now on, my love?")

"*Pour toujours, cher.*" ("Forever, cher.")

"Wherever we are, whoever we're with, when we look at the moon, we'll think of each other, promise?"

"*Oui.* That be good."

"Audrey wasn't scary or weird or anything like what you hear about readers, was she?" Elizabeth asked.

"Nah, nah, nice lady."

Elizabeth was moved by talk of the moon. She backed Peck against the door and kissed him again, this time leaning on him. She lifted her head back and smiled into his eyes, her hand reaching down and feeling William through his jeans.

"It still there, cher?" Peck asked.

"Oh, it's still there."

"The Bistro?" Peck asked. "Can we go eat now?"

Elizabeth playfully squeezed William.

"*Peut-être que Peck va me nourir avec ça?*" ("Maybe Peck will feed me this?")

"Bistro, cher. Take us there and we'll eat and talk."

Elizabeth laughed and held his hand as they walked. They chose a sidewalk table at the bistro.

"Would you want wine, Peck?"

"Nah, nah. Can you tell Peck what's good to eat here, my chef frien'?"

Elizabeth ordered calamari they would share and two Hawaiian chicken and pineapple barbeque wraps. Elizabeth drank Chardonnay and Peck drank water. They relaxed and spoke of the city; of the beautiful LSU university campus; of Peck's New Orleans, and of night school at Tulane. They spoke of Millie and her baby doll Charlie and of Peck's devotion to her, and how important it was to learn of his past.

"Your boo, cher. Is he good to you when he's not on the oil rig?"

"He's a good man, Peck. He works hard, long hours when he's out there. It takes him some time to rest up when he comes home."

"Do you have the good times?" Peck asked.

"We'll go for walks. We sit in the park and watch people. Sometimes we pack sandwiches and wine."

"Is he, how you say—romantic?"

"It's more like we're good friends and we fuck, Peck. Understand?"

"*Je comprends*," Peck said. ("I understand.")

"He's a nice man and he'd be a good father."

"Hokay."

"I wouldn't say he's romantic."

"Dass good. That he's nice."

"With me in cooking school he knows one day I may be going to New York or Paris to try to be a chef."

"Would he go with you?"

"We've talked about it."

"What'd he say, cher?"

"He said he'll have to cross that bridge when we come to it. He said there were rigs in Europe."

"Would he be upset if he knew about us?"

"He'd be hurt. He'd probably understand, but he would be hurt."

"*Oui.*"

"Would you be hurt if Millie made love to another man?"

"Peck would be surprised a lot...and hurt, *oui*. I would come to you and ask for advice."

"I would say come to Paris," Elizabeth said.

"Peck would maybe go, but Millie loves me so, we are meant to be."

"She sounds perfect for you, Peck. I'm happy for you both."

"Is there a library we can get maps Audrey wants us to get?"

"A few blocks away. Let's get a dessert and split it."

"Good," Peck said.

They ordered key lime pie.

"Peck, are you okay with being with Audrey tomorrow?"

"*Oui.*"

"What's going through your mind about it?"

Peck lifted the tarot cards from his pocket and began to fan them out on the table, faces up.

"These are so good to look at, but so mysterious, *Gris Gris*. Are they good?"

"Each one is supposed to tell a story of where a mind and soul are the day they are turned over. We'll see how you think about them tomorrow."

"I think sometime if I'll ever know'd if my foster nanna just finded me or did somebody didn't want me and just gived me to her when I was born. I just think sometime I'll never know."

"Maybe you can find her and she'll tell you things. She must have loved you. Was she nice when you were there with her?"

"I don't remember. I know she let gator man slave me, carrying bait shrimp, and he make me gator bait is all I remember. So, I runned away to Carencro."

"Did your foster nanna know what gator man was doing to you, about how badly he was treating you?"

"Nanna would say to mind him—he was church-goin' and teaching me things to make me a man. She didn't like to talk too much. Told me to go with gator man and mind him."

"Tomorrow, then?" Elizabeth asked.
"Tomorrow?" Peck asked.
"Tomorrow maybe Audrey can help."
"*Oui*. Maybe."
"Finish the pie, Peck. We'll walk to the library, then to the grocer for tonight."
"Hokay."
"I'm doing a special chicken tonight, a light lemon butter sauce and capers."
"I like shicken, cher."

Chapter 11

ORDER IN THE COURT," the bailiff announced. "All rise. Section M of the Criminal District Court is now in session. The Honorable Judge Lindsay Fontenot presiding. Silence is commanded under penalty of fine or imprisonment. God save this state and this honorable court. Please be seated. There is no talking in the audience. Good morning, Judge."

The district attorney stood in this magistrate court and waited as the bailiff spoke.

"The State of Louisiana calls Captain Gabriel Jordan, US Army retired."

Gabe stood. The bailiff approached.

"Captain Jordan, raise your right hand and place your left hand on this bible. Do you swear that the evidence that you shall give shall be the truth, the whole truth and nothing but the truth, so help you God?"

"I so swear." Gabe said.

"Captain Jordan, I have read you the charges. Are they clear to you?" Judge Fontenot asked.

Lily Cup nodded.

"They are clear Your Honor," Gabe said.

"The defendant has plead not guilty to the charges," the judge said. "This preliminary hearing is to determine probable cause. We're here to determine further disposition."

Judge Fontenot was adjusting her microphone while the bailiff was taking a seat. Gabe and Lily Cup at their table and across the aisle, Lieutenant Gaines (Larry) the DA and assistant DA were in the front tables. Seated behind the DA were three people unknown to Lily Cup. Gabe leaned over.

"Who are those three?" Gabe asked.

"I don't know," Lily Cup said.

District Attorney Holbrook, Counselor Tarleton, a sidebar please?" the judge asked.

Lily Cup stood and stepped into the aisle and waited while the district attorney lowered the lid of his briefcase, stepped into the aisle and joined her. They walked to the judge's right side of her bench. The judge pushed her microphone away and leaned in with a modulated voice.

"Don't look now but three news networks, two civil rights group representatives, the New Orleans' Visitor Association, a Tulane professor and an author writing a mystery novel have joined us today. The police are at the door, prepared to remove demonstrators."

"Why all the hullabaloo, Judge?" Lily Cup asked.

"The New Orleans Film Festival always draws a crowd of hungry news people," the district attorney said.

If this goes smoothly, it will be thanks to you, Counselor Tarleton," Judge Fontenot said. "And to you District Attorney Holbrook."

"Excuse me?" Lily Cup asked.

"Counselor, you asked for a pretrial conference before we began. District Attorney Holbrook agreed. Any other setting and a lock-out wouldn't stand their speculations and we couldn't have avoided the press."

"Thank you, Judge."

"District Attorney Holbrook and Counselor Tarleton, this is the million-dollar question. Have the past thirty-six hours been helpful so we can move this forward?"

"We'll know soon enough, Judge," the district attorney said.

"Ms. Tarleton?" Judge Fontenot asked.

"Your Honor, I am honored to work with a court with grace and compassion and a district attorney with such integrity and caring for the benefit of the community. I'm speechless."

"It appears you have found the words, counselor. Such a pleasant way to open a day."

"I agree, Judge," the district attorney said.

"Before we run off to Tipitina's for some Zydeco dancing, I have something to share, and I'll let you two decide," Judge Fontenot said.

Lily Cup and the DA stood, waiting.

"District Attorney Holbrook and Counselor Tarleton, with the thought of containment of, shall we say, prying media eyes with jaundice on this particular case with its racial overtones, you might consider meeting the press after we've concluded."

"It would appear you've done some homework, Judge," the district attorney said.

"I'm thinking about New Orleans and the Black Lives Matter theme," Judge Fontenot said. "The last thing this town needs is unfounded *Gris Gris* becoming headlines for months to come and messing up our private walks in the park."

"I agree, Judge," Lily Cup said.

"Are you ready?"

"Your Honor, speaking for the state, I believe we can present a case in a manner that will leave no question unanswered," the DA said.

"Counselor Tarleton?" Judge Fontenot asked.

"I agree, Judge."

The district attorney and Lily Cup took their places at the tables.

Lily Cup leaned into Gabe's side.

"Stay cool, Gabe. Today we're going with the flow. It's the DA's show, just be patient and let's see how it goes."

"I'm ready for anything," Gabe said.

"District Attorney Holbrook, call your first witness," Judge Fontenot said.

"Your Honor, the State of Louisiana calls the assistant district attorney from Lafayette, Louisiana, Ms. Berkin."

The Lafayette assistant district attorney stood and walked to the stand and waited for the bailiff to swear her in.

"What's this about? Why Lafayette?" Gabe whispered.

Lily Cup looked at Gabe with a look as if be still, and to not over react to things.

"Ms. Berkin, do you know why you're at this preliminary hearing?" the district attorney asked.

"I believe so," Ms. Berkin said. "I'm here to offer witness to Captain Jordan's physical and mental state."

"And why would the defendant's physical and mental state be important at this hearing."

"I assume to find if he was disturbed in any way—to the point of being prone to violence."

"Can you share with the court when you first met the defendant, Captain Jordan?"

"I can," Ms. Berkin said.

"Would you tell us the time and circumstance?"

"It was a nine months ago. Our offices received an anonymous call about a suspected homicide in Opelousas," Ms. Berkin said.

"And was it a homicide?" the DA asked.

"The call was referencing the defendant. It seemed that the defendant was not victim to homicide as the caller thought but he had collapsed on the side of the highway and was taken by a good Samaritan to a doctor in Carencro. In fact, two persons had witnessed his lying on a roadside and called it in as a suspected homicide."

"Was the defendant taken to an emergency room?" the district attorney asked.

"It was a hospice in Carencro," Ms. Berkin said.

"Was there a reason why the good Samaritan chose a hospice, Ms. Berkin?"

"The good Samaritan was a friend of a doctor at the hospice, so that's where he took the defendant."

"What happened then?" the district attorney asked.

"Two things," Ms. Berkin said. "The first was that it was almost fortuitous that the good Samaritan had taken the defendant to the hospice, as it seemed three months before this incident, the defendant had been diagnosed with stomach cancer and given two months to live by the staff at the VA hospital in Pineville."

"What was the second thing?"

"Because we learned that the defendant had run away from the VA hospital in Pineville, I took it upon myself to investigate his background for criminal records or mental issues that might be threatening to the general public."

"Can you share with the court what you found?"

"I only found that the defendant had been diagnosed with stomach cancer and had voiced a weariness of the treatments the VA was administering to him," Ms. Berkin said.

"Anything else?"

"From the accounts of witnesses at the hospice, the losses of his wife and only son weighed on his mind, and these witnesses felt the defendant was in a state of depression."

"Do you know the circumstances of how the defendant lost his wife and son, Ms. Berkin?"

"What do you mean?"

"Were their losses of natural causes or—"

"Are you asking me if they were violent deaths?"

"Are you aware of the circumstances of their deaths, Ms. Berkin?"

"The defendant's wife died of a heart attack in her midsixties. I'm not certain of the date. His son was lost in Iraq—Desert Storm."

A tear came to the corner of Gabe's eye. He lowered his head.

"Ms. Berkin, was the defendant clinically tested for depression, to determine if he needed confinement?"

"No," Ms. Berkin said.

"Excuse me? Are we to understand that the investigation of the defendant who was deemed suicidal didn't include a clinical evaluation and diagnosis?"

"Suicidal?"

"The defendant refused any more treatment, Ms. Berkin. Isn't it true he actually ran away from the VA hospital and their treatments?"

"Maybe he just accepted the inevitable," Ms. Berkin said. "It's not all that uncommon for terminal patients."

"Explain why you couldn't test him for depression, Ms. Berkin."

"I never got an order for an evaluation but had I— by the time the order would have come, Captain Jordan had run from the hospice."

"Run away?"

"Yes."

"Wasn't he free to leave?"

"When a patient carries opiods—"

"Narcotics?" the district attorney asked.

"Yes."

"Hospice care includes a responsibility to have a more watchful eye and security to protect their patients. How was it possible he just ran away without anyone knowing, Ms. Berkin?"

"At first we suspected foul play."

"Please continue," the district attorney said.

"The yard maintenance man was seen with heavy amounts of blood on his hands the same day both he and the defendant disappeared from the hospice."

"What took place then?"

"We were asked to investigate for a possible kidnap and homicide."

"The defendant, Captain Jordan, is here with us today, looking alive and well, Ms. Berkin. Might we assume the matter of the disappearing duo and the bloody hands has been resolved?"

"They are," Ms. Berkin said.

"And can you describe for this hearing how it was resolved?"

"Captain Jordan apparently wanted to run away to Newport, Rhode Island, and the gardener employed by the hospice offered to help him get there."

"Does the defendant, Captain Jordan, have relatives in Newport?"

"I don't know."

"What was the attraction?"

"We were told he wanted to listen to the jazz at the Newport Jazz Festival. The gardener arranged to get him there."

The courtroom seemed to pause and take a deep breath in quiet reverence for a story of a dying man's last wish.

"Assistant District Attorney Berkin, were there any findings of a criminal nature in Captain Jordan's past?" Judge Fontenot asked.

"Your Honor, the defendant had no criminal record, no lawsuits or liens, no unpaid traffic tickets. We found he was decorated four times—twice in Korea, once in Vietnam and once again on his retirement—for exemplary service to his country."

"Thank you," Judge Fontenot said.

"Thank you, Ms. Berkin. Your witness, Counselor Tarleton," District Attorney Holbrook said.

Lily Cup stood.

"Ms. Berkin, for the benefit of this hearing—was there ever any explanation offered for the blood seen by witnesses on the gardener's hands the day he and Captain Jordan disappeared from the hospice?"

"There was."

"Can you tell the court?"

"The first thing the gardener was known to do when he came to work on his day to mow, was prepare, bait, and throw a trotline into the bayou behind the hospice. He would catch fish and turtles he would later trade for money or food. The hospice administrator had given him permission to do this. The morning they disappeared he had cut his hand trying to remove fishing hooks that had stuck into his hand. That explained the blood to our satisfaction."

"Ms. Berkin, do you know the whereabouts of this gardener today?"

"Yes."

"Where might he be?"

"The defendant has unofficially adopted the gardener and is now putting him through college," Ms. Berkin said. "I learned that from the hospice administrator and according to her the gardener lives with the defendant."

"Thank you, Ms. Berkin, no further questions," Lily Cup said. She turned to the judge. "Your Honor, for the record, Captain Jordan underwent major stomach surgery while he was in Rhode Island, and the result was the total removal of his cancer."

"A serendipitous outcome—his surgery during a Newport Jazz Festival," Judge Fontenot said. "District Attorney Holbrook, call the next witness."

"The state calls Lieutenant Larry Gaines, of the New Orleans Police."

Lieutenant Larry was sworn in and took the stand.

"Lieutenant Gaines, how long have you been with the New Orleans police department?"

"It'll be a total of fourteen years this October."

"What do you mean, a total of, Lieutenant?"

"I was on the Storyville patrol as a police officer for six years before the second Iraq war. I enlisted and served in 2011 and 2012, and I rejoined the New Orleans police department when I was sent home."

"Thank you for your service, Lieutenant—to our nation and to our city," the district attorney said.

There was no response.

"What position do you hold today, Lieutenant?"

"I'm full detective. I've been a detective for two years."

"Were you called in on this case, Lieutenant?"

"Actually, I was on vacation, still am for ten more days. Our chief called me at home and asked me to assist in any way I could. He said it was an important matter that needed to be cleared up."

"Can you share with us the process you went through and what you found and whether or not you came to any conclusions, Lieutenant?"

"That's why I'm here."

"Thank you, Lieutenant. Please continue."

"The first thing I did was watch the Walmart security videos to get a look at both parties. I knew this wasn't relevant to the day, almost three weeks later, of the killing, but I wanted to see if the videos offered any clues."

"Would you explain to the court the Walmart security videos, Lieutenant—they've not been brought up before?"

"Yes. There were security videos that captured a confrontation between the defendant and the victim—a confrontation that took place three weeks before the homicide in question."

"I can see these videos you speak of as not being admissible in a trial, Lieutenant."

"I agree."

"So why would you bring them up?"

"They show that the defendant and the victim knew each other."

"So, are we to understand the defendant knew the victim for several weeks?"

"According to the security tapes, yes."

"What did you see, and what could you conclude from watching the tapes, Lieutenant?"

"The defendant was having keys made and the victim had visibly accosted him, he badgered him, demanding the defendant give him the use of a credit card."

"Was that it—a verbal threat?"

"On the second video, taken outside the store, the victim brandished a long blade knife and was jabbing it at the air in the defendant's direction. He was jabbing it aggressively. The store manager could be seen running toward the young man and his escaping on a yellow bicycle."

"Were you able to conclude anything from this, Lieutenant?"

"Two things. It did help me narrow my focus—I concluded that the young man was violent, aggressive, appearing to be without conscience at the time this happened in Walmart."

"And number two, Lieutenant?"

"The defendant did have a possible motive. Revenge."

"Would premeditated murder be a possibility, Lieutenant?"

"It's possible."

"What the fuck?" Gabe whispered to Lily Cup.

Lily Cup elbow nudged Gabe's arm.

"He's setting the stage," Lily Cup said.

"Please continue with the investigation's findings, Lieutenant," the district attorney said.

"I was aware the defendant pled innocent to second-degree murder. I was asked by the commissioner to step in as the arresting officer and to investigate the homicide. I asked to meet the defendant and his attorney, Ms. Tarleton, to see if I could question him."

"For what purpose, Lieutenant?"

"Speaking with the accused I find helpful. It was my own coroner's inquisition, you might say," the lieutenant said.

"And were they cooperative?"

"Most cooperative, District Attorney Holbrook. We met the first time for breakfast."

"You interrogated a murder defendant over a public breakfast table with beignets and cinnamon?"

"No, sir. At breakfast I told him the seriousness of the charges and that it was in his interest to help me prove his innocence."

"And the defendant's attorney agreed to his cooperating with you?"

"She did."

"Lieutenant Gaines, did you read him his Miranda Rights?" Judge Fontenot asked.

"I did, Your Honor. His attorney was witness to it."

"And both Captain Jordan and his attorney agreed to cooperate?" Judge Fontenot asked.

"They did, Your Honor. They were aware that with no eye-witnesses coming forward the defendant's innocence was in question knowing the young man was—well, a young man—and that Captain Jordan was an experienced, battle-proven army man…and…"

"And what, Lieutenant?" the district attorney asked.

"There was no knife at the scene."

A grumbling rolled about the gallery. Judge Fontenot slammed the gavel three times.

"Order in the court," the judge said.

"In your opinion, were the store's videos a help to the defendant's case?" the district attorney asked.

"They could help him, but without a knife not so much," Lieutenant said.

"Can you elaborate?"

"As I said before, if they were admitted into evidence the security videos could help, by demonstrating that the young man was an aggressor—an armed aggressor at that."

"Go on, detective Gaines."

"The video could also suggest motive for Captain Jordan."

"And if the defendant 'sought' revenge, that would be premeditated murder."

"Yes."

"While the defendant has only been charged with second degree murder."

"Yes."

"You were at breakfast, Lieutenant. Please continue," the district attorney said.

"My instincts told me that from his many years in the service, the defendant knew and understood the army way of investigation—and that was to duplicate the details of the entire day from the minute he woke up until the moment he was handcuffed and taken into custody."

"And what would prompt these instincts, Lieutenant?"

"I was an officer in the army and...well..."

"You were an officer in the army and what? I didn't quite hear you, Lieutenant."

"And, like the defendant, I'm a black man," the Lieutenant said.

You could hear a pin drop. Papers were not being rustled. The whoosh of the ceiling fans seemed silent. The district attorney stepped back and looked at Lieutenant Gaines.

"The people for the state of Louisiana are colorblind, Lieutenant, I don't see a relevance—"

"If you were a man of color, Mr. District Attorney, you would see the relevance."

"Although I appreciate your candor—your insight," Judge Fontenot said. "There are few places other than in our beloved New Orleans where many cultures are more respected. It's a respect that has grown over a century of living and working together that bring us to the same family supper tables. Our blend of cultures is what make us one in mind and soul."

"I agree there's an effort," the lieutenant said. "Your Honor, there is a tolerance between our cultures, but it's natural that each culture understands their own with an innate sensitivity."

"Please go on, Lieutenant. This is not a trial and the court will keep our interruptions to a minimum," Judge Fontenot said.

"We went to the defendant's home and waited for the exact time that he left the house the day before."

"The day of the incident?" the district attorney asked.

"Yes. From there he walked as he had done on that day and we followed him, to St. Charles Avenue and turned left—east. In the middle of the block he crossed the avenue and walked to the streetcar stop and waited. We rode the streetcar to St. Joseph's just as he had done two days before. I questioned him about what he did next, what he saw. We repeated each step and he told me everything he could remember seeing. He was most cooperative."

"Go on."

"It was the way he described coming across the street when I felt his innocence was a definite possibility," Lieutenant said.

"You stated that you had taken the streetcar to St. Joseph's. Did you get off there, Lieutenant?"

"Yes."

"This should be interesting, Lieutenant. A man crosses the street and it indicates his possible innocence?" the district attorney asked.

"It's the way he was crossing the street."

"So, you're telling the court the defendant made an impression by simply crossing the street—I take it the street is St. Charles Avenue."

"Yes."

"Please continue."

"He was crossing the avenue while blowing his nose," the lieutenant said.

"Would you repeat that for the court, Lieutenant Gaines?"

"The defendant was blowing his nose," the lieutenant said.

"Would you favor the court with the significance of a man's blowing his nose with his not committing murder, Lieutenant?" Judge Fontenot asked.

"Your Honor, to cross the street while blowing his nose, his cane had to be tucked in under his arm, elbows close to his body, with both hands on the handkerchief or tissue. He had sneezed five times, two times standing by the track when he got off the streetcar and three times while crossing St. Charles Avenue at St. Joseph."

"Is there a point to this?" the district attorney asked.

"There is. It seems natural that if a man were blowing his nose all the way across the avenue, he couldn't have been in an aggressive posture, especially one that would result in the death of another. He was wiping his nose, probably not looking up, and my theory is he never saw the victim until he was approached on the sidewalk at knifepoint and threatened."

"Sound detective work, Lieutenant, but there has to be more," Judge Fontenot asked.

"Your Honor, according to the defendant when the young man threatened with knife thrusts and demanded his money and wallet, I think I can prove my theory that the defendant went into a self-defense mode, brandishing his cane as a weapon as he had been trained to do—and I think I can prove he dropped the assailant to the sidewalk with one blow to the upper side of his back calf."

"Did he strike the victim's head?" the district attorney asked.

"Other than a defensive attempt to poke him in the eye, no, not at that time. He put the young man on the ground with one blow to his upper calf, just as he was trained to do, and then it was his intent to leave as quickly as he could."

"Continue," the district attorney said.

Lieutenant Gaines lifted a property bag that held the torn shirt with the missing button.

"The young man grabbed the defendant's shirttail, making it difficult for him to break away—and according to the defendant he kept stabbing up with the blade. You can see that the button was not pulled from the shirt. He cut the button thread clean from the defendant's shirt and slashed the shirt four other times. It was his own pulling of the shirt away from the defendant's torso that may have saved the defendant from being cut with the knife."

"Had Forensic examined your evidence and the scene?" the district attorney asked.

"They had. I worked Forensic a year and a half, so I returned to the scene several times and examined it as well."

"What did you find?" Judge Fontenot asked.

"On the first time I went, I found the button that was cut from the Captain's shirt. I found it under some leaves."

"Without the proper lab work how could you possibly know the button was from the defendant's shirt, Lieutenant?" the district attorney asked.

"I called in a favor from a friend at the state troopers lab in Baton Rouge who reported that the button had the victim's blood on it, and a partial print of his thumb. I drove it up and waited."

"Some favor," the Judge said. "Lab work usually takes weeks."

"It was a Super Bowl bet he owed me, Your Honor. I traded it for an early lab result."

"Please continue," the DA said.

"I believe the victim cut his own thumb when his blade cut the shirt button off. It was his blood on the button which indicated to me he did have a knife. I also found seven cigarettes stepped out in the same spot more than thirty feet away from the scene. Every cigarette had the victim's fingerprints on them."

"What would that tell you—spent cigarettes, Lieutenant?" the district attorney asked.

"It proves nothing but, gathered as they were and with his prints it suggested to me that the victim could have been loitering near a corner he knew was a popular corner for people going to the WWII Museum. I imagined his standing there smoking for a long period of time, lying in wait for a prospective score, and when he recognized the defendant stepping onto the sidewalk, remembered his face, a man who he knew had a wallet filled with credit cards, he approached the defendant to rob him."

"You've presented an intriguing case to the benefit of the defendant, Lieutenant."

"It's only my theory, Your Honor," the lieutenant said.

"Were there any discoveries leading to a self–defense?"

"My theory went a long way to pointing me toward self-defense—I went over everything a hundred times but I needed more."

"What you've presented is impressive—that it was likely not a random act by the defendant, Lieutenant. But the people still see no weapon the victim was purported to having used," Judge Fontenot said.

"Where's the knife?" the district attorney asked.

"I still didn't have a knife."

"Are you implying, since there was no knife, the people should see a probable cause?" the district attorney asked.

"Not yet. What I had was either the Captain's word, or my own investigative experiences—a gut sense if you will—of the purposes of the clues I found—like the cigarettes—the button with the victim's blood on it."

"Without a knife, Detective Gaines, I don't see a strong case for self-defense."

"I knew I needed a knife, but I needed more."

"A knife alone would go a long way, what more would you need?"

"I needed to bring theories into credibility."

"Go on."

"I needed to corroborate the defendant's account he was crossing St. Charles Avenue, while sneezing, wiping his nose and in a non–offensive posture. As a trained military man, it could be self-serving for him to tell me he was sneezing and distracted while crossing the street."

Lieutenant Gaines lifted an evidence bag.

"I'd like to present this into evidence. I found it under a bush between the building and sidewalk—on the complete other side of the sidewalk from where the captain had stepped up."

"What is it?" District Attorney asked.

"I found this handkerchief with the initials GJ sewn into it. With his initials monogrammed on it, it would appear it belonged to Captain Jordan, but it can be tested for DNA. Where I found it convinced me the defendant was sneezing as he told me and couldn't have been in an aggressive posture, or an offensive stance before he threw the handkerchief toward the building and he was threatened the moment he was in the middle of the sidewalk."

"The handkerchief tells you that, Lieutenant?"

"The positioning of the handkerchief does. As a good soldier, he knew to throw the handkerchief out of the way to do battle without distraction or impediment."

"And that's when he killed the victim?"

"I believe he put the man down and tried to walk away."

"Please tell the court what you think this means, Lieutenant," Judge Fontenot said.

"Your Honor, the defendant was trained for 'civil' self-defense, not for a military defense. It was 'man on the street' cane and walking stick self-defense training 101, Your Honor—put the aggressor down and leave quickly."

"The man is dead, Lieutenant," the district attorney said.

"The attacker wouldn't let the defendant retreat. He grabbed and held his shirt as he attacked him with swipes of his knife. As a soldier, Captain Jordan defended his life by striking his attacker twice, once in the head, once at the knife."

The lieutenant lifted Exhibit #1, Gabe's walking stick, in the air.

"This is the walking stick Captain Jordan used to strike the victim. If you examine it closely, although it isn't a new stick, it shows no wear. Captain Jordan even admitted he had only started wearing a cane or carrying a walking stick since his scare at Walmart. If you look at it, the walking stick that looks new has a quarter-inch gash in it. By first impression it's as if a knife had struck it and cut into it."

The lieutenant set the walking stick on the table.

"On a hunch, I went back to the scene just before dusk. I wanted another look."

"You have us on pins and needles, Lieutenant," Judge Fontenot said.

The lieutenant lifted a property baggie in the air.

"I'd like to enter this into evidence, Your Honor. It is the knife, and it does have the victim's prints on it."

A murmur swept the courtroom. The judge answered with three gavel knocks.

"Order."

"Your Honor, the lab confirmed the knife is tipped with a drop of the victim's own blood."

"How did the knife mysteriously reappear?" the district attorney asked.

"My combat training, District Attorney Holbrook."

"Your combat training found the knife?"

"It was my hand-to-hand combat training that reminded me of self-defense tactics with a rifle or stick. My hunch was the victim didn't cut the cane with his knife which was my first theory or impression."

"What changed your mind?"

"The gash in the stick was too deep for a swipe of a knife."

"Are you an expert on such matters as to probabilities involving physics, Lieutenant?" the district attorney asked.

"I'm not."

"But you state it was a knife cut on the stick, Lieutenant."

"My combat training tells me it was Captain Jordan, the defendant, who used his stick to hit the knife out of the victim's hand as opposed to the knife striking the stick offensively. The defendant followed his military training by knocking the knife out of the victim's hand with his walking stick. Following that hunch and looking everywhere, I found the knife on the second-floor balcony of the house behind the scene."

"The lab has determined the knife you found is the knife used in the attack?"

"Yes. Blood and prints."

"So, your testimony is the defendant struck at the knife with his walking stick like he would a bat or a golf club?" Judge Fontenot asked.

"Exactly, Your Honor, the knife landed on the second-floor balcony of the house close by."

"That is impressive detective work, Lieutenant. Any more?" the DA asked.

"The victim was not an unarmed man. This is the weapon we needed. I believe there is substantial evidence that the defendant was only protecting himself."

"Thank you, Lieutenant. He's your witness, Ms. Tarleton."

"We have no questions, Your Honor," Lily Cup said.

"I would like to call my last witness, Your Honor. I would like to call Mr. Chris O' Sullivan, coroner for the city of New Orleans and Orleans Parrish."

The coroner fumbled papers in his hands while walking to the stand. He was sworn.

"Coroner O' Sullivan, have you examined the body of the deceased in question?" the district attorney asked.

"I have, superficially," the coroner said.

"What do you mean superficially?"

"I have an autopsy scheduled for tomorrow. I only had time to examine the body for external wounds."

"What did you find?"

"A severe trauma to the head was the probable cause of death. Death by homicide. Just under the right eye there was trauma, but it was not life-threatening. There was a fresh knife cut on the left thumb of the deceased."

"Could that cut be from cutting himself when he cut off the button of Captain Jordan's shirt?"

"I wasn't told the circumstance or the bloodwork results, but if the blood matched the deceased's blood it could be the result of being cut by his own knife."

"Would you say that the blow to the head was pretty conclusive as to cause of death, Mr. O'Sullivan?" the DA asked.

"I would."

"Anything further before I turn you over to the defense?"

"We were served with a court-ordered request from the Dallas County District Criminal Court in Texas, asking for exhumation rights of the body. They need the body to settle several cases in Dallas, Texas," the coroner said. "Their legal system allows for exhumation, if a violent crime was involved."

"If a body is evidence in a murder trial here, Judge, I'm thinking we hold precedent and can hold the body?" the DA asked.

"Before I answer, District Attorney—Mr. O'Sullivan sir, do you have a copy of the order from the Dallas Criminal Court?" Judge Fontenot said.

"I do, Your Honor."

"Would you please read the 'several cases' portion of it?"

The coroner put his reading glasses on and lifted the page from his file folder.

"'*Kenneth Bauer's prints were found on three empty wallets and one empty purse in downtown Dallas dumpsters and alleys. His print was found on the eyeglasses of a man who was stabbed to death and robbed while entering his car in a downtown parking lot a block from city hall. There is video of him following the man. In the video the man was carrying a briefcase. There was no briefcase at the scene.*'

That's about it, Your Honor."

"Who would pay to ship the body to Dallas?" Judge Fontenot asked.

Lily Cup stood and raised her hand in the air. "If Dallas doesn't pay it, I'll pay it," she said.

Lily Cup sat down and gently knuckled the side of Gabe's thigh.

The judge reached for her gavel.

"District Attorney Holbrook, you asked if Dallas Criminal Court could do that—request a body for examination for five crimes, one being murder?"

"I did, Your Honor."

"It would seem they have," Judge Fontenot said. "District Attorney Holbrook, I find no probable cause for second-degree murder here. Now what say you?"

"Your Honor, at this time the State of Louisiana will not be moving forward for an indictment against Captain Gabriel Jordan."

"Clerk of courts, you may release the body to Dallas. If it's necessary please arrange billing the expense of sending the body to Dallas to Counselor Tarleton," Judge Fontenot said.

"Yes, your honor," the clerk of courts said.

"Captain Jordan, your case is dismissed," the judge said. "Your bond obligation is extinguished. This case is closed."

Her gavel fell a decisive knock.

Lily Cup and Gabe stood.

The press emptied the room into waiting cameras in the hall.

"You are quite a woman," Gabe said. "Best attorney I've ever seen, and I've seen a few."

"Gabe, I can't do lunch. I have a lot of paperwork and the DA and I have to meet with the press. You go home and rest. I'll pick you up later. We'll go to Charlie's Blue Note and celebrate."

"Will you tell Sasha?"

"She's busy with closings all day today. I know she's dying to know what's going on, but let's surprise her together, tonight," Lily Cup said. "Peck too, later."

Gabe gave Lily Cup a long embrace.

"Thank you, little sister."

"Go get some rest, Gabe. You must be exhausted from all of this. We'll party tonight."

CHAPTER 12

NOT LONG AFTER Gabe walked out of the criminal court room in New Orleans, Peck and Elizabeth had walked from lunch at the Bistro. Peck was reading public notices pinned on the Baton Rouge Library bulletin board while Elizabeth spoke with a librarian at the front desk about procedure.

"The lady said we can use any of the reference materials here, but we can't take anything home unless we have a library card," Elizabeth said.

"I have a library card, cher," Peck said.

"It's for New Orleans, not Baton Rouge." Elizabeth said. "It won't work here. Let's just look around and see what we can find. We can make copies to take home."

"Copies be good."

As they walked between the shelves full of books, Peck occasionally reached his hand out to touch the spine of a book with his fingers. Elizabeth wasn't quite certain where to start. She circled back around, reading off the nameplates over each door. She held Peck's arm.

"Peck, let's sit down a minute and talk."

They sat at an empty library table. She gathered her thoughts while looking around the room.

"In cooking school, they teach us that the first time we try to do a menu item we don't experiment—we follow the recipe. After we know what we're doing we can experiment."

"Oui, cher—like baiting a snood. First time you watch and learn from somebody, then you know."

"Something like that, so I'm thinking if you only remember this foster nanna and then there was gator man, I'm thinking we should maybe look at maps and see what you can remember from them."

"Maps is what Miss Audrey say we was to get her, remember?"

"That's right she did, didn't she?"

"Maps, she say to get maps."

"You have a good memory Peck. I wish you could remember more."

Peck leaned into Elizabeth with a nuzzle.

"I remember your neck, cher."

He kissed her neck.

Elizabeth scrunched her neck and shoulder in a "now don't get me started" gesture and stood, looking about for a room where maps might be. She pulled atlas map books and Louisiana reference books from shelves and stacked them on the table.

They sat together as she turned each page.

"Look at this one, Peck. Didn't you say Gabe came from Pineville?"

"*Oui.* He stayed at a VA hospital in Pineville. He runned away from there."

"Look at this—see this dot right here? It's Opelousas. I think you said that's where they found him. Imagine that distance. He walked almost seventy miles."

"He fell down is when somebody bringed him to the hospice."

"Here's another one. Does the Mississippi River make you think of anything when you were young, Peck?"

"Nah, nah. I heard stories but never see'd it until after I runned away."

"Does the Atchafalaya River mean anything?"

"Yes," Peck said.

"What does it mean?"

"I been on that, the Atchafalaya, I think with gator man."

"*C'est un bon debut,*" Elizabeth said. ("This is a good start.")

"Bayou Chene too," Peck said.

"See this water, Peck? Does Lake Maurepas mean anything to you?"

Peck sat tall, as if he bristled.

"Maurepas Maris. *Oui.* Frenchman Settlement, Killian. *Je me souviens d'eux,*" Peck said. ("I remember them.")
"You really remember?"
"I remember floater house."
"You mean houseboat?"
"Oui. Péniche." ("Yes. Houseboat.")
"Does she live on the houseboat?"
"Oui."
"And did you live on it too?"
"*Oui.*"
"Did the houseboat have a motor, Peck?"
"Nah, nah. A pole, cher. A pole would push the houseboat around."
"Did you travel in it?"
"Nah, nah. It was tied to a willer tree—tied tight."
"You were a little boy. How can you remember it was a willow tree?"
"Mamma Nanna would say to Peck, she say it was a sad tree. It, how you say…?"
"Weeps?"
"*Oui*, cher—weeps."
"Willow weeps?" Elizabeth asked.
"*Oui.*"
"It's like the song," Elizabeth said.
"Hanh?" Peck asked.
"*Saule, pleure pour moi,*" Elizabeth sang. ("Willow, weep for me.")
"Peck, I know Audrey is going to have you do this tomorrow, but shall we peek at the tarot cards? Would we be in trouble?"
"She tolded me to touch them. I don't see no trouble."
"Take the cards out of your pocket and spread them on the table."
Peck turned the deck face down on the table.
"*Leur eventail.*" ("Fan them out.")
Peck spread the cards in a two-foot trail.
"Okay, now one at a time, when I tell you, pick one," Elizabeth said.
"Hokay."

"Go ahead, pick one and turn it over."

Peck turned a card. It had an angel in the sky blowing a golden horn and naked people on the ground with their arms outstretched.

"Hmmm," Elizabeth said.

"What it mean, cher?"

"*Je n'ai pas la moindre idée, mon ami,*" Elizabeth said. ("I don't have the faintest idea, my friend.")

"Humph," Peck said.

"Turn another card."

Peck turned a card with a knight on a white stallion. The knight was a skeleton in full armor and there was an archbishop on the ground praying over what looked like a dead body with a little girl fainting.

"*Merde,*" Elizabeth said. "Put them away, Peck, hurry. Turn them over and put them away. We'll make a copy of these two maps and then go to the grocery."

When they got to the apartment, Peck put sacks on counters, then lifted his phone, indicating he was going in the bedroom to call his Millie. Elizabeth looked at her watch and motioned approval, and that she would cook.

Peck took his shoes and jeans off and stretched out on the bed, pressing call keys on the phone.

"Hello?" Millie asked.

"How you are, my Millie?"

"Hold on, sweetie. Let me get out of the shower and grab a towel. Don't go away."

Peck smiled.

"Is this my darling, my superhero?" Millie asked.

"I'm anything my baby want, cher. Peck misses you so much."

"If I think of how much I miss you, Peck, I would not get my schoolwork done so I could come this summer. I take a lot of cold showers."

"Do it good. Schoolwork makes you smart to run our farm."

"I can't wait. Chickens and a garden."

"When you sleep, you think of Peck?"

"Always. Where are you now?"

"Baton Rouge. I spend'd time at the library. We looked up books—maps and things."

"I was at the Baylor library today. They scolded me for keeping books too long. I tried to explain to them I was madly in love, and I could not be held responsible for my tardiness with their books—as time had absolutely no meaning to me anymore."

"Ha," Peck said.

"What are you going to do tomorrow, Peck?"

"I see Audrey."

"Audrey?"

"Audrey, this lady who reads what you call tarot cards and tells Peck things."

"Tarot cards—I've seen them do that at a UT party in Austin."

"You turned the tarot cards?"

"I don't think Baptist girls are allowed to play with tarot cards. I'm not sure."

"Are Baptist girls allowed to be with Cajun French fishers?"

"This one is. Do you have anyone in mind?"

"I have something in mind, cher."

"You little diablo, you. Are you talking naughty?"

"My William make Peck do it—talk dirty."

Millie laughed. "You don't like it called William. What makes you talk about William now? Are you being a bad boy?"

"Peck is perfect gentlemen. It's William is so bad."

"William is so good," Millie said. "Don't be picking on him."

"So, Peck will call tomorrow and tell you what the Audrey lady say, hokay?"

"I love you, Peck."

"I love you, cher. Study hard."

Peck got up from the bed and in his briefs and T-shirt walked out to the kitchen where Elizabeth was talking on her phone. She raised a finger over her lips, indicating "be quiet." Her boo was on the phone.

Peck went to the refrigerator next to the counter Elizabeth was leaning on. He opened the door and looked through and behind on its shelves and lifted out a bottle of iced tea. He stood beside her, removing the cap. He held the bottle out, offering her a sip. She shook her head *no* while reaching a hand out and pulling the top of his briefs away from his stomach. She looked down in at his prize, rolled her eyes and let it snap closed, smiling.

He stepped into the living room, plopped on the sofa and picked up his *Cannery Row* novel. He opened the chapter where the brothel owner, Nell, saw Doc in the general store. Peck read each word to himself while Elizabeth finished her phone business and prepared a candlelight dinner of chicken in butter cream sauce with capers and thin asparagus Hollandaise.

As Peck turned the page he learned that brothel owner Nell was telling Doc that he worked too hard and was living alone. He needed to get out more. She had a new girl at the house, Suzy, that he might be interested in. "She don't quite fit in, she don't belong there—just needs the work, Doc. She ain't like my other girls, Doc."

Peck turned another page to see if Doc makes a decision to go meet the girl, Suzy, and add some fun to his life of collecting sea urchins and frogs for science labs in schools.

Peck read until Elizabeth called him to dinner.

CHAPTER 13

ABOUT THE TIME Elizabeth and Peck were sitting down for dinner in Baton Rouge, in the alley off Frenchmen Street, Lily Cup was pushing the door to Charlie's Blue Note open to slam with an attention-getting irreverence.

"A round of drinks for everyone, Charlie—the boys in the band get two, and where's my box of cigars?" Lily Cup asked, as Gabe stepped into the room behind her.

She lifted his arm as though it were after the fifteenth round of a heavyweight prizefight.

"Ladies and gentleman, the winner and champion, let's hear it for our own Captain Gabriel Jordan," Lily Cup said.

Sasha, in a gray business suit, reached over the bar and grabbed a fresh cigar and a clean ashtray. She climbed from her stool, pranced toward Lily Cup and handed them to her. She turned to Gabe and hugged to a round of applause from Charlie and four at the bar, the eight sitting at tables with their bowls of red beans and rice, and four on the dance floor. The band stopped a piece of jazz and counted into "When Sonny Gets Blue," knowing it was Gabe's favorite. The three joined arms and walked like musketeers over to Gabe's table by the band.

"Don't get me wrong, darling, you look fresh out of Bloomingdales, but what's with the business suit?" Gabe asked. "This is Frenchmen Street."

"Forget the suit. Didn't I tell you she was one incredible attorney? Didn't I tell you?" Sasha asked.

"You did indeed, and just watching her two days ago and today and how it all came down could bring me to happy tears. I could not agree with you more," Gabe said. "What a ride it's been."

"What is with the gray suit?" Lily Cup asked.

"I just came from a closing and didn't want to miss you guys if you came here and your phone is off, thank you very much."

"Was it an agent's closing or your own closing?" Lily Cup asked.

"One was mine, a place in the Garden District on Coliseum Street. It's a redo. Four and a half million, my listing, my client, my sale," Sasha said.

"Gabe, our queen of the strapless gown here just made more coin today than everyone in this alley will make all year combined."

"You do pretty well yourself," Gabe said.

"Not if I keep handling pro bono bums like you, I won't," Lily Cup guffawed.

"I'm not pro bono. I'm paying you, little sister."

"No, you aren't. It's on me. Shut up and have some fun tonight."

"Tonight, we celebrate," Gabe said.

"I'll go get our drinks," Sasha said. "We'll do beans and rice later."

"And grab a couple more cigars for me," Lily Cup said.

"Isn't smoking banned in restaurants and bars, counselor?" Gabe asked.

"You are correct, my friend. Cigars are absolutely banned from bars and other confined spaces…"

"I thought I read that somewhere," Gabe said.

"But you didn't read the fine print, Captain. Cigar bars in New Orleans existing before the smoking law are grandfathered."

"And Charlie's Blue Note is a…?" Gabe asked.

"I personally took the matter into my own hands. I set up the corporation for Charlie ten years ago. It's Charlie's Blue Note and Cigar Bar, Inc." Lily Cup said.

"You are something else, little sister…something else," Gabe said.

"You're talking to a fucking visionary, Captain. Half my clients, half the judges—even the DA's people—smoke cigars. This is New Orleans."

"Sweetie pie, you can smoke all the cigars you want tonight," Sasha said. "You saved Gabe, you genius best friend all my life, and otherwise nice person who I'll love until I die," Sasha said.

"Lily Cup, we've never danced. Would you do me the honor?" Gabe asked.

Sasha removed her suit coat and rested it on the back of a chair.

"Behave, you two," Sasha said, smiling and walking away.

A three-piece band took stage in a break for the jazz band. The music was a boogie-woogie Sewanee River on a lap piano, snare drums, and fiddle. Gabe stood, held his hand out for Lily Cup as she reached for an ashtray.

"Keep the cigar with you, little sister. You've earned that privilege," Gabe said.

She stood, smirked and strolled to him while bending over with a jazz step and hip motion, cigar in her fingers. Gabe took her free hand, pulled her to him and held her waist. Then he faked a jerk with his hips, then one with his shoulders, then back and forth and a step forward and back. The two were in perfect sync on their row down the Sewanee River with the band. As the music faded with a violin landing and bow removed, Gabe stood motionless, put his hands tenderly on each of Lily Cups cheeks.

"Thank you, little sister," Gabe said.

"My pleasure, poppa bear," Lily Cup replied.

"Make room for the tray," Sasha said.

Lily Cup stepped away from Gabe and moved her ashtray to the corner of the table.

"The lady can dance," Gabe said.

"What do you think we've been doing here at the Blue Note for ten years? Arts and crafts?" Sasha asked.

"Now don't get me started, darlin'. I've heard about the days on Magazine Street. Woman, you can't put one over on old Gabe, here."

Sasha put her hand on her waist, braced up with a smirk.

"Whatchu talkin' 'bout, dancin' man?" Sasha asked.

"You know what I'm talkin'. I'm talkin' the Victoria's Secret brassiere you saved up for and the shows—I'm keeping it clean—the shows you put on in those back sheds on Magazine Street," Gabe said.

"Lily Cup, you are such a blabber puss," Sasha said.

"Gabe and I were making conversation over chicory coffee, girlfriend. Thought I'd tell him how your girls could quench a hot afternoon's free-time boredom on school days."

"The Brewster kid—remember him?" Sasha asked.

"That's the one. Gabe, we took his virginity, took him around the world, and I convinced him to ask Mrs. Conklin how to spell *ménage a trois*—that she would be so impressed she would give him an A."

"You two have a book to write," Gabe said.

Lily Cup threw back a swallow of rye. "Gabe, can I ask you something?"

"Anything, my heroine."

"It's personal," she said.

"I have no secrets at this table, little sister."

"It's something that's been kind of, you know, gnawing on me, inside…and I was trying to figure out how to ask."

"So, ask already," Gabe said.

"I started thinking about it in the courtroom today when Lieutenant Larry was telling the judge that because he was black he could understand your messages. He said he could communicate with you better than others, because it was a black to black, a culture thing," Lily Cup said.

"He was right. Just as a man can't talk good menstrual, a white can't talk good black," Gabe said.

"We communicate on the dance floor, baby," Sasha said.

"We do, and that ain't no lie," Gabe said.

"Gabe, when you said—I don't know—I think it was right after Larry told the judge the Walmart videos could make you look like you had a motive for murder…you leaned over and said to me, 'I'm ready for anything.' Do you remember saying that? Did you mean that?"

"I remember and I meant it," Gabe said.

"What did it mean?"

"It's a black thing. Now you two, of all people, know ole Gabe here don't dwell on being black. But what you may not be able to see is being black dwells on me and my brothers for all our lives. We don't all go through life with chips on our shoulders, but we do go through our lives with a clear understanding that the Declaration of Independence, where all men were created equal, was written by a man who owned slaves until the day he died. We know what it's like, in most cities, when we cross a street and we can sometimes hear car doors lock."

"Are you saying you expected the worst and were ready not to fight...just give up?"

"I was."

"I'll be damned."

"Sorry."

"But why? You knew it was self-defense."

"Yes. I did, and you did, and the chief of police did, and the DA did. But—and you even said it—the media upset the Visitors Bureau, and it then became second-degree murder."

"Let me ask. Did OJ expect the worst just because he was black?"

"OJ was guilty. He expected it...and maybe his murder trial was just another Tuesday night NFL game for him—who knows?"

"How about Bill Cosby?"

"I think he expected a public lynching."

"But he gave them pills."

"He admitted to giving them Quaaludes years before the trial. He was a big star. I wouldn't be surprised if he had a bowl of pills and a pile of cocaine on his dresser. You don't go to a man's bedroom to have tea."

Gabe lifted the bottle and swallowed some scotch.

"Cable changed the world. It's divided us. It's now the court, judge, and jury," Gabe said.

"Your case wasn't a race case," Lily Cup said.

"I know exactly what it was, little sister. It was a case of all eyes on New Orleans, and tourism had to cover its ass by whupping mine. Nothing personal. My being black only helped ratings. Pundits had five victims for stories—me being black for one, me being an old man, me being military, and don't forget the homeless white boy."

"Television changed everything," Lily Cup said. "I had to take six hours of crisis management on handling media. Nothing is local anymore. It all goes global."

"Pavarotti has left the building," Gabe said.

"You mean Elvis?" Lily Cup asked.

"Pavarotti," Gabe said.

"The opera singer?"

"Our lesson of any sense of world-class humility we had was watching an entire world at war when eighty million people died. Showing respect for others was a given; it was how we were raised. Good behavior was drummed into us in the sixties and seventies, when the world was still young and Pavarotti lived and set the example on the world stage. When Luciano Pavarotti died, little sister, with his broad smiles and long scarves; with his hand-sewn tuxedos with black ties and white ties and a passion for brilliance...When he died it just seemed feeling good about the simple, respectful dressing up to go out and the saying of *please* and *thank you* eroded from our culture. It was as if our sense of world class took a bow with him and exited, stage left," Gabe said.

"Will you two give it a rest? Dance with me, Gabe," Sasha said.

"Absolutely," Lily Cup said with a hiccup. "I have to pee. I'm going to call Peck and tell him."

As Lily Cup got up, Gabe stood and offered his hand to Sasha. The bass slap–strummed the beat, brushes on a soft snare offered the way...and the riff began. Gabe pulled Sasha in full circle. He didn't know the tune, but he knew the right moves. The clarinet took him back to Benny Goodman, and they swayed in a syncopation of celebration—not of court battles, not of life going by. It was a celebration of New Orleans. For the bad that happened in this particular bend in the Mississippi river, there were two things good that happened, and there was the music.

"Hello?" Peck asked.

"Hey Peck, I have good news," Lily Cup said.

"You sound like an echo, cher. Where you are?"

"I'm in the restroom. We're at the Blue Note."

"A restroom?"

"I had to pee. Now can I tell you my news?"

"Tell Peck."

"Gabe got off. He's free as a bird. We're celebrating at Charlie's."

"That is good news. You the best."

"It happened with you telling me about the videos, Mr. Investigator. You're the brains behind this whole thing."

"You plenty smart. T'ank you for helping my frien'."

"Hey, Peck."

"What?"

"My panties are around my knees. Want a selfie?"

"You drinking that rye again, cher?"

"Is there any other drink?"

Peck laughed.

"I was just fooling with you. If I took a selfie like that it would probably wind up on Facebook in an hour."

"Cher, tell Gabe I'm happy? Tell him for Peck?"

"I will."

"T'ank you."

"Is that Elizabeth gal helping you?"

"Yes'm, she is big help. Tomorrow we go see Audrey. She's a tarot lady."

"Where are you?"

"I'm in Baton Rouge."

"Be careful, Peck."

"I be careful, dass for true."

Lily Cup flushed the toilet.

"Shit, I didn't want you to hear that," Lily Cup said.

"Hear what?"

"Never mind. Keep us posted?"

"Hanh?"

"Bad connection. Just let us know how it's going."

"For sure, cher."

"Night, Peck. Good luck."

"Bye."

CHAPTER 14

THE BEDROOM WAS DARK, and the time was somewhere between bar closings and when the brushes of street washers would sweep through the streets of downtown Baton Rouge. A city sound, a siren, wailed in the distance behind buildings in another neighborhood. In a deep sleep, Peck mumbled with a restless roll, and he turned over with a flop, facing the center of the bed. Now they sleep as friends, not the lovers they once were but as he rolled over, his arm followed him like a boa, the back of his hand landing on the heat of a warm blend of soft satin and silky–smooth skin. His hand turned from back to palm instinctively inquisitive, feeling the warm buttock, and it met the touch with an unconscious squeezing and Braille–like feel. This awakened Elizabeth's curiosity and she rolled on her side, her back to him. Her head on her pillow, eyes open, she looked up at a ceiling she couldn't see. Peck's free hand went from the flat of his stomach it was resting on down into his briefs, and William was pulled summarily from a restless sleep and directed between the hidden warmth of Elizabeth's crotch from behind. Her legs straightened and flexed her buttocks, holding her thighs together like a vice. William began pumping between her legs, slowly at first, teasing the awakened but hidden lips of her island while rubbing the softness of their satin gatekeeper.

"Peck," Elizabeth whispered, as if she didn't want him to hear her.

William thrust slowly.

"Peck."

William's motion between a heaven-sent triangle of thighs and a warm, satin-covered crotch became more deliberate, upper thighs softly slapping her buttocks. A sleeping hand fumbled in front of her like a lost puppy in search of breasts.

"I'm not Millie."

William was relentless.

"Peck, wake up."

"Hanh?" Peck asked.

In the dark of night, Peck woke, and as if he saw the light of what he was doing on the backs of sleeping eyelids, he pulled his hips away, freeing William into the night air and rolled on his back. He rubbed his eyes and cheeks and raked stiff fingers through his hair in a scratch.

"Peck's got to stop drinking the wine, cher, dass for true," Peck said.

He tucked William in his briefs.

Elizabeth was silent as she smiled, still looking toward the ceiling in the darkened room.

"No more wine for me."

Elizabeth rolled toward Peck and nuzzled his neck.

"*Mais le poulet et les câpres ètaient bons, non?*" Elizabeth asked. ("But the chicken and capers were good, no?")

He thought for a moment, and with stomach muscles contracting, broke into a silly laughter.

"What time is it?" Peck asked.

"It's three–thirty. We should sleep."

"What time does Peck have to see Audrey?"

"Ten. I'll show you where to catch the bus and when to get off. I'll write it down."

"You go with me, cher?"

"I have to be at the cooking school at ten. I'll be back here at three. You should be done by then. Want me to cook tonight, or want to eat out?"

"Bistro?"

"*Parfait!*" Elizabeth said. ("Perfect.")

"We'll meet here and then go to Bistro," Peck said.

"Oui." Elizabeth said. She kissed Peck on the neck. She knelt up in the dark.

"*Tu veux que je retire ma culotte?*" ("Do you want me to take my panties off?")

"*Peck doit être bon, cher,*" Peck whispered. ("Peck need to be good, cher.")

She pulled her T-shirt up over her head and off, flipping it to the bureau. She leaned in, felt around for William and kissed it a quick goodnight through his briefs and lay down, her bare back to Peck, tucking a pillow between her legs and falling asleep.

When Peck stepped out of the shower he could smell coffee. He toweled his hair, wrapped a loosely knotted, dry towel around his waist and walked the hall to the kitchen for a cup. Elizabeth was barefoot in her chef school pants with no top. Bell-shaped breasts flexed as she reached into the upper cabinet for cooking utensils and then into the refrigerator for eggs. Peck watched her nipples, likely remembering the first time they met, and he saw them through her yellow T-shirt so many years ago.

"*Bonjour,*" Peck said.

"*Bonjour,*" Elizabeth said.

"*Tu as l'air reposè. Tu as bien dormi?*" Peck asked. ("You look refreshed. Did you sleep well?")

Elizabeth smiled.

"I was sleeping so well until this naughty boy with a big, long broom handle molested me," Elizabeth said.

"I was dreaming. You are so lovely in the night, I could not resist touching you in my sleep. Ha ha. Don't be upset with Peck, cher."

"You were more fun when you weren't in love," Elizabeth said. "You finished things you started back then."

Elizabeth poured a cup for Peck, dropped two teaspoons of sugar in it and stirred. She held it out.

"*C'est tellement triste, cher,*" Peck said. ("It's so sad, then, cher.")

"Why sad?" Elizabeth asked.

Peck took the coffee from her hand.

"It's so sad because Peck won't ever finish with Elizabeth, ever. So sad."

Elizabeth reflected and smiled at the oral embrace. Her eyes felt good about it. She reached and with her thumb and finger loosened the knot and let his towel drop to the floor, exposing skillet flat abs, carved pecks and a resting, chubby, William. He smirked, not moving a muscle. He nonchalantly sipped of his coffee.

"*Oh mon dieu, on dirait que notre ami a eu une attention particulière dans la douche peut-être?*" Elizabeth asked. ("Oh my, it looks like our friend got special attention in the shower, maybe?")

Elizabeth put a pot under the faucet and turned the water on.

"Our friend has a name, cher. Don't be rude," Peck said.

"A name? What name?"

"William. He is William."

Elizabeth grinned, turned the faucet off, lifted the pot to the stove and turned the gas flame on.

"I would shake William's hand, but I'm certain he's exhausted from being in the shower with you."

They continued their repartee with smiles and grins, and it reminded them why they had been such good friends for so long a time.

"I'm going to shave. I'll be right out. Will Elizabeth have breakfast with me?"

"I'll have toast, but then I have to leave. We eat what we cook, and I'll get so fat if I eat more now. Go shave."

Peck sipped his coffee and turned down the hall. Elizabeth watched him walk away and then turned to crack the eggs into the three ceramic coddlers. Peck came out dressed and ready to start his journey.

"Do you have money, Peck? You have to pay Audrey."

Peck took a debit card from his pocket.

"This?"

"That will work. She'll take a card. Do you have bus money?"

"*Oui.*"

"Don't forget the tarot cards."

"I have the cards."

Peck twisted the lids off the coddlers and peppered the contents of the first, and with a spoon enjoyed its sunken treasures for the palate. Elizabeth liked watching the adventure in his eyes. She was happy for him with his new love and continued education. Sometimes she would wonder if Peck and her man should meet, and if they did, how it would be arranged.

"Here's a spare key. Hang on to it. I'll see you when I get home."

"T'ank you, cher."

Elizabeth went back into the bedroom and came out buttoning the top of her cooking school chef uniform. It was a heavily starched white. Her nametag was pinned to it. She walked over to where Peck was sitting and nudged her knee into his thigh so she could sit in his lap. He turned and she sat on his lap sidesaddle.

"Don't be afraid today, Peck."

"I'm not afraid."

"Audrey will tell you what she sees in the cards, but it's what she thinks she sees, so don't be afraid."

"I'm not afraid, cher."

"It's good to listen to her, though, so listen to her and remember what she tells you."

"Peck is a good listener. Have to listen for turtles."

"Turtles don't make noises. Why do you listen for turtles?"

"Frogs make noises when they jumpin' away from snappers, cher. Crawfish snakes chase after frogs."

Elizabeth put her arms around his neck and smiled into his eyes. She found great warmth, a security in knowing how closely her friend communed with nature.

"Will it be all right if I kissed you goodbye, Peck?"

Peck sat there without speaking.

"Well?" Elizabeth asked.

"I'm thinking," Peck said.

Her right hand lifted from his neck to the top of his head and grabbed his hair and pulled his head back. Her open mouth plunged his smile with a morning kiss of passion between friends. Her hands held his ears as they kissed. She kissed his lips, his chin and sat up with a happy sigh.

"Now good, cher?" Peck asked.

"Needs more pepper," Elizabeth said. "Use the white pepper on the other coddled eggs, Peck."

With that she stood, clutched her bag of books and notepads and headed to the front door.

"*Au revoir, mon ami,*" Elizabeth said.

She left for school, and Peck was not far behind. His phone showed he had an hour to be at his appointment with Audrey, so he decided to walk. He would walk to South Tenth Street and go from there.

Audrey was waiting for him. She opened the door and invited him in. She then hung a "do not disturb" sign on the door, closed and locked it behind them.

"Let's step into the next room, Peck. We'll be more comfortable there."

With the exception of a strand of blue LED lights hanging over a velvet-draped table and a burning wax candle, the room was darkened.

"Have a seat, Peck. I use these few lights and one candle so we are not distracted by things in the room."

"I understand."

"Would you prefer I use your given name, Boudreaux Clemont, or Peck. I want to use what is comfortable for you. Do you have a preference?"

"Peck is good."

"Did you bring the tarot cards?"

"Yes'm."

"Before we begin, would you shuffle them?"

Peck shuffled the deck of cards in several different manners before setting them on the table.

"Now fan them out."

Peck ran the palm of his hand tightly over the deck and dragged them into a trail of about two feet.

"Do you have a number you feel most comfortable with? It may be what some call a lucky number...or a number you think of more than other numbers?"

"Eight."

"You feel good with the number eight?"

"Eight hooks on a snood. Eight fingers, no thumbs. Eight is good."

"One at a time, Peck, slowly run your hand over all of the cards and pick eight cards you feel may be sending you a message. Take the time you need. One at a time, hand them to me."

The first time, Peck ran his hand over the cards and selected one card and handed it to Audrey. She held it face-down in her palm. The second and other times he put his left hand on the left end of the card trail, closed his eyes and ran his right hand over the cards and picked one at a time and held it out for Audrey. With each card he selected, he became more concentrated on the task at hand.

Audrey picked up the remaining portion of the deck and placed it on the wooden shelf behind her. She fanned the eight cards in her hand.

"Pick one of these cards, Peck. The card you select will tell us the road before you that destiny has willed you to travel. Let the card speak to you. Be patient."

Peck placed his palm under her hand holding the fanned cards. He held his other hand over them. He closed his eyes and moved each hand back and forth slowly. His index finger came down and touched one.

"This one," Peck said.

He pulled it from her hand and held it out for her. Audrey placed it face-down in front of Peck. She then placed the remaining seven cards face-down and side-by-side in the middle of the table.

"We first reveal a lead message, and then we will turn one message at a time and see in what direction they lead the journey," Audrey said.

She took the first card Peck had selected and turned it over.

"Your hand selected this first. It's the Death card. Death means change in your future. It could be any aspect of your life. It might be something you learn about yourself. It could be something about someone you love. Death means a complete severance from the past and future. Do you wish to hear more?"

"*Oui.*"

"The change in your life will be painful. It will be permanent. You must have death before you can move on to a new phase of your life. Something has been approaching you. It will arrive soon. You are about to lose something valuable to you."

"Foster nanna, I think," Peck said. "She's coming, I t'ink."

"It could be a person, but it could also be a thought, a dream."

Audrey placed her hand on his. "Do you wish to continue?"

"*Oui.* Continue."

She turned another card.

"This is the High Priestess card. You possess good judgment and have strong intuition. You will be rewarded if you maintain discipline. Although this is a time of renewal for you, you need help from someone."

"Elizabeth," Peck said.

"Would you like me to continue, Peck?"

"*S'il tu plaît, ne me demande plus. Je n'ai pas peur d'entendre ça,*" Peck said. ("Please don't ask me again. I'm not afraid to hear this.")

"Ahh, the Justice card. A very good card if you are kind and fair, or if you've been a victim. For the unjust it is a warning, for you it is a blessing. You are going to receive an outcome you truly deserve."

Peck clenched his fists and held them to his lips in heavy thought.

"This one is the Strength card. You have chosen cards well, my friend. This shows you have the rawest of power. You have a balance of mental and physical strength. It does come with advice. You shouldn't turn down any offers that will change your future."

As if he were waiting for the nibble on his trotline that would feed him that day, Peck gazed at the remaining cards.

"Oh my. This is the Hanged Man card. With it comes two interpretations. Either the old must die to create the new, or it lets you let go from a past—a sacrifice. The Hanged Man is a metamorphosis."

"I runned away once. Do I run back now, maybe?" Peck asked.

"Time will give you the answer, Peck."

She turned another card.

"This is the Lovers card. Love comes to you in many forms. You will come to two paths. One of them will take you to a good place. You have a conflict approaching. Choose wisely."

"Between Millie and Elizabeth, you mean?" Peck asked.

"No. I think you'll have to choose between love and a career. I'm not certain."

"I pick love," Peck said.

"I believe you can pick both. I just think the card is telling you to keep a balance."

"D'at is good then," Peck said.

"Now, third from last of the cards you picked—the Fool card."

"Hanh?" Peck asked.

"Oh, but it's a most powerful card, the Fool card. It's a new beginning. It means something is going to change in your life. You ran from home when you were nine. Imagine the risks you took. It has only brought you success."

"Millie, Gabe, Peck's frien's so good," Peck said.

"There are two more cards. You must select carefully now. The card you select will anoint your journey. But the one left on the table—the last one—will seal the fate of all that is meant for you in the days ahead. Choose carefully. Take your time."

Almost without thought, his hand, like a darting eel, reached and grabbed a card and held it out for Audrey.

"Oh my, you have a strong will. Let's see what you selected."

Audrey turned the card.

"Interesting. You selected the Judgment card. It tells of the transition we speak of. It tells that it's been long in the making and it is coming to a fruition. It also says you will have to make decisions."

"*Si seulement Peck ètait plus intelligent, Mlle Audrey. Je pourrais mieux comprendre, je pense,*" Peck said. ("I wish Peck was more intelligent, Miss Audrey. I could understand better, I think.")

"It will come to you in time, Peck. It's important that you're pure of thought and true to those around you. Follow your heart."

"Yes'm."

"Now there is one more card. It is a window on your destiny. Are you ready?"

"*Oui.*"

"Peck, try to think of your entire life. In this lifetime, what one thought or dream have you turned to time and time again, for balance, for warmth, for hope?"

"My mamma, cher. I talk to my mamma."

"Turn the last card, Peck."

Peck turned the card, looked at it and set it on the table as a tear formed in his eye.

"The Moon card, Peck."

"I know," Peck said.

"Something in your life is not what it seems."

"My mamma, maybe?"

"The Moon card is a strong indicator that you must rely on your own intuition."

"The moon is my mamma, I know for true."

"Your understanding of the past is distorted."

"It's my mamma for true, cher."

"Peck, the moon is your imagination. Don't ever lose that."

"I'll never lose the moon, cher."

"That's the end of our reading, Peck. How do you feel?"

"So much to t'ink about. I feel like there are so many—how you say—doors to open now?"

"That's a perfect description. Yes—doors that need opening."

"Thank you, Miss Audrey."

"Peck, is it possible that you come back in the morning and bring Elizabeth with you?"

"*Pourquoi?*" Peck asked. ("Why?")

"I want her to be a part of a decision that has to be made. I'm thinking a hypnotist can help you now. I think you're ready to open some of those doors, and your subconscious has many of the keys."

"I'll ask Elizabeth and if she say yes, I bring her. What time?"

"Same time. It won't take long. After that I'll set an appointment with the hypnotist."

Peck dug in his pocket and pulled out his debit card.

"Pay me tomorrow, Peck. How do you feel about today?"
"I feel good. So many things to t'ink about."
"Good."

As Peck walked to the apartment his cell phone rang. It was Lily Cup.
"Hey, cher. How you are?"
"Peck, I'm in Baton Rouge. I have meetings in the courthouse until four. Can you have dinner with me?"
"Elizabeth in school to three o'clock. Maybe all of us for dinner?"
"Perfect," Lily Cup said.
"So, you will call me later, cher?"
"I will. Pick your favorite restaurant," Lily Cup said.

Peck put the phone in his pocket and smiled as he crossed a street. He would go to the apartment and call his Millie and tell her of the day, and then he would read more chapters of *Cannery Row* until Elizabeth came home.

A traveling cloud seemed to block the sun, but only for a moment. The air cooled as it passed over. Peck enjoyed walking through downtown Baton Rouge.

Chapter 15

NOT KNOWING PECK'S MOOD following his tarot reading, Elizabeth took care to unlock the apartment door quietly. The living room and kitchen were empty, and the bathroom door was ajar. Through the hall she could see his bare feet on the bed. He was sleeping on top of the bed cover on his back in his briefs and no T-shirt. His arms wrapped around a pillow pulled over his face. She took her cooking school chef uniform top off, checked it to see if it needed laundering and hung it in the bedroom closet.

She stood bare-breasted and watched Peck sleeping in his briefs, the John Steinbeck novel beside him. She quietly pulled a drawer, removing a yellow-gold T-shirt with LSU's, "Tiger Bait" imprinted on it in black. She dropped the T-shirt on the bed and began untying straps holding up her school chef pants. She lowered them enough to realize she was *sans* panties that day, pulled them up and refastened the strap. She took a hairbrush from atop the bureau and placed a knee on the T-shirt at the edge of the bed as she crawled on over it and sat beside Peck. She ran her fingers gently around his chest.

"Ma cheri?" Elizabeth asked.

His body didn't move as he lifted the pillow from over his face and rested it behind his head.

"Brush my hair?" Elizabeth asked.

Peck opened his eyes at the sound of her voice and without moving he looked at her eyes, at the brush in her hand, and at her breasts.

"*J'aime comment tu me brosses les cheveux*," Elizabeth added. ("I like how you brush my hair.")

"Run the tub hot, cher," Peck said.

Elizabeth grinned, her eyes awakened with a twinkling. The tub had been a special place for all the years they had been friends. A hot bath usually followed good sex, sometimes bath time led to it, but whichever way the compass pointed, a tub was their secret place, their tree house.

Elizabeth would say the tub was special because they would take the time to talk while he brushed her hair or she washed his back or clipped his toenails. Peck held his secret from Elizabeth that she had taken his virginity when he was almost nineteen and fresh out of their first tub bath, and Elizabeth held hers from him that she knew. Peck would say the water was good when it was hot like a bayou swamp but without alligators or snappers. Elizabeth would say her time with Peck in the tub bonded them together like the Holy Trinity of Cajun cooking –onion, celery, and bell pepper.

Hearing the faucets turned off, Peck got up and stepped into the bathroom and dipped a toe into a full tub. He pushed the curtain to the far left, out of the way. Elizabeth reached and pinched either side of his briefs, pulling them to the floor and he stepped out of them.

"Get in," Elizabeth said.

He did and sat down. She handed him the brush, dropped her chef uniform pants to the floor and stepped in the tub in front of him, sitting between his legs. Peck took her hair into one hand and brushed it down from her scalp and off the end into his flattened hand. He would pull brushstrokes with an endless patience, like a fisherman casting his line from a lonely reef.

"*Qu'as-tu cuisiné aujourd'hui, cher?*" Peck asked. ("What did you cook today, cher?")

Elizabeth pouted her lips. Her voice cracked.

"*Le chef Elizabeth a cuisiné de la merde aujourd'hui. J'ai brûlé le saumon, brûlé une sauce au beurre, et j'ai râpé une putain de carotte et pas julienne. Merde, merde, merde,*" Elizabeth said. ("Chef Elizabeth cooked shit today. I burned the salmon, burned a cream butter sauce, and grated a fucking carrot and not julienne. Shit, shit, shit.")

"Anyone can burn a salmon."

"Not when it's supposed to be poached, they don't."

"Oh?"

"Yeah...oh."

"Your hair is so pretty, cher."

"Don't make me ask. Tell me what Audrey said."

"She told Peck the moon was my frien', and she say there is change coming in my life. She say not to be scared, but I need somebody to go with me when I go to my past."

"Did she say who?"

"And she say that the death she saw is for changes in my life, and that something always had to die to make, how you say, room for the new thing—at least I think dass what she had to say."

"Who will die, did she say?"

"Your salmon is dead, maybe that counts, cher."

With a grin in her eyes, Elizabeth's pouting lips bristled a tight pucker.

"Do you think butter sauce dies?" Peck asked.

Elizabeth reached behind her back with her hand, threatening to grab William or his personals, but she paused and rested her arm on his knee.

"It didn't frighten you, the things she said?"

"Nah, nah."

"Did she say who should go with you?"

"No, but she ax if you could come with me to see her tomorrow, same time. She say to bring maps."

"Peck, I can't be the one to go with you. You know that, don't you?"

"So, I tell Audrey you have cooking school and can't come see her with me."

"No, I don't mean that. I can go tomorrow. I just can't be the one that goes with you wherever it is you have to go in your past."

"I know that, cher. You have your boo on the rig. I've been thinking maybe Millie should go with me."

"Your Millie? Interesting. Do you think she could handle the swamps and things you might see and hear?"

"My Millie can handle it. I just don't want to disappoint her maybe."

"How could you possibly disappoint her?"

"What if I'm a nobody bag dare where I grow'd, cher?"

"Tell me about Millie. What's she like?"

"Millie ax me if I could watch her t'ings on the bus that time. She had to go to the *salle de bain* (bathroom) and I saw her eyes good, and I knew there was something about her come over me. When she come out she sat with Peck, and we talked about her boyfrien' what cheated on her all the time and how her daddy was a reverend and strict. She has a little doll, you know, like a baby ever since she was three or two. Peck not sure how old it is now, but she keeps it with her. It's her baby Charlie."

"She had a boyfriend when you met her?"

"No. She told him goodbye when she got on the bus to go bag home in Tennessee from university. Dass when I meeted her. On the bus."

"Is she pretty?"

"Oh, *oui*."

"When did you know you were in love, Peck?"

"On the bus. When she ax me to watch her t'ings, dass for true, cher. It was magic."

"C'est tellement beau, Peck. Je suis contente pour toi," Elizabeth said. ("That's so beautiful, Peck. I'm happy for you.")

"Do you know why Audrey wants to see us both tomorrow?" Peck asked.

"I'm certain she wants to let me in on her thoughts while we're both in the room. I told her stories about what you went through with the gator man and with the foster nanna you ran from."

"You told her all dat, for true?"

"And more."

"What more?"

"I told her you are one of the most romantic men I've ever known."

"Dass for true?"

"For true," Elizabeth said.

"Ta Millie vous rend tous les deux si chanceux. Garde-la et ne la laisse jamais partir," Elizabeth said. ("Your Millie makes you both so lucky. Hold her and don't let go.")

"If Millie come here, would it be good or bad if she meeted you, cher?"

"I would love to meet Millie. What would you tell her about us?"

"Millie and Peck so much in love, I wouldn't have to tell her anything."

"What kind of woman would she think I am, cheating like I do?"

Peck stopped brushing and set the brush on the tub rail.

"You don't cheat."

Elizabeth paused, squeaking the tub floor with her bottom as she turned around and looked into Peck's eyes.

"I'm a cheater on my man, no?"

"You have to be in love to cheat, cher. Elizabeth not in love."

Their gaze into each other's eyes churned memories of nearly ten years of nights together. Ten years of Elizabeth watching Peck grow up and years of Peck knowing he had the privilege in lying with a masterpiece not yet painted. He knew Elizabeth was a woman with destiny, and it comforted him in knowing they would always be the closest of friends.

"You are such a lovely, lovely man, *mon ami.*"

Elizabeth raised up and stood over Peck in the tub, soap suds melting down her thigh. They looked into each other's eyes with understanding that the change in their lives was happening, and they could feel it. Peck looked up at her perfect body, waiting to be sculpted in his dreams of her and in her own fulfillment of life's adventures.

"*Qu'est-ce qui va m'arriver, cher?*" Elizabeth asked. ("What will happen to me, cher?")

"Elizabeth will become a chef in Baton Rouge, this red stick city with an x at its heart, and then she will go to Paris where the big wheel is, where the tower glows at night and the wine is good—the Paris you told me stories about—and she will not kill the salmon or burn her butter sauces anymore."

"And what will happen to my man out on the rig?"

"He is just a man on a rig. He is not your man on the rig. He will find someone who is right."

"Will I ever again be held like you hold me, Peck?"

"*Oui.* A lucky man will see your eyes and find you and he will hold you forever."

"For true, Peck? How can you be sure?"

"Paris will hold you, cher. He will follow."

Elizabeth cupped her island with a palm almost as if someone had walked into the room.

"Cher, it do no good to hide yourself. Won't do no good."

"I don't know what you're saying. I'm not hiding anything."

"You are. It'll do no good."

"Why won't it?"

"Peck has memorized all of you to his brain—dass why."

Elizabeth laughed, stepped from the tub and wrapped herself with a towel.

"My frien' Lily Cup called Peck today. I forgot to tell you, cher, she wants to take us someplace for dinner."

"Lily Cup?"

"Dass for true. Lily Cup. She's a frien' of mine and Millie too. Her daddy named her Lily Cup when she got born. You'll like Lily Cup."

"Where do you know her from?"

"Lily Cup is a lawyer in New Or-lee-anhs. She helped me one time and I clean her offices. She comes to the capital for business, I t'ink. She's in Baton Rouge and wants to take us to dinner."

"We'll have to go someplace where nobody knows me," Elizabeth said.

"Why?"

"My man? The rig? Remember?"

"Today Audrey showed Peck the Hanged Man card. She say it meaned upheaval and change. What does upheaval mean? Can you tell me?"

"*Oui.* Upheaval means your salmon is dead and the sauce is merde and the carrot is a joke."

"Ahh. Well we go to any restaurant we want with Lily Cup, then. Audrey say upheaval is so good. We do it for me, and for Paris, for my good frien' Elizabeth."

Lily Cup was standing outside Ruffino's when Peck and Elizabeth walked up. Peck hugged her and introduced Elizabeth while pulling the door open. The maître d' sat them at a corner table. Lily Cup handed him a twenty and asked for a bottle of his driest Bordeaux, and if he didn't have French, the driest Italian red in the cellar. She instructed him to have it decanted, to awaken it in the night air.

Elizabeth looked about for faces she knew but settled in and hung her purse strap over the back of Peck's chair.

"So, you are Elizabeth?" Lily Cup asked.

"*Oui—Mademoiselle?*" Elizabeth asked.

"Peck, she is as beautiful as you said she was. Every bit."

"Cher," Peck said, looking at Elizabeth. "I didn't tell…"

"He certainly did. He told Sasha when they were in Memphis just how beautiful you are—and he was right. You are."

"Ha, I forgot to tell you Lily Cup and the Sasha she speaks of are best friens' since like six years old," Peck said.

"And we have absolutely no secrets," Lily Cup added.

"Tell me about Gabe," Peck said.

"The judge made us work with a detective and the district attorney's office to study what happened that day…well, you know. The detective proved Gabe was acting in self-defense, just as you said, Peck. They dropped the case. He's home free."

"Elizabeth, Lily Cup is the best lawyer in the state of Louisiana. She the best."

"That reminds me," Lily Cup said.

She opened her bag and pulled out three one-hundred-dollar bills and put them in front of Peck's bread plate.

"I owe you this. We won."

"Nah, nah, cher. You don't owe—"

"If we had lost you are paid, but we won, and you get a bonus for your research. Take it. You earned every penny."

Peck raised an arm and motioned for the maître d'.

"May I be of service, sir?"

Peck held up the three bills.

"Will this be enough for a bottle of what Miss Lily Cup just ordered? The wine?"

"More than enough, sir."

"Well, bring the bottles it will pay for, and don't open them until we say."

"Yes, sir. Right away, sir."

"Well, well, well...just look at you, Mr. Boudreaux Clemont Finch. Elizabeth, I believe our friend is propositioning us to party tonight."

Elizabeth nodded. "That's how it looks, for certain."

"I'd better get a hotel room. I'll be in no shape to drive back tonight," Lily Cup said.

"Stay at my apartment. I can make coffee later."

"And crepes?" Peck asked.

"It's settled. We'll have crepes with cream and jams for dessert, of course," Elizabeth said.

They celebrated and talked about life, and of friendship and of Acadiana charms and of its hoodoo and full moons. Lily Cup told the many bad things she learned while practicing criminal law and how Peck must take care and not be followed, and to be cautious of who he talks to and what he says— to never leave a trail of clues when he travels back into the swamps and bayous.

Peck told Lily Cup how proud he was to be her friend, and maybe they would dance when they next go to Charlie's Blue Note, and Elizabeth talked of Paris and how one day she would like to perhaps have a breakfast spot or a bakeshop of her own. Lily Cup talked of Peck and how genuine he was, and she asked Elizabeth if he had introduced her to William, and Elizabeth told her that she and William were once close friends, but lately he's been standoffish and like "*un poisson froid*," ("a cold fish") as she put it.

They laughed and they sipped wine and shared the tastes on each of their many plates, and the candle burned out to a stream of smoke and a new one was lit.

"Why did you pick Baton Rouge?" Lily Cup asked.

"Cooking school, why?" Elizabeth asked.

"I don't know, it's something about Baton Rouge."

"What about Baton Rouge?" Elizabeth asked.

"New Orleans is where food is celebrated worldwide, honey."

"Why don't you like Baton Rouge?" Elizabeth asked.

"I think it's the way the Mississippi River cuts through the middle. It's like Baton Rouge is the vulva of the whole country."

Elizabeth lifted her glass with a grin.

"To the vulva," she said.

"Peck, don't let me forget," Lily Cup said. "I brought papers that might help you. I have your birth certificate and other things in my briefcase. I'll give them to you later."

"Thank you, cher."

Peck hiccupped and leaned over to Lily Cup. "Lily Cup, can I ax you something?"

"Don't you just want to squeeze him? He is so cute the way he talks sometimes," Lily Cup said. "What do you want to ask, sweetie?"

"Millie is maybe wanting to do research, like she say—maybe work for you during summer, or for a judge—I don't know."

"First, let me ask you something, Peck—and no bullshit," Lily Cup said. "Was it true, you know, what I heard about how you caught the guy who stole Gabe's pills a year ago, under that bridge?"

"For true, cher."

"Like did Millie really follow you and carry your bag when you killed the dog with the baseball bat?"

"Dog was Rottweiler, attacking us, dass for true. I bonk him dead."

"And she saw the whole thing and didn't scream or run away?"

"She saw more, cher. She saw Peck fight the knife man who had a machete and Peck tie him up in his trailer."

"And she wasn't afraid?"

"She was plenty afraid, but always by my side, and we did it good, with the pill stealer tied up."

"Did it? You mean—what do you mean? Like, you did it? Right there?"

Peck lifted his glass of wine and smiled.

"Whoo hoo!" Lily Cup said.

Elizabeth gasped. "The, how you say, bad man was watching while you made love?"

Peck clicked his glass on her glass, then on Lily Cup's.

"That settles it. I'm hiring the bitch. Give me her number. I'm going to have her meet you here and help you do research—help you drive while you're looking around."

Peck looked at Elizabeth for an opinion.

"Invite her to stay, Peck. Millie is welcome to stay with us."

"Won't that be a little awkward with your man?" Lily Cup asked.

"You know about…?" Elizabeth asked.

"Peck, Sasha, Memphis, remember?" Lily Cup asked. "I think she got him drunk. He told her everything."

"Perhaps I can explain two people, like a couple, quite easily. Explaining only one would be hard," Elizabeth said.

"She's smart, Peck. Hang on to her friendship."

"Peck always will."

"So, what's next with tarot lady?" Lily Cup wanted to know.

"We're both going in the morning to see her," Peck said.

"You have an empty sofa, Elizabeth?" Lily Cup asked.

"I do."

"I'm going with you both in the morning. I want to meet your tarot reader, Peck. Maybe I can help."

Lily Cup picked Peck's cellphone up from the table and scrolled through it. She pushed a button and put it to her ear.

"Hi sweetie," Millie said.

"I'm not your Peck, Millie. This is Lily Cup."

"Hi, I was thinking of you, and…"

"Peck told me you want a summer job."

"Yes, oh that would be so good."

"You're hired. I'll wire travel money. Where are you, anyway?"

"I'm in Waco, Texas."

"Do they have an airport in Waco?"

"I catch a bus to New Or–lee–anhs."

"I want you to catch a bus to Baton Rouge. I'll call you tomorrow to explain."

Lily Cup gave Millie her cell number.

"Text me your full name so I'll have your number and can send money, and I'll be in touch."

"Thank you, thank you," Millie said.

"We're out at dinner. We'll be late. Peck'll call you tomorrow after we have a meeting we have to go to, and I'll call you when I get back to New Orleans tomorrow afternoon."

"Tell Peck I love him."

"I'll tell him—and he loves you too, sweetie. Night, night."

Lily Cup smiled at Peck and set the phone down in front of him.

"Now, then," Lily Cup said. "That's out of the way, and we have a bottle and a half left, and we have the promise of crepes with cream and jam – what say you both we head to the apartment for our treats?"

"*Ça m'a l'air bien,*" Elizabeth said. ("Sounds good.")

"*Oui,*" Peck said.

The dinner's finale of pear salad with Roquefort was put before each of them, and they celebrated future great adventures with a toast and a salute of salad forks.

Elizabeth smiled at the fun of an evening out with real people who talked to each other and shared thoughts and ideas, having real fun.

Lily Cup told stories of cases she has solved and of criminals she has gotten off of death row.

While Lily Cup distracted Peck with her tales of the law, Elizabeth would lift the bottle of wine and fill three glasses.

They traded stories, Lily Cup of defending a gambler of shooting a card cheat, Peck of getting bitten by a snapper and Elizabeth of burning a poached salmon. They broke into laughter and thought of more stories and the ice was broken. After their salads they stood, locked arms and followed the Louisiana moon on their walk to the apartment.

Elizabeth switched a lamp on in the living room and then the kitchen lights. She rummaged two cabinets looking for seasonings and her crepe pan. Peck went back into the bedroom.

"This is a nice apartment, right downtown," Lily Cup said.

"It's close to my school, and now my work," Elizabeth said. "I like it."

Lily Cup asked where the bathroom was and managed to find it in the dark hall and bedroom.

"Peck's conked out on the bed with one shoe in his hand," Lily Cup said. "He's out like a light."

"Oh my, he'll blame the wine," Elizabeth said.

"Do you have any cognac?"

"I do."

"What's say we forget the crepes and sit on the floor with some cognac and talk?"

Lily Cup removed her jacket and set it on the arm of the sofa and they kicked off their shoes and squatted on the floor like campfire girls holding snifters of cognac and they talked about Baton Rouge, about what a sous chef does and how hard it was to get into law school.

"Are you in love with Peck?" Lily Cup asked.

"I love him, but I'm not in love with him, if that makes sense."

"It makes perfect sense. How long have you two known each other?"

"Oh my, it's been maybe seven years, maybe more. I met him when I lived in Anse La Butte."

"So, he was a babe in the woods?"

Elizabeth blushed.

"Do you think you were his first?"

"I definitely was. I could tell."

"You popped him? Yum! So how was it? Like how did it play out first time? Was it a quickie and he fell asleep, or was there a big seduction scene?"

"We got in the tub together, I washed his back and he told me stories. I let him watch me shave my legs."

"Your legs and…?"

"Yes."

Lily Cup raised her snifter and clanked the one in Elizabeth's hand.

"Did he go bananas?"

"Banana might be the wrong, how you say, expression—but yes, William showed a great deal of interest."

"Did you do it in the tub?"

"No. He looked big and I wasn't sure if I could take it without some practice."

Lily Cup guffawed. "So you both decided to go to a gym and work out?"

"I toweled him down."

"By down you mean?"

"How you say, blow dry?"

"Oh, a girl after my own heart."

Elizabeth nearly choked on a sip in her mouth. She swallowed, set the glass down and went through a silent giggle with lips pursed.

"Well we have Peck in common just between us girls. I had him the first night I met him too, but I was drunk," Lily Cup said.

"When was that?"

"Last year."

"And he seduced you?"

"Well, it was more like he asked me where the men's room was and I took him to the lady's room and seduced him on the sink."

They poured more cognac and discussed calorie counts of shellfish and seafood. By 2:00 a.m. they had emptied the bottle and were on to finishing the open bottle of wine with two glasses left in it, and they spoke of how Elizabeth was going to go about breaking up with her man on the rig.

By 2:30 a.m. Lily Cup had to pee and she reported that Peck was asleep in his clothes and wouldn't it be polite of them to take his clothes off?

In the dark, with only the hall light on, they had him down to his skivvies when his eyes opened enough to see them both standing there. He rolled over and closed his eyes again.

The ladies looked at each other.

"Rock, paper, scissors?" Lily Cup chided.

"Let's drink cognac," Elizabeth said.

By 3:34 a.m. they were asleep, and from that moment forward, on this particular bend in Huckleberry's Mississippi River, not even the gods of night could predict what legends were seeded from quiet secrets shared in a second-floor apartment in Baton Rouge.

Chapter 16

AUDREY, I JUST WANTED YOU TO MEET my good frien' who helps Peck," Peck said.

Peck introduced Lily Cup to Audrey. He described a special good friend who has helped him in the past and how she is worried about him and asked if she could meet Audrey to talk. Lily Cup offered her hand.

"Hi Audrey—Elizabeth has said nice things. I wanted to meet and maybe have a few words before you got started today and I drive to New Orleans," Lily Cup said.

"Nice to meet you. Peck and Elizabeth, why don't you go to the kitchen, take a seat and have some coffee or there's fresh squeezed orange juice while we chat out here," Audrey said. "I'll come get you when we're ready."

Peck followed Elizabeth through the house.

"Peck, maybe orange juice for you. It's in the fridge. Coffee is a stimulant. Best you don't drink any more coffee this morning," Audrey said.

Lily Cup had picked up and was admiring a set of oyster-shell pink plastic rosary beads from the shelf holding a statue of the Virgin Mary.

"You may keep it," Audrey said.

Lily Cup opened her purse, pulled a ten and set it on the table. She held the rosary in her hand, rolling beads between her thumb and finger.

"My best friend and I sit on the roof under full moons and star-gaze and wonder about the supernatural. I'm no expert, but I do believe in it," Lily Cup said.

"It's always been a wonder to me. I find searching for answers fulfilling somehow," Audrey said. "How can I help you?"

"I've been a criminal attorney for some time," Lily Cup said. "I'm conflicted between what I've learned about the darker side of some of the regions in Acadiana over the years and the journey Peck is about to head out on."

"Let's sit over here," Audrey said.

"There was that serial killer who lured his victims with the promise of sex, tied them up—I don't remember how many, twenty or so—and cut their throats or strangled them," Lily Cup said.

"How tragic," Audrey said.

"I hear it all in Angola prison. One, I heard was a wise guy disposing bodies on carnivore feral pig farms. Another, when in the old days they would execute enemies with their feet in cement and drop them overboard—now victims being pushed out of low-flying airplanes deep into swamps after the advance plane signals an alligator congregation below."

"What a morbid world you must witness," Audrey said.

"I picked it, it didn't pick me," Lily Cup said. "If I can help one innocent person break the shackles of so many misunderstood public perceptions of what poverty actually is and that it is not a disease but a symptom of despair, it makes my effort worth it. Being poor does not mean a person is criminally oriented."

"And the criminals?" Audrey asked.

"Being a criminal doesn't preclude you from being defended."

"You're worried about Peck going back into these swamps?" Audrey asked.

"In New Orleans, most violence is drug-related. Peck would avoid that world. But there is a *Gris Gris* in the swamps by their almost prehistoric nature, and it's the bayous where there's a frightening anonymity. I live in a world that is reminded of the silt and darkness of the bayou and swamp. I hear about it in Angola."

"Are you suggesting you don't want me to help Peck explore his past because of the physical dangers in the swamps?" Audrey asked.

"I think what I'm trying to say is it frightens me to see Peck exploring. Exploring can be fraught with danger. If he doesn't know where he's going he'll be exploring," Lily Cup said.

"But if we can give him specific destinations to go to, there would be less danger?" Audrey asked.

"Yes. Exactly," Lily Cup replied.

"I understand," Audrey said.

"Can this be done, or am I deluding myself, hoping for the impossible?"

"With hypnosis, I believe it can be a definite possibility. I've seen it work many times, and I think Peck would be a good candidate for it. There is something eternally spiritual about him. He's of the mind."

"I've heard Peck described quite like that in different words. You express it well. I see him as a man of nature, of God and of the wind and the rain," Lily Cup said. "While we would hide from lightning, Peck would be of a mindset to lean against a tree or fence post and watch thunder and lightning split a sky open and he'd wait through it for the full moon to once again reappear."

"Do you believe in tarot?" Audrey asked.

"I believe in spiritual magnetism and of the windows that tarot opens to little rooms in our brains making us think. So yes, I do."

"The last card Peck selected yesterday was a destiny card. What card do you suppose he selected?" Audrey asked.

"Will I faint?"

"He picked the Moon card."

Rosary in hand, Lily Cup blessed herself.

"In the name of the Father, Son, and Holy Ghost," Lily Cup said.

"He told me the moon is his momma," Audrey said.

"Is that all he told you it was?"

"Yes."

"Let me tell you things for the hypnotist. By the way, will the hypnotist be a medically licensed psychiatrist?"

"If his budget would allow, it could be," Audrey said.

Lily Cup handed Audrey a business card.

"Make that happen and send me the bill. I'll get it paid."

"Very good."

"I don't know any of the circumstances of his birth, but I do know his birth certificate says race unknown. I'm not certain what he will remember from back then. I do know there was an Alayna Prudhomme somewhere near Bayou Sorrell and Choctaw. I believe she was what he called a foster nanna, but there are no records of an adoption or of his being in foster care. I do know from his own account he was chained under a back porch by some fisherman with a padlocked dog collar and he would look up at the full moon and talk to his momma by way of the moon. I also know they would tie his hands and drag him behind boats trolling for alligators when he was a child. They'd tape his mouth to keep him from screaming."

"I find it interesting that you know of this Alayna Prudhomme, and yet he's never mentioned that name to me. He's only mentioned a foster nanna," Audrey said.

"In eight months he's learned to read and write and he gets his GED this month. I could see why he'd block out his childhood," Lily Cup said.

"In eight months he learned to read? Such a passion he must have. We should be so lucky to have such a passion."

"He has an amazing mind," Lily Cup said. "I sometimes wonder if it's wise to encourage him to learn about his past."

"He'll always wonder, and until he knows, it could haunt him if he didn't at least try."

"Has he mentioned Millie?"

"He's mentioned her, yes. Are they close?"

"He's flipped for her—almost a year now. She was the start of this whole thing. She asked him if she could meet his mother."

"I'm certain her asking wasn't meant to be spiteful."

"I'm sure. They're talking about getting married. Most any girl would ask the same thing."

"Yes."

"How about my idea of Millie traveling with him to help with research and the driving?" Lily Cup asked.

"I think it could go a long way to build a strong, lasting bond between them, if the girl is meant for him and it would protect him and allay your fears."

"How would it protect him?"

"By virtue of his nature he'd go out of his way to protect her. That would keep him from being distracted. It would help keep him from putting either of them in harm's way."

"You're very good," Lily Cup said.

"I majored in psyche at LSU. I don't practice, I enjoy tarot insights."

"You are good because you care."

"I've been at this for some time now. I can always tell the differences between the couple who come in on a date like I'm a carnival reader, wanting to hear that they will live happily ever after if one of them would commit. I also know when there is a depth to my work when it comes to persons in situations like Peck or Elizabeth. There is much reward deep in my soul for helping people like them."

"And the rosary beads and the blessed Virgin Mary? Do you tie religion in?"

"Religion isn't an occult here when I read. By displaying my Catholicism, I try to project a message that a guide for happiness is the Ten Commandments—and in any religion – Christian or Jew or Hindu, whatever."

"Elizabeth is a beautiful woman," Lily Cup said.

"Such a beauty, inside and out," Audrey agreed.

"I wonder why they aren't together?" Lily Cup asked.

"Peck means the world to Elizabeth, and he means so much because he's comfortable knowing exactly what he is to her. Two closer friends you will search long and hard to find…but both he and Elizabeth know he is one color on her palette, and he knows that Elizabeth is an artisan of a world that will discover her one day."

"One color," Lily Cup said. "I like that Peck is secure in his own skin. It's so refreshing."

"That one color, his, will always be on her palette. He will always be a part of her life."

"Always goes such a long way, doesn't it?" Lily Cup asked.

"She speaks of him almost with reverence. They are blessed to have found each other. It was in the stars for them," Audrey said.

"In the moon?" Lily Cup asked.

Audrey started and held her hand to her mouth, looking at Lily Cup in awe for the depth of her perception.

"The Moon card," Audrey said.

"I feel good," Lily Cup said. "Elizabeth did well finding you, Audrey. Let me go say goodbye to them and be off."

"Do come by whenever you get to Baton Rouge. You are a most interesting woman. We can do lunch."

Lily Cup made her way back into the kitchen. Peck was sitting with a glass of water; Elizabeth had a cup of coffee. They both stood when she walked in.

"She's fabulous. She's a caring reader with real depth. I may have her read for me some time."

"I like coming to her," Elizabeth said.

"Peck, you be patient. She's getting an appointment with a doctor who might be able to hypnotize you and bring you the information you'll need for going back. I'll see Millie comes to go with you."

"Is she coming here?" Peck asked.

"No, New Orleans, first."

"Does she know? You say last night Baton Rouge."

"I'll tell her about this when we can sit down and talk. I don't want to just throw it at her over the phone."

"Good idea, cher."

"I'll call her when I get to my office and have her come to New Orleans first. She can stay at your place with Gabe. I'll put her to work in my office for colleagues until you have a better grasp on where it is you have to go. Then I'll drive her up and drop her off, or Sasha will."

"Peck drank too much wine last night. Dass for true," Peck said with a sheepish grin.

"Do you remember anything about last night?" Lily Cup asked.

"Nah, nah," Peck said. "I remember eating is all, and you calling Millie."

"Then I'd say you had just enough of the wine—right, Elizabeth?"

Elizabeth smiled.

"*La prochaine fois, c'est moi qui cuisine,*" Elizabeth said. ("Next time I cook.")

Lily Cup kissed Peck on both cheeks. He kissed hers in return. She did the same with Elizabeth. They followed her into the reading room and waved goodbye.

"Did you remember to bring maps, Peck?" Audrey asked.

Peck pulled three copies of maps from an envelope and set them side-by-side on the table.

"Let's sit at the table," Audrey said.

"May I ask what we are to do today?" Elizabeth asked.

"Today I'd like to make a list of words that might stir memory in Peck's subconscious. Words the hypnotist may or may not use in helping Peck remember," Audrey said.

"When we do it?" Peck asked.

Audrey brought her cellphone from the side table drawer and turned the volume up. She pressed a button.

"Dr. Price's office, may I help you?"

"Audrey here."

"Oh hi, how are you?"

"Doing well, thank you. I have a man who I need to set an appointment for a hypnotherapy session as soon as possible. Can one be arranged?"

"What's the patient's name?"

"Boudreaux Clemont Finch."

"May I tell Dr. Price what the nature of your concern is, Audrey?"

"He's twenty-five. I think it would be easiest to say childhood abuse."

"One moment please, I'll check his schedule."

"Thank you."

"Audrey, would tomorrow between twelve-thirty and three p.m. work for you? Dr. Price would want to meet with you from twelve-thirty to one p.m. and with Mr. Finch from one to three."

"That will be perfect."

Audrey ended the call. "It's set then for tomorrow."

"Will I need to be there?" Elizabeth asked.

"Not unless you want to. Right now, I want to make the list of words for Dr. Price. Can you help?"

One by one, Elizabeth listed the words and names she had learned from knowing Peck almost ten years and from several hours in the library with him.

"Carencro, nanna Prudhomme, Atchafayalaya River, Lake Maurepas, Frenchman Settlement, Killian…"

Audrey patiently waited as they thought, and she wrote down each word, occasionally looking into Peck's eyes sympathetically. After Elizabeth had exhausted her memories, she paused.

"Bayou Chene," Peck said.

"Oh—and weeps," Elizabeth said.

"Weeps?" Audrey asked.

"Yes—like the song—Willow weeps for me," Elizabeth said.

Audrey made a note of it.

They chatted a while, Audrey jotting things down and describing what Peck might expect in tomorrow's hypnotherapy. Peck paid what he owed, and he and Elizabeth walked home without speaking. She splashed her face and changed into her chef school uniform and headed to school.

"Want to do Bistro tonight, Peck?"

"*Oui*, cher."

"Why don't you get some rest? We were up late last night."

Elizabeth smiled and closed the door behind her.

CHAPTER 17

HELLO?" Peck asked.

"Were you ever going to call me?" Millie asked.

"We just gotted home, Millie. How you are?"

"I'm lonely."

"I'm sorry."

Peck unbuttoned and unzipped his jeans, preparing to take a shower.

"Seems like I've been waiting for hours."

He sat on the sofa, stretched to reach a side pillow and folded it behind his head as he lay back.

"We talk now. All you want."

"I'm happy Lily Cup called me last night about working for her. Won't it be fun?"

"She happy too, cher."

"If you show me how, I can cook for you and Gabe."

"I can show you. Gabe knows too."

"I can't wait to see you. I'm looking at bus schedules to Baton Rouge after I go to the library."

Peck knew Lily Cup had a change of plans and was going to have Millie go to New Orléans first, but as he wasn't certain, he decided not to confuse Millie by opening it up.

"I'm nervous," Millie said.

"Don't be nervous, cher."

"I want to make a nice impression—do a good job."

"You will, no worries."

"Like what does she wear to the office?"

"Lily Cup dresses good—business clothes, lady suits, ya know."

"So, not jeans, things like that?"

"Nah, nah—dressy."

"Mommy will send things."

"Wait for Lily Cup to call you," Peck said. "She just left Baton Rouge and should be in New Or–lee–anh soon."

"I got a C in French, Peck. Will you just hate me?"

"Nah, nah."

"I'm so embarrassed."

"Peck will larn you French."

"You mean teach me French."

"See? Already my Millie teach me English, so I teach you the French."

She asked about Elizabeth and was he alone to talk, and she learned which jams were best on crepes and how to get a perfect lace in a crepe without burning it by gently rocking the pan above the burner. They spoke of Steinbeck and *Cannery Row* and of soft-shelled crabs and would chickens eat the okra seed if the garden wasn't fenced and how rice came from wet paddies called marshland and not swamps and how crawfish could be farmed with rice.

They mused about baby names and whether Peck would walk or drive to Tulane. Millie's schoolwork was important to her sense of worth, just as Peck's keeping his promises of growing and learning were to him. It would be another year before she could live with him full-time. He told of the x in downtown Baton Rouge, and did she know Baton Rouge meant *red stick,* and she suggested colors for curtains in Peck's room in New Orleans.

The warmth of the call wasn't the small talk or the sounds of voices, and it wasn't the topics. It was being together, like logs on a fire, if only by phone, that made them feel whole. They expressed their love with a softness in tone as if their heads were on the same pillow, and Millie stalled saying goodbye until her clock told her she had to go to the Baylor library to return books and Peck nodded off with his jeans below his hips.

Peck was in the shower washing his hair after shaving when Elizabeth came into the bathroom bare breasted and lowered the chef pants and white cotton panties to her thighs and sat on the commode.

"It's me, Peck."

She stood, dropped the pants to the floor and stepped out of her panties. She pulled the shower curtain aside just enough to step in behind Peck and put her hands on his shampoo-covered scalp and massaged it with her fingers.

"*J'ai pensé a plus de mots,*" Elizabeth said. ("I thought of more words.")

"*Mots?*" Peck asked. ("Words?")

"For tomorrow, in case you need more. Want to hear them?"

"Nah, nah, cher, not now."

"Give me the cloth," Elizabeth said.

Peck picked a cloth from the soap dish and handed it over his shoulder to her. She began at his shoulders and created suds and washed his back slowly.

"Are you frightened about tomorrow?"

"I don't know."

"Hypnosis doesn't hurt, Peck. I had it done once. It doesn't hurt. It's like you're asleep."

"Nah, nah—what if I die, cher?"

Elizabeth bolted. She pulled Peck's arm around until he was facing her.

"*Mon dieu,* you are not going to die. Hypnosis does not make you die, Peck."

Peck clenched his jaw, his eyes closed to keep soap away.

"What is it you're afraid of, Peck? Please tell me."

"Audrey say this man will, how you say, put me under like asleep, right?"

"Yes, and he only talks to you. He sits a distance away from you, so he can't hurt you."

"Audrey say I will remember t'ings, like being chained under gator man's porch."

"I'm sure you'll remember some things, yes. That will be good if you want to find your foster nanna."

"So, Peck could die—dass for true."

"*Je ne comprend pas.*" ("I don't understand.")

"English, cher."

"What do you mean you could die?"

"I can see the porch where he chained me again?"

"Maybe."

"I can see gator man again?"

"Maybe, but he can't hurt you."

"Gator man can tape Peck's mouth and tie my hands and pull Peck behind his pirogue looking for gators?"

"I guess, but…"

"Then Peck will die, cher. I maked myself die when he did that."

"I don't know how it works Peck, but I think you're allowed to ask the doctor to wake you so you don't have to be tied up. Ask him before you do anything. Then decide if you want to go through with it."

Peck raised his head back to rinse under the shower.

"Peck needs wine."

Elizabeth laughed. "You don't like wine, remember?"

"Peck need the wine tonight."

"Bistros, wine, and dinner, and maybe…"

"Maybe what?"

"Maybe I talk to the owner and he gives me a job as sous chef—or on salads."

"That would be good, *non*?"

"That would be good, *oui*. And we can talk and you tell me about your Millie, and we'll drink the wine and we get in the pool tonight?"

"No gators or snappers?"

Elizabeth reached and took William in hand with firm pulls and strokes.

"Only wild women with much wine."

Peck turned full circle in a final rinse and stepped out of the tub onto the towel on the floor. Elizabeth tied her hair in a knot on top of her head and let the shower splash her face.

"I feel like meat tonight."

"Lamb chops with herbes de Provence. You will like them, Peck. You ever had lamb chops?"

"Nah, nah."

"They're good."

"Bistro?" Peck asked.

"*Oui*, very good."

While dressing, Peck saw that he had two calls from Lily Cup. He pressed the return button.

"Hey Peck," Lily Cup said.

"You in New Or-lee-anh, cher?"

"I've been here an hour or so, stopped over and saw Gabe. We talked about Millie coming and about the party for Sasha's engagement. He gave me a key for Millie."

"You need me?"

"I wanted to let you know Millie will be here late tomorrow night. The bus ride from Waco is about twelve hours. I'm only bringing her here just until you feel you are ready to go to wherever it is you have to go."

"Is that why you called me?"

"Sort of. I also wanted to ask you if you thought it would be a good idea or a bad idea for me and Sasha to have a talk with her. Give her some background about before you ran away when you were a kid."

Lily Cup paused and waited for a reaction.

"We wouldn't do it without your approval, Peck. Do you want to think it over and call me back when you decide yay or nay?"

"You plenty sm'at, dass for true, cher. I think you know'd what to say, so it would be good. I think it be hokay."

"I think it would be best this way. We don't want to scare her the minute she gets up there," Lily Cup said.

"*Oui.*"

"That's what I called about."

"Cher, do you read the tarot cards?"

"Sasha can—not so much me."

"Maybe she read cards for Millie before she comes here, maybe?"

"Does Millie drink?"

"She likes the frozen daiquiris."

"We'll take her to the roof and have a séance. Don't worry about a thing."

Peck finished the call and he and Elizabeth left the apartment to walk to the Bistro. The night air was dry and warm, the stars were there, hidden by an occasional streetlamp. Elizabeth asked the host to send the owner or manager to the table when they had time. Their table was in a corner and the unlit candle was lighted and placed in the center. Elizabeth opened the menu and started to speak in French.

"Oh, *oui*, English...sorry," she started.

She ordered a bottle of red Bordeaux, escargot for two, and a plate of cheeses and French bread for starters. The server expressed his approval and stepped from the table. Elizabeth watched him walk away, and then she folded her arms on the table, leaning in.

"Peck, it's time."

"It's time?"

"I'm going to tell him."

"Hanh?"

"My man on the rig. It's time I tell him."

"You mean...?"

"It's over between us. I think he knows it. I know it. It has to be said."

Peck reached for her hand.

"You're not doing this for Peck?"

"I'm doing it for me. I want to be free to do things I want to do. I'm going to be a good chef. I want to travel."

"When will you call him?"

"I respect him too much for that. I'll wait for when he comes back."

"Dass good."

"I really think he knows. We hardly talk on the phone anymore. He'll tell me the weather offshore or I'll tell him what I'm cooking at school."

"Where will you live?"

"The apartment is in my name. I paid the deposit and six months in advance when we moved in. He'll move. Probably to New Orleans. He would like that better."

The wine was opened and a sample poured and approved. Peck lifted his glass.

"À ma meilleur amie courageuse. Ma deuxiéme cousine pour toujours," Peck said. ("To my brave best friend. My second cousin always.")

"You mean kissing cousin, don't you?"

"Ahh *oui, oui* – kissing cousin."

They sipped their wine.

"Peck, know what I want to do tonight?"

"What?"

"First I want to enjoy the escargots."

"*Oui.*"

"Then Peck will have the lamb chops herbes de Provence and Elizabeth will have the duck."

"This is your night, cher. Anything tonight for my frien'."

"Will you swim with me later, Peck?"

"*Oui.*"

"*Nue?*" ("Naked?")

"Is there any other way, cher?"

Piping hot garlic butter, for dipping the crusts of baguette to best savor the snails was the perfect start to a beautiful evening. Elizabeth putting the rig out of her mind and Peck putting tomorrow from his. Tonight, they celebrated the death the tarot cards predicted. They knew that with it came a new life, a new vision. It was all good. Tonight, they belonged to the stars.

CHAPTER 18

PECK WAS IN THE WAITING ROOM while Audrey and Dr. Price visited in a small conference room. When they came out, Audrey kissed Peck on both cheeks and said goodbye.

"Have Elizabeth call me," Audrey said.

"Yes'm."

Dr. Price shook hands with Peck. "Audrey tells me you go by Peck, while your given name is Boudreaux Clemont Finch," Dr. Price said.

"Yes, sir," Peck said.

"Do you have one you are more comfortable with, may I ask?" the doctor asked.

"Peck is hokay, Doctor," Peck said.

"Tell me, does Peck date back to your childhood or was it a nickname you took on as you got older?"

"Don't know," Peck said.

"That'll be fine, then. Peck, it is. Let's step into our small conference room and talk."

It was a comfortable room with pictures of honeybees on red roses and birdhouses on the side of a tree—–decorated to not arouse either suspicion or angst. Peck handed the doctor a sheet of paper Elizabeth had printed out from her computer—the words that might be of help to the doctor. Dr. Price studied them without comment. He set the paper on the table face-down.

"Peck, I think a good start would be for me to tell you a little about me, and what I hope to accomplish today...and how we go about it. I would like you to ask me anything. It could be things you're concerned about, or just things or procedures you want to know more about."

"Yes, sir."

"My name is Dr. John A. Price. I'm well aware the word *doctor* might intimidate some, so it's not necessary that you call me 'doctor.' 'Mr. Price' will do. I studied medicine at Tulane Medical University and got my medical degree at LSU, right here in Baton Rouge."

Peck started and sat up straight. "You go to Tulane, doctor? Dass for true?"

"I did."

"Peck is going to Tulane night school, in New Or–lee–anh, start in June," Peck said.

"That can only mean one thing, Peck."

"What?"

"Us Tulane men have to stick together. From now on you call me John. Okay with you?"

"Hokay with me."

"Okay with me, John," the doctor said.

Peck beamed.

"Hokay with me, John."

"This is a good start. Now Peck, hypnotherapy is just a big word for trying to get you to relax."

"Relax?"

"Do you sometimes take a nap in the middle of the day? Other times you just stretch out on the bed or a sofa and take a nap?"

"Yes."

"Well, hypnotherapy is trying to relax you so you can take a nap."

"I can did that," Peck said.

"But the difference between hypnotherapy and the everyday nap is that I'll try to get you to talk in your sleep."

Peck listened with an inquisitive eye.

"You see, when a person talks while they are wide awake, that's their conscious mind helping them remember things and what to say. But when a person talks in their sleep, that is their subconscious mind talking."

"What does sub mean?" Peck asked.

"Sub means lower, or deeper. Subconscious means to go deeper into your memory. Like a submarine goes deep in the water."

Peck stiffened.

"I said submarine and you reacted, Peck. Does that word, submarine, bother you in some way or remind you of something bad?"

"Gator man tied my hands and threw me in the bayou and pulled me with his pirogue for gator bait. Dass for true. Peck died ever' time, dass for true."

"Well this is a different sub than what you're describing, Peck. This sub will only be in your brain, not in any water, bayou, or swamp. You have my word."

"For true?"

"For true, Peck. If your subconscious even so much as puts your toe near the water, I'll simply wake you and we'll start all over another time if we have to."

"So, Peck won't die?"

"Not on my watch, Peck."

"So good. Peck is good. You can do it."

"Shall we get started?"

They stood, shook hands, and went into a room with a leather-upholstered chaise for the patient with a leather chair beside it. Peck asked about the pictures on the walls and if John had to take English at the university. Doctor John talked about trying to learn how to fly-fish and he was pretty good with English and words because he had to take so much Latin, but he couldn't spell.

Peck lay on the chaise with his eyes closed. In thirty to forty-five-second segments each, the doctor asked Peck to tighten his feet and toes and then in about a minute relax them; then tighten his calves for a minute and relax them. Then his thighs, his stomach muscles, his chest, and each hand and arm in turn. The doctor asked him to tighten his lips and hold for a minute, and then his brow for a full minute. When the doctor said to relax his brow, Peck fell into a deep sleep, as though he was floating on a feather cloud. The room stayed silent while the doctor watched.

"Peck, I want you to go back to the earliest you can remember. Travel back through your mind to the first thing you can remember."

"*Je suis la,*" Peck said. ("I am there.")

"Where are you, do you know?"

"*Je ne sais pas.*" ("I don't know.")

"Peck, can you tell me what you see?"

"*Maman.*" ("Mamma.")

"You see mamma. Do you see anything else?"

"*Je vois la lune.*" ("I see the moon.")

"Peck, can you look around where you are?"

"*Oui.*"

"Look carefully. Are there any words you can see? Words on books you see, envelopes, on signs or maybe wall calendars."

"*Il fait somber.*" ("It's dark.")

"Do you see any words at all, Peck?"

"*Oui.*"

"What words do you see?"

"*Ward, je vois ward.*" ("Ward, I see ward.")

"Are you saying *word*?"

"Ward."

"Can you tell me how to spell *ward*, Peck?"

"W-A-R-D."

"I want you to go to another place now. I want you to go to a place where you see mamma and the moon again."

"*Saule pleureur.* Peck see'd the willer tree."

"Is the willow tree an important tree, Peck?"

"Mamma nanna houseboat tied with rope to tree."

"Peck, are you on the houseboat with your mamma nanna?"

"*Oui.*"

"What are you doing?"

"Highchair."

"You're in a highchair?"

"*Oui.*"

"Are you eating?"

"Nah, nah. Mamma nanna has mail from man come by."

"The mailman?"

"*Oui.*"

"From where you're sitting, can you see any mail? Letters? Envelopes? Can you see any words from where you are? On books, on walls?"

"*Oui.*"

"What can you see? Can you tell me?"

"A paper."

"A paper. Is there anything on the paper?"

"Killian National Bank."

"Killian National Bank. Very good. Does it say anything else?"

"Alayna Prudhomme."

"Alayna Prudhomme. This is good. Does it say anything else?"

"Maurice Pontelban. It say Maurice Pontelban."

"Peck, now this is important. Can you tell me how Pontelban is spelled? Can you see it well enough?"

"p-o-n-t-e-l-b-a-n-m-d."

"Peck, look at that word again and tell me how it is spelled one more time."

"p-o-n-t-e-l-b-a-n-m-d"

"Now Peck, take your time and look about where you are right now. Just look about."

The doctor could see Peck's pupils rolling under his eyelids.

"Peck, when you're ready, you can wake up."

His eyes opened.

"How do you feel, Tulane man?"

"Peck feels good, cher...oops, I mean...?"

"Cher will do fine—or John. Whatever suits you. I'm going to my office to jot down a few things. Take your time. When you're ready why don't you go to that small conference room area and have a seat? I'll be in in a minute and we'll talk about what I've learned."

"Can I see if Elizabeth is here, and can she come with me?"

"Is it important to you that Elizabeth be with you?"

"Oh, *oui*. She my good frien'. Elizabeth got me to go to Audrey."

"By all means, bring her in, if she's here. There's coffee somewhere. Ask the girl at the desk. I'll be no longer than fifteen minutes or so."

Peck stood and tightened his belt buckle. He stepped out into the waiting room where Elizabeth was standing, arms outstretched. She wrapped them around Peck and nuzzled his neck in a complete silence.

She lifted her head back.

"*Comment vas-tu?*" Elizabeth asked. ("Are you okay?")

"I'm good, cher. So good."

"And you didn't...you know?"

"Peck didn't die. Not ever today."

"Do we leave now?"

"No. He wants to talk and he say it good you come too. Hokay with you?"

Peck led Elizabeth into the conference room. He passed on getting coffee, as none would come close to his Cajun chicory home brew. Dr. Price came into the room, shook Elizabeth's hand and sat.

"Peck, I feel good about our session today. How about you?"

"So good."

"I want to start by telling you that from my experience, if one approaches to find the seed first, the plant will grow on its own accord. What this means is I think if I can tell you the beginnings of your life as your subconscious remembers it, that alone will give you the tools internally to slowly remember more...and you will discover more each day."

"Peck didn't die?"

"Peck didn't die, and the fact is you didn't see this gator man fellow—not a pirogue and definitely no alligators."

"So good."

Dr. Price handed Elizabeth a small spiral pad and a pen.

"You may want to take some notes for your friend, Elizabeth."

He looked at Peck.

"Are you ready?"

"Peck is so ready."

"It's important you understand that what I tell you are my interpretations of what I think I heard listening to you answer my questions while you were under. Do you understand that?"

"*Oui.*"

"Peck, I have a feeling the woman who raised you is named Alayna Prudhomme."

"Dass for true. Mamma Nanna."

"Peck, I have a feeling this Alayna Prudhomme is your real mother."

Peck started. His fists clenched. He waited for more.

"Peck, I knew of your talking to the moon as if it were your momma."

"*Oui.*"

"And the moon would give you great comfort, especially when you were stressed or felt abandoned?"

"*Oui.*"

"Peck, you weren't saying momma nanna. You were saying *mamma* nanna."

"*Quoi?*" ("What?")

"You said *mamma*, and you could see the moon. Peck, mamma means a mother's breast— milk for her baby. You said the room was dark. You were suckling and could see the moon. When you see the moon, you think of your mother."

A tear grew in Peck's eye. His head dropped. The tear rolled down his face as Elizabeth clenched his hand.

"Peck, you mentioned a Maurice Pontelban. You spelled it p-o-n-t-e-l-b-a-n-m-d. The MD at the end meant this Pontelban fellow was a doctor. You also mentioned the Killian National Bank. I called the bank and they said Maurice Pontelban was a doctor at a hospital near Choctaw."

"Choctaw. I know'd Bayou Sorrell and Choctaw."

"The banker told me that Dr. Pontelban passed away four years ago."

Peck wiped his eyes with his wrist.

"Peck, you saw the word *ward* when you spoke of your 'mamma' nanna. Dr. Pontelban worked at a woman's mental health hospital near Choctaw. The hospital was for women with mental issues. They first called it an insane asylum. Peck, you saw a sign that read 'Ward.' It was likely a psychiatric ward and your mother was breastfeeding you at night by a window—the woman who you call mamma nanna. I'm afraid your mamma nanna and Alayna Prudhomme are the same person—a patient in the mental hospital. You could have been born in that hospital."

Peck couldn't have been more stunned if an alligator had taken a leg off. Elizabeth held his arm with a hug.

"Peck, will this help get you started?"

"It will help, *oui*. T'ank you."

"If you want to meet with me on a regular basis to work out some issues, I'm here for you, at any time."

Peck stood and shook the doctor's hand.

"Thank you, John."

Doctor Price smiled. Peck and Elizabeth went into the hall and rode the elevator in silence and stepped out onto the sidewalk. They crossed one street at the corner and came to a park with a tall bronze statue of Governor Huey Long, stopped and gazed.

"Can we go to Maison Lacour tonight?" Elizabeth asked. "My treat."

"Where Lily Cup taked us?"

"*Non, non, c'est un bon restaurant français,*" Elizabeth said. ("No, no, this is a fine French restaurant.")

"Will you order for me, cher?"

"Can we swim again? A long time tonight, and perhaps a shower and maybe crepes with jam?"

"And whipped cream?"

"*Mais oui...mais oui.*"

They held hands like school children and Peck walked briskly, running his fingers against the wrought iron fences they passed by like they were playing cards in a bicycle wheel, Elizabeth skipping from time to time. They didn't speak of it but they both knew change was coming for them both—good change. Peck now had a mother that he didn't know he had, and he knew where to go to find out more—and where to find her. Elizabeth was happy for Peck, while sad about some things he learned. But any answers to a lifetime of questions had to be good for the soul.

Tonight, she would celebrate her commitment to a new freedom and she would shower and wear provocative perfumes and her alluring imported black Chantilly lace bra and perhaps garter straps and sheer hosiery.

Tonight, Elizabeth would lasso a sensual encore of flavors for the palate and the whirling tornado that was now in Peck's brain—and she would ride the night wherever the winds pointed their sails.

Chapter 19

STANDING ON THE SMALL BALCONY in Baton Rouge, Peck watched the setting sun rest on the Mississippi River in a quiet moment of glassy calm; the crawling waterway was that one vein Peck imagined physically connecting him to Millie this night. His Millie, whose bus was just now driving through the city traffic into the soul of New Orleans. It was as if mythical candles were being gathered along the shoreline by spirits for a special lighting.

Something was in the air. It was like how we feel on the last day of school, or after a first prom, a first kiss; how it feels when you sit by the window while your plane lands in a brand-new city. This evening was spoken for and with it was a promise of the biggest full moon ever, just to match the mood. Acadiana and Southern Louisiana was about to celebrate Millie's arrival in a big way, a Sasha and Lily Cup way in the heartland of jubilee, the Big Easy, while miles away Elizabeth and Peck, in downtown Baton Rouge, would be savoring herbs of their new life awareness with fine Bordeaux and decadent chocolate souffles with Grand Marnier Cordon Rouge.

In the apartment on Baton Rouge's South Fourteenth street, the shower was recently turned off to a drip, but sink and door mirrors were coated with a steam of concealing opaque, while Elizabeth stood in the tub, her hair wrapped in a towel, shaving her legs and her lovely. Peck was now in the living room finishing his hundredth pushup on the floor. He could always think at his best while doing pushups.

By watching his face, one couldn't discern if he was thinking of the road ahead to finding his mother, or of the mischief he saw in Elizabeth's eyes when she stepped into the bathroom. It was the inviting smile in her eyes that caught his imagination. Add to that the blind embossed, ivory-toned gift box wrapped in ribbon on the coffee table with his name on the card. In its tissue papers lay an imported black Mouline fabric shirt with black onyx buttons. Peck held the shirt and felt the texture of its collar and buttons with a look on his face as if it was likely that this was to be a joyous evening of *adieu, mais pas au revoir.* (farewell, but not goodbye.)

As he lifted the shirt and unbuttoned its collar button it dawned on him this special evening could only end one way...at dawn. Peck set the shirt on the sofa and dropped to the floor for fifty more.

On Loyola Avenue in New Orleans Sasha parked her light blue Bentley convertible with top down in front of the bus depot and waited, listening to jazz while Lily Cup went in to find Millie. They came out with Millie pulling her bag. Lily Cup opened the car door and Millie climbed into the back seat.

"It's so good to see you," Millie said.

"One bag for the whole summer?" Sasha asked.

"Mommy is sending my things for work."

"Did you bring your baby Charlie?"

"Charlie's in my bag," Millie said.

"My Teddy still sleeps with me," Lily Cup said. "He's pushing forty."

"I promise I'll look presentable soon," Millie said.

Sasha pulled the Bentley into traffic and toward Canal Street with a wry smile.

"You'll be presentable tonight, darling. You're in good hands," Sasha said.

"You thinking what I'm thinking you're thinking?" Lily Cup asked.

"Saks Fifth Avenue?"

"I thought so."

"I do have some nice things, I promise," Millie said.

"Honey, there's a full moon tonight and we have a séance planned on a rooftop. We three must look our best in the light of the moon," Sasha said.

"For alone and on a rooftop?" Millie asked.

"For after, love, for when we go to Frenchmen Street and dance," Lily Cup said. "Gabe will be there."

Millie shrugged a relenting grin and sat back with her arm rested on the opened car window ledge.

"This is such a beautiful city," Millie said. "It's filled with so many chapters, like in a picture book."

"Driving through N'Orleans is like crawling through an attic," Lily Cup said. "Every neighborhood is opening another box of something timeless—something that was once a part of someone's life, that got stored and tucked away like memories of better times."

"That's beautiful," Millie said.

They bantered and laughed and spoke of architecture and of the sounds and how music on street corners reminded passersby that life was good, and they talked of how many different streetcar lines there were in New Orleans.

In Saks Fifth Avenue, Sasha did a beeline to Women's Wear with Millie and Lily Cup in tow like children on a field trip.

"Shoe size?" Sasha asked.

"Seven," Millie said.

"Dress?"

"Three."

"Bra?"

"Thirty-two C."

"Lily Cup, take our Miss Millie to a fitting room and camp there while I look. I'll hand things over the door for her to try for fit."

"But I—" Millie started.

"Save your breath," Lily Cup said. "Sasha is in Saks, and something always comes over her when we're in Saks. It's like she's rabid or something. That's how she is. Just go with the flow. Strip."

"Huh?"

"Strip."

"Everything?"

"Honey, strip to what you would be wearing if you were alone with Peck in the bedroom."

Millie grinned and pulled her T-shirt over her head and was unfastening her bra when two hands came over the top of the fitting room door, one hand holding a large plastic cup with rye on the rocks and the other a large, frosted frozen daiquiri. Lily Cup took them in hand and held them up like prizes.

"The only large every woman prays for in a fitting room," Lily Cup said.

Millie dropped her jeans to the floor and kicked them aside.

Lily Cup handed the daiquiri to Millie and settled on the stool by the door, sipping her rye. There was a hook holding empty hangers above her head.

"Lose the panties," Lily Cup said.

"Huh?"

"Off."

"Why?"

"Trust me, I just saw Sasha head to the lingerie counter. It's a mile long. This ain't Target." She pointed her cup at Millie's midsection.

Millie looked down at her panties.

"Drop 'em."

Millie hesitated, looked in the large cup in her hand and belted back a swig and followed that with another quick swallow that would keep her awhile. She handed the cup to Lily Cup while she took her panties to the floor and stood with her feet pigeon-toed, as if by holding her knees together she could hide her girl power. Lily Cup glanced over the beautiful, freckled body with perky, full young breasts and her eyes rested on Millie's pelvis.

"What's with the lady garden?" Lily Cup asked.

Millie jerked her hand to cover her crotch. "Well, one day I'll be on a farm, and I didn't think..."

"You were going to grow a bird nest for the farm?"

Millie started to giggle uncontrollably. She reached for the daiquiri and took another slug, this time spreading her legs to keep from falling. Three sets of panties and bras flew over the door.

"How're your drinks? Need anything?" Sasha asked from outside.

"We could use a weed-wacker," Lily Cup said.

With that, the New Orleans' night was broken open like a Humpty Dumpty cracked egg, and the ladies were ready for any omelet it might serve up. More drinks were followed by more laughter and more fittings of gorgeous lace undies, Parisian hosiery and Chanel evening wear, with and without straps.

Millie exaggerated poses in the mirror and admitted she had a lovely cleavage, but opted for conservative sexy, the shorter skirt and thigh-high look, and Lily Cup confessed she couldn't help, as her own taste was mostly in her mouth, and Sasha had dressed her since high school and hated the diamond brooch she wore and the white Nike driving shoes.

When Millie finally stepped through the fitting room door, her cinnamon hair combed back neatly with a Jeffersonian flair and tied with a black and red striped ribbon, she looked as an Audrey Hepburn with freckles might look in the same black Chanel cocktail dress, hand-sewn, black lace stockings and Prada's finest red satin heels with ankle straps.

"You are such a beauty," Sasha said.

"She doesn't dye her hair," Lily Cup said.

Sasha picked from the four handbags in her hand and handed Millie a red satin Chanel bag as the fitting room door closed behind her.

"Didn't you have braces last time?" Lily Cup asked.

"I got them off three weeks ago," Millie said.

"You are a beauty."

"This has been so much fun, but my debit card has a limit, and I don't think—" Millie started.

"The outfit is a wedding present," Sasha said.

"For me? But Peck and I—"

"My wedding," Sasha said. "You'll look smashing walking down the aisle as my bridesmaid."

They first drove to Lily Cup's house.

"See you in an hour?" Sasha asked.

"I'll be there."

Sasha drove home to the Garden District.

While Millie explored the art and bric-a-brac in the living and dining rooms, Sasha dressed and made an entrance, delicately sliding her palm on the wrought-iron handrail of a winding staircase. In strapless Chanel she stepped from the bottom stair with a smile and fabled cleavage, setting a tone that the night was young, the moon was full, and it was meant for a dry martini and how lovely they both looked. She handed Millie a sealed deck of tarot cards to bring to the séance. Millie glanced in every mirror or reflective glass window or picture frame she could. She felt like the million dollars she looked like when they stepped from the house into a waiting limousine.

"Parking in the Quarter is such a pain," Sasha said.

"Is that where the rooftop is?" Millie asked.

"Yes. It has an umbrella table with chairs that won't rip our dresses and a box of candles. It's cozy."

"Do you like know somebody who lets you on their roof?" Millie asked.

"I do."

"That's awfully nice of them."

"Lily Cup," Sasha said.

"Lily Cup?"

"Lily Cup owns the building. My realty office manages the rentals."

Millie pulled a lighted mirror down from the ceiling and checked her makeup.

"I would have drinks for us in here, honey," Sasha said. "But dry-cleaning Chanel costs a mortgage, so I take no chances drinking in moving vehicles."

Millie sat up like royalty and watched through every window, catching lights and motions in a New Orleans night with a determination in her eyes that she would take in every minute, every sight, every sense and sound and enjoy every drip of it.

"When we go to Charlie's later, do you think someone will ask me to dance?" Millie asked.

"Count on it," Sasha said.

In Baton Rouge the maître d' let Elizabeth examine the Bordeaux label and then uncorked it.

"Do you mind decanting it?"

"Not at all, Miss."

Elizabeth explained to Peck that a decanted dry red was smoother because it breathed deeper breaths of air, or so it seemed to her. Once the ceremony was completed and they felt alone in the room filled with chatting, laughing lovers, and other patrons, Elizabeth lifted her glass in toast. Peck followed suit.

"To my new job at Bistro," she said. "You happen to be dining tonight with the brand-new sous chef."

"Oh, cher, this couldn't be better news. Everything is changing for us, dass for true," Peck said.

"*Ce soir, je me sens comme une femme,* Peck," Elizabeth said. ("Tonight, I feel like a woman, Peck.") Tonight, I feel fresh and flavorful and a bit sassy. Isn't it wonderful?"

"It is so wonderful. Such a day."

"And to think, I'm sitting at this table with all the lovely silver and wax candles and fine linens—across from such a sexy thing."

"Aw."

"Oh, not you, Peck. Did you think I was talking about you? *Mais non, mais non*! William. I was talking about William."

They guffawed and snorted and sipped their wine and lifted cheeses to smell the piquant and their cheeks would puff with a bite of baguette as they tried to finish a sentence, sometimes their own. The food moved from plate to palate and they talked of Paris and of how long cooking school was and of Tulane.

"Will you bring Millie to Paris?"

"Nah, nah. You say yourself Peck is, how you say, chopped liver? You only speak of William."

"Well, you're important too."

"I am, for true?"

"But of course, you are, you're William's driver. You're his portage." She giggled.

There was an air about the table that everything was fine in the world. Elizabeth could taste Paris and her corner café or bakeshop with the crepes and jams and French country mushroom soups with the richest of creams. Peck knew now his momma was in sight of the moon not far away, and he and Millie would see her soon, and didn't Elizabeth look like heaven, her green eyes inviting him with lips, glistened with a buttery hollandaise, closing on an asparagus stalk she held delicately in her fingers.

The French Quarter was busy with people in the streets milling about, listening to street performers or looking through the windows of antique shops. The limo stopped a block away from a group sitting in a circle in the center of the street playing Dixieland for a growing crowd. Each musician had a can or jar on the ground before them in case anyone wished to show appreciation for their sounds.

Sasha's leg stepped out and with a hand from the driver she stood and adjusted her bodice and waist. To the onlookers' delight, Millie bounced across the back seat to the door almost as if she were in her shorts, and with an awkward step out her leg revealed red panties that matched her shoes and bag, fine hosiery, and a delightfully freckled bare thigh. She was none the wiser for the stir she caused and read the smiles on faces in the crowd as official welcomes into the Quarter. In a certain sense, they were.

Lily Cup's building in the Quarter had two elevators. One was installed with the building in the late 1930s. The other was Lily Cup's private elevator, less than ten years old. This private elevator required a key only three people had—Lily Cup, Sasha, and a neighbor's housekeeper, who cared for the plants on the roof garden. The two walked arm-in-arm and stopped to hear a riff of Dixieland by the performers. Millie clapped her hands to the beat and rhythm with a delightful grin and bright, excited eyes, and Sasha swayed her hips, while looking through her purse for a fifty.

"Which can is for all of you," Sasha mouthed to the clarinetist.

The player, a young lady, lifted a finger from her clarinet and pointed to the large can in the center of the circle.

"Oh, can I do it?" Millie asked.

Sasha handed Millie the fifty. Millie added a ten from her bag and stepped between the tuba and trombone in grins, bent over with her Chanel doing a proper job of showcasing a delectable hint of bare thigh above exquisite French hose. The elevator door opened and they stepped in and pushed the button with the arrow pointing up.

"Lily Cup is here," Sasha said.
"How can you tell?"
"Smell the perfume?"
"I do."

The door opened to find the candle in its proper holder on the table, but unlit. Lily Cup was standing by the rail looking down into the street with her phone to her ear. She was in black tights with four-inch, black, sequined heels and a shimmering sleeveless top. She turned and held her index finger up to be patient while she finished a call she didn't seem to be talking on.

"Sit where the moon is to your best advantage," Sasha said.

Millie stepped behind one chair, then another and selected the second, pulled it and sat. Sasha lit the candle.

"Do you have the cards?" Sasha asked.

Millie took them from her bag and handed them over. Sasha broke the seal and took them out. While standing, she leaned and shuffled the deck four times on the tabletop and set them there.

"Okay, I'm ready," Millie said.

Sasha pulled a chair and sat down.

"My, but don't you two look absolutely gorgeous," Lily Cup said.

"You look pretty amazing yourself," Millie said.

Millie opened the door of a small refrigerator and pulled out a plastic tray with three drinks on it. She held it for Sasha and Millie to take theirs, and she set hers in front of the empty chair.

"No trial tomorrow, no clients to bail out of jail. Tonight we party and dance," Lily Cup said.

"We're dancing tonight," Sasha said. "Gabe is probably at Charlie's already, so let's get started."

"I'm ready," Millie said.

Sasha raised her martini in toast. Lily Cup and Millie followed suit.

"Millie, it's been a whirlwind year for you. It was just about nine months ago you came into our lives like the most welcome child a family could ever have," Sasha said.

Millie started to tear up.

They each sipped to the thought and set their drinks on the table.

"Millie, I want you to take your mind back a whole year. If you do, you will see your life before Peck and us, your family here—and you will have it to compare with your life now."

"I can do that."

"As you do, I want you to think of the most important number you can think of—the first number that comes to your mind."

"Easy," Millie said.

One at a time she pointed at each of her friends at the table.

"One, two," Millie said. "Two is the number."

Sasha placed her palm on the tarot deck and fanned them across the table.

"Pick any two cards, Millie. Take your time. We have all night. But pick two and slide them out of the deck. Don't lift them."

Millie used the index finger of both hands and lowered them both to the fan of cards and pushed two cards at the same time to the tabletop. Sasha picked up the remaining cards and handed them to Lily Cup to put back in the case.

"Two cards will tell us a story tonight. A story of our sweet Millie and what lies ahead for you."

Millie reached to her right and took Lily Cup's hand and held it for security. Sasha turned both cards over and left them side-by-side, face-up.

"Oh my," Sasha said.

"Is that good?" Millie asked.

"Well this one is the Lover card. That looks pretty good to me."

"What does it mean?"

"The Lover card tells you that in the coming days and years you will have strengthening of an existing love relationship."

Millie beamed, holding fingers over her mouth to cover braces she had forgotten were no longer there.

"Peck?" Millie squeaked.

"Seems like," Sasha said.

"Watch the moon, everybody," Lily Cup said. "Let's watch for a shooting star."

Millie sat tall, her eyes embracing the thought of a lifetime with Peck and her body lurched when a star raced across the heavens, and she bounced in her chair while pointing up.

"There's one! I see one!"

"A shooting star," Lily Cup said. "So, it will all come true."

Millie's palms touched her cheeks, tears in both eyes, evaporating in the gentle night's air.

"The second card is Nine of Pentacles," Sasha said. This is a most enlightening card."

Millie leaned in to take a closer look at the card.

"What does it mean?" she asked.

"The Nine of Pentacles means you have reached a point in your life where you are feeling self-confident and self-sufficient."

"Are you feeling more self-confident, Millie?" Lily Cup asked.

Millie reflected, shoved her chair back, stood and pulled her dress up to her hips, displaying a red garter belt, matching thong panties, young bare thighs and hosiery that cost more than three graduate school textbooks.

"Why, I wouldn't know. Whatever would give you the impression I lacked self-confidence? Well, I mean, I just wouldn't have the foggiest idea how you could ever..."

Roaring in laughter, Lily Cup spilled her drink on the table, Sasha snorting three, four, five snorts, slapping a flat hand on the tabletop. Millie stood stoically, lips clenched to keep from laughing. Just as the laughter subsided, Millie went into act two. She reached with both hands and pulled the front of her top and the bra beneath down.

"And my tits are pretty confident too!"

Almost as soon as act two was over, Millie's face turned a beet red in embarrassment, but grinning as she covered her girls. Sasha, still laughing almost to tears, picked the two tarot cards from the table, reached and stuck them under the thigh strap of Millie's garter belt. They sat and enjoyed the moment and the friendships. Such a day it has been and such a celebration the night promised. At what she thought was the right moment, Lily Cup interrupted.

"I heard from Peck," Lily Cup said.

"What'd he say?" Millie asked.

Lily Cup looked at Sasha and nodded a wink.

"Millie, do you remember how I told you I want you to go with Peck to see about finding his mother?"

"Yes, why?"

"What if you find her, and she's not well? Or maybe she has dementia, or it could be anything? What then?" Lily Cup asked.

"His mother is his mother. I would love her just for that. Why? What did he tell you?"

"I didn't talk to him, but he left a voicemail for me this afternoon. I was listening to it when you both came up here tonight. Would you like to hear it?"

"Yes."

"It's a long one."

"Please."

Lily Cup pressed the voicemail button and the speaker button and set her phone on the table.

"Lily Cup, I see'd this doctor John today, and he did good, I t'ink. He say my mamma I see'd in the moon is what I thought was my foster nanna, and she been my mamma all along. He told me where to go to ax a banker where she lives and I see'd it on a map, so I'm ready to go. I want to ax you somet'ing, and I do what you say, but I got to ax, or I can't live with myself. Lily Cup, when I runned away from home and my foster nanna, I was running from my own mamma, and dass for true. Lily Cup, what kind of man runs away from his own mamma and don't stay to take care of his own mamma? I need you to tell Millie what kind of a man I am and tell her Peck understand should she never want to see me again ever. Would you tell her, please, for me please? I'm going to turn my phone off until tomorrow, then I'll call you back."

The message beeped to a close.

Sasha and Millie were in tears. Millie was sobbing. No one spoke. The moment was for thought, for garnering strength. Millie dabbed her face with a sheet of paper towel.

"I love that man more than I dreamed I could ever love someone," Millie said.

Sasha and Lily Cup waited to react.

"You okay?" Sasha asked.

"Lily Cup, will you drive me to Peck tomorrow, please?"

"Damn straight."

"Millie, Millie, you are so fucking perfect for Peck. You go girl!" Sasha said.

"What now?" Lily Cup asked.

Lily Cup and Sasha looked into Millie's eyes. It would be her call. Millie looked at them, and a smile broke into a grin through the tears. She pushed her chair back, stood and pulled her skirt up over her hips for an encore.

"If all this doesn't get me a dance with a drunken sailor tonight, nothing will. Let's go girls!"

Sasha and Lily Cup stood and howled and applauded.

Millie lifted her cell from her bag and held it up as she pressed the off button.

"I'll turn it on when we get to Baton Rouge tomorrow. Tonight I'm Catholic."

"Ha ha, you are such a Baptist. What's with the Catholic trip?" Lily Cup asked.

"Southern Baptists aren't supposed to drink or dance. You Catholics can drink on the dance floor." She blessed herself. "Look out tonight."

Lily Cup called Uber and arranged a pickup spot.

In Baton Rouge the dinner and conversation carried to closing and a walk to the apartment was settling. Peck was feeling his wine and opted not to swim, so he sat on the floor, leaning back on the sofa, as Elizabeth stretched on the sofa, her head near his, and told him it had been a perfect evening. Peck asked about wild mushrooms and if there was a market for them and what Lily Cup was going to tell Millie when he tells her he's ready to go meet the banker so he can find his mamma. His head fell back from time to time. Could have been the drink, could have been all that was on his mind.

He turned and looked into Elizabeth's eyes and told her he would always love her, and maybe if he sold enough crawfish and soft-shell crab, he and Millie will come to see her in Paris, and she could make crepes with jam. Elizabeth leaned over as though to kiss him, but she reached her arm around his waist, sliding her hand in behind his opened belt buckle. She found William, and she held it firmly and could feel the head on her wrist and Peck began to grind his hips and her hand held the skin tightly and William moved up and back, up and back in the sheath of nerves and she kissed his neck, his hips thrusting William again and again. She nibbled his ear and licked it with her warm tongue and his pelvis held and quivered, his butt lifted from the floor and then down. Elizabeth left her hand on William, tenderly feeling the wet warmth of his still firm love and Peck turned his head to her and smiled. She spoke softly into his ear.

"*Nous devons dire au revoir a Peck avant que ton Millie ne vienne,*" Elizabeth said. ("We need to say goodbye, Peck, before your Millie comes.")

"Goodbye, cher?" Peck asked.

"Make love to me Peck."

Peck unzipped his pants and pushed them down first with his hands and then with each foot pushing a pantleg off, his back resting against the sofa. Elizabeth stood in her black, sleeveless French cocktail dress and stood over Peck, straddling him while facing him. She lifted her skirt briefly to show she was without panties and then she reached down and she held the sides of his head for leverage as she lowered herself to just above a still glistening William. Her hand between her thighs guided it in with a slow compression down to its base, every centimeter a lighted fuse of nerve endings about to burst. Their friendship would not wane, but just this once, an electric au revoir.

Was she thinking of her lonely nights without him or of the first time he walked her home stepping backwards in front of her because they couldn't take their eyes from each other? Was he thinking of how being held by her took him from the nightmare of carrying bait buckets and sleeping under saw blades? She kissed and sucked on his lips as her buttocks would rise and lower with a passionate squeeze and flexing a conjuring of so many memories of so many empty nights filled. She came while kissing him and then soon again with still another kiss until his hands reached under her dress and grasped her buttocks, now lifting and lowering her on William to share a final, long-lasting climax they both needed before they went their own separate ways. The kiss lingered patiently, their bodies at rest. Elizabeth lifted her head back. She wasn't quite ready to get up and end the physical connection. She leaned in and whispered in his ear?

"*Un bain chaud*, Peck?" ("A hot tub, Peck?")

"*Oui.*"

They held each other while the tub filled and they stepped into it like it was their private tree house where it all began.

CHAPTER 20

THE DOORBELL RANG. Gabe stood from his easy chair.

"Is she up?" Lily Cup asked.

"I haven't heard a peep. How late did you stay at Charlie's?"

"You and Sasha left, what—at midnight?"

"About then."

"We closed the place. Twinkle-toes in there danced with two different guys. One couldn't keep his hands off her."

"I saw the one with the Saints hat. I didn't see the other."

"He came in after you left. She told Sasha the Saints hat was a sexy guy and made her want Peck."

"The other?"

"He was the all hands, kept feeling her. She even asked Sasha what to do about him besides slap him or not dance with him."

"And?"

"Sasha asked her if he was a good dancer and when Millie said he was the better dancer of the two, Sasha told her to tell the guy to wash his hands. The dress was twenty-eight hundred bucks."

"That's our Sasha," Gabe said.

Gabe brought in a cup and the pot of coffee for Lily Cup. He poured.

"Has anybody told her?"

"Told her?"

"About the jam I was in. She has the right to know she's living with a..."

"Knock it off, Gabe. Get a grip. I'll tell her before I take her to Peck today."

"She has a right to know," Gabe said.

"I'll handle it. Put it out of your head."

"Let me hear the voicemail," Gabe said.

Lily Cup picked up her cellphone and pushed the voicemail button and the speaker button. Gabe listened to Peck's voice talking through his experiences with the psychiatrist.

"This is pretty heady stuff," Gabe said.

"What do you think?" Lily Cup asked.

"I'm not worried about the boy. The life he's lived would have broken most men. He hasn't so much as flinched or yelled uncle one time since he was nine. He's fed himself and kept a roof over his head, and he's done it with honor. I'm not worried for a second for him or for what he's going to find in those swamps."

"Is this one of those black epiphany moment things you were telling me, Gabe?"

Gabe chuckled. "Actually, it could be. There isn't one of my brothers or sisters who couldn't go back in time and not find ghosts and spirits haunting the barns and haylofts and church steeples in alleys of pain."

"What the hell does that mean?"

"I'm Creole—you think I wouldn't find slaves in my bloodline if I went back far enough—maybe a family of slaves? Maybe a great, great uncle whose body was dropped in chains overboard when he died from scurvy or something at sea on his way over. Maybe a grandmother who jumped overboard or ran into a burning barn to kill herself after she was raped by a slave trader or owner."

"Jesus."

"What?"

"Do you sit up at night dreaming this stuff?"

"It's like our chicken pox, little sister. Something we're born with...sorry. You have your *Goldilocks and the Three Bears*, we have our, 'don't be lookin' the Massah in the eye, les' you want to get a whuppin', boy.'"

"Christ, Gabe, you're depressing me."

"You asked me what I thought."

"Can't you at least tell me you're in a happy place now—that you're a happy man, and all that crap is behind you, and you're going to go out in style with a smile on your kisser with us as your friends and family?"

Gabe looked at Lily Cup. He grimaced a smile and reached his cup over to click on hers.

"To the end, my friend," Gabe said. "To the end."

"Damn," Lily Cup said. "If I didn't have to drive Millie to Baton Rouge I'd go buy a fifth of rye."

"You'll tell her?"

"I'll do it before I take her to Baton Rouge."

"Wasn't that something in the voicemail about Peck, mammas and the moon?" Gabe asked.

"It gave me chills. He told Sasha since he was a kid he would talk to the moon, thinking it was his mamma. It had Sasha and Millie in tears. Now that's the real hoodoo, in real time."

"I'll make a fresh pot, go see if Millie is awake. I have Danishes and crumb cake."

"I feel like I need another fucking shower," Lily Cup said.

Lily Cup and Gabe shared a grin.

"Try to get it out of your head, Gabe. Life's too short. He would have killed you. You protected yourself. End of story."

She followed him to the kitchen, took an empty coffee mug from the shelf.

"How does she take it?" Lily Cup asked.

"Two Splenda. It's on that shelf over there, and a bit of milk."

Lily Cup prepared a cup and quietly pushed Peck's bedroom door to find the sleeping Cinderella. She was lying on her side, facing the window, the sheet and blanket over her head, blocking sunbeams coming in. Lily Cup stepped around and adjusted the blinds to deflect the sun. She sat on the side of the bed and just nestled in the fold of Millie's stomach and thighs. A voice came from under the sheets.

"What time is it?"

"What's it matter? You're out of school."

"Where am I?"

"You're in a hotel room off Canal Street. Some guy wearing a Saints cap just left your room, counting the money in his wallet."

Millie slapped the sheet and blanket from her face; her eyes blinked a grin and focused on Lily Cup's eyes.

"Who are you?" she demanded, just before she giggled and turned on her stomach.

"I'm your worst nightmare. I'm your new boss and this is your first day of work and you're already two hours late. I'm thinking of canning your ass."

Millie turned and sat up.

"You never told me when to come to work."

"Here, drink some coffee."

Millie took the mug and had a temperature sip.

"What time is it?"

"We'll have a Danish and I'll show you my office, and we'll do some things before we head on up to Baton Rouge."

"Did Peck call?"

"His phone is still off, but I left a message we'll be there by two."

"Who'd you leave a message with?"

"I texted Elizabeth, and she texted me back that he was sleeping and she would leave a note for when he wakes up."

"He's still asleep?"

"My accountant says I should intern you. Would that be okay with you?"

"Of course. Do whatever you want. Do you think Peck and Elizabeth are having sex?" Millie asked.

"What brought that up?" Lily Cup asked. "You heard the message and how much he loves you."

"I know, but he's been with her a long time this week. Who is she to him anyway?"

"So, tell me—who was the better dancer last night, the Saints hat guy or the grabber stud?"

"Larry…"

"Larry? Oh, really? Larry? Aren't we getting a bit personal?"

"He was sweet. He has a girlfriend in Jackson. He was only in New Orleans on a job interview. He danced like a gentleman. I didn't mind so much that he wasn't a good dancer."

"Now I get it little lady, you're feeling guilty about your Larry last night so you're thinking Peck is hiding the salami in Baton Rouge?"

Millie did a doubletake at the concept and broke into a giggle, which ended with her head down on the pillow and a sigh.

"Well, it's not about Larry," Millie said.

"So how was Curley? Or was it Moe? The grabber?"

"He's a really good dancer. He pinched and grabbed, which was a pain, but he was such a good dancer."

"Aha," Lily Cup said. "He's the guilt trip you're having."

Millie looked up with a sheepish smile.

"Ain't that a bitch? The good ones are always copping a feel."

"That's not true. Gabe doesn't grab Sasha."

"Well did the grabber get his hands on the lady garden?"

Millie turned her head away.

"He did, he copped a feel of your kitty."

"He didn't get under my panties and it was only once...twice. I told him to stop and he stopped. I feel so bad, I've got to tell Peck. I was drinking."

"He was a hunk. Did you get his name?"

Millie reached into her red Chanel purse on the side table and pulled a business card from it.

"Here's his number. Keep it."

Lily Cup looked at the card.

"Well, what do you know about that?" she asked.

"What?"

"His name really is Curley," Lily Cup said.

"Shut up," Millie said with a giggle.

"Curley Moe, that's his name."

"Shut up."

"How's his willie, did you get a grab of his willie?"

"What!?"

"Aha, you did, I can tell."

"He knew all the song names to the music we danced to."

"So, you had to feel his baton."

"Shut up."

"Don't you just hate that? The grabbers are like that. They know all the words."

Millie handed the coffee mug back to Lily Cup, lifted the sheet and crawled to the other side of the bed and stood in her new, red satin panties.

"At least you were sober enough to take your garter belt and stockings off."

"I wasn't that drunk. After the first one on the roof and one at Charlie's I just sipped. I'm a stupid drunk."

"Plus, the two you had at Sak's and it was two, not one, on the roof," Lily Cup said.

Millie donned a T-shirt, and they went into the kitchen, and she told Gabe how embarrassed she was to get a C in French and that she was studying about crawfish farming online, and would her new dress be protected from the elements better in a closet or at a dry cleaner? They spoke of Peck's trip and how Gabe wanted her to use her phone and always find a hotel room if they had to stay over and to not stay with strangers or sleep in the truck. They lifted and bumped fists and he took her hand.

"You could be going into some dark waters, darlin'. You going to be okay?" Gabe asked.

"I watched him kill the dog," Millie said.

Gabe hesitated, wrinkled his brow and remembered. The other knife man's dog—the thief who stole Gabe's pills under the bridge the year before. Peck killed the dog when that knife man told his dog to 'sic 'em' and it sprung into attack.

"You're a good woman."

Millie grinned, lifted and dropped her shoulders with pride.

"What's on the agenda for you ladies today—besides taking Millie to her Boudreaux Clemont Finch?" Gabe asked.

"I'm going to show her my office and where her desk is. Then we're meeting Sasha at Coquette for an early lunch, and after that she and Millie are hitting the Ritz-Carlton spa for a mani-pedi and a mow."

Millie broke into a red-faced grin at the "mow" and Gabe, ever the gentlemen, held his coffee cup up with a silent approval.

"Will I see you before you leave for Baton Rouge?" Gabe asked.

"Probably not," Lily Cup said. "I have to be back by four. Best you get your hugs in before we leave here."

Gabe lifted the lid on the box of Danish for the ladies to see, turned and went to his easy chair to finish the morning paper.

"Help yourselves."

In Baton Rouge, Elizabeth, in her morning garb of chef school pants and bare top, was in her usual ritual of gathering dishware and utensils for the dishwasher when Peck came from the bedroom in his briefs.

"You up for good? I want to make the bed before I leave for school," Elizabeth said.

Peck didn't say a word. He walked into the kitchen rubbing his face and leaned against the counter to her left. Elizabeth started the dishwasher, and sidled over to Peck and leaned against him, skin on skin, folding her arms around him. They let their body language say good morning.

"That was beautiful, Peck. Thank you," Elizabeth said.

"I can make the bed, cher. Gabe teach'd me how he did it in the army. I'll make it," Peck said.

"I want to change the sheets," Elizabeth said.

"They look clean."

Elizabeth raised her head and looked Peck in the eyes.

"*Ta Millie arrive aujourd'hui, et tu voudras lui faire l'amour passionnément, non?*" Elizabeth asked. ("Your Millie is coming today, and you'll want to make passionate love to her, no?")

"*Oui.*"

"*Des draps propres, alors. Une femme sait ce qu'il faut faire dans ce cas,*" Elizabeth said. ("Fresh sheets, then. A woman knows these things.")

Peck ran his flat hands down under her chef pants waistband and grasped a buttock cheek in each hand and gently squeezed.

"If we don't speak English, Peck will be forty when I graduate Tulane."

Elizabeth lifted her head and smiled.

"When will you and Millie be leaving to find your mamma?"

"Tomorrow."

"Tonight, you take her to Bistro, and I see you get free wine and a beautiful dinner, and you bring her here after your chocolate souffle and make love. I'll sleep on the sofa."

"You're good to Peck, cher. T'ank you."

Elizabeth stood.

"You go shower. I'll make the bed and pick things up. I can't be late for school. Come to Bistro at six. There will be a table for you."

As Peck was stepping into a morning shower in Baton Rouge, on Carrolton Avenue in New Orleans, Lily Cup was touring Millie through her law offices and to her private office.

"We all get our own coffee here."

"This is beautiful," Millie said.

"Before the summer's out, you'll learn your way around all these files and cabinets, and you'll know who's who around here."

"Why are those files against that wall red and the ones on that wall green?" Millie asked.

"Very observant, young lady. You must have some Peck in you…"

Lily Cup started a second as they both realized what she had said. They did double-takes at the double entendre and guffawed.

"Simple. The red filing cabinets are for violent crime case files. The green ones are for nonviolent felony case files. We have everything on computer, but it's easier to take files into meetings or to court."

"Have you had any murderers for clients?" Millie asked.

Lily Cup turned and hesitated. She reached and took Millie by the arm.

"Come with me. We have to talk."

They went into her office, and Lily Cup pointed to a chair for Millie as she stepped around and plopped into her leather wingback.

"Push the door," Lily Cup said.

Millie obliged and sat down. Lily Cup leaned in, elbows folded on her desk.

"Millie, ever pinky-swear a secret?"

"Duh?" Millie asked.

"And duh is?"

"I'm a southern Baptist girl. My Daddy is a southern Baptist minister and my mother is a Baptist Evangelical missionary to the poor."

"And this means exactly? Help me out here."

"They still don't know I started on birth control pills my freshman year at Baylor, and I could make frozen daiquiris for my thermos by the time I was nineteen. I can keep a secret."

"Good, because there's something I have to tell you, and I need you to keep it a secret always."

"I can do that, I promise."

"Peck, Sasha, Gabe and I have been trying to come up with a way to tell you something, and they asked me to spill it as I knew all the facts."

"Should I be worried?"

"It's nothing like that, It's just something that happened, and we want to make sure you heard the whole story so you can decide for yourself."

"Now I am worried."

"Millie, do you know what self-defense is?"

"I do. I took two law courses."

"Well about a week or so ago, somebody down at Lee Circle tried to rob Gabe with a knife."

"Was Gabe hurt?"

"Gabe had to fight the man with his cane."

"I remember something about self-defense—"

"And Gabe hit the man when he tried to stab him with the knife."

"Did he stab Gabe?"

"No, but Gabe hurt him really bad when he hit him."

"What is it with Louisiana and men with knives? Peck was attacked with a knife too. Remember, we caught the guy?"

"I do remember, and it was in Mississippi."

"Oh, that's right, sorry. Well, if the crook with the knife got hurt by Gabe's cane, it's just too bad for him. He deserved it."

"He died."

"Oh."

Lily Cup kept silent to let it all play out in Millie's mind. She knew if she dealt with it in her own way, it would be more lasting than if she were "sold" the rationale.

"Is Gabe okay?"

"He was sad about it—almost in a stupor for a while. It was like a depression when the man died, knowing he did it, but he was frightened for his life. He had to defend himself."

"Yes."

"Like he would defend you or me or anyone."

"Yes."

"It's just that we try not to talk about it. It still upsets him, and he's an old man, and we try not to bring it up. That's why I'm telling you so you don't learn it from some stranger, or by looking in our files."

Millie placed both hands on the edge of Lily Cup's desk. She lowered her head and rested her forehead on the back of her hands and meditated, motionless. When she lifted her head she sat tall.

"If the thief is found breaking in and is struck so that he dies, there shall be no bloodguilt for him…" Millie was quoting scripture.

Lily Cup sat in awe, with gaping mouth. She started, shook her head awake and came to life again.

"You're one amazing kid," Lily Cup said.

Millie lifted her hand, pointing a curved pinky finger.

"Pinky-swear, I won't tell," she said.

Lily Cup lifted both hands, with both pinky fingers out and curled.

"Two pinky-swears—one for the secret about Gabe, and one for you're one amazing kid."

They clasped pinkies on the swears, and Millie sat back. She lifted a comical twisting of her index finger to her cheek to the "kid" remark.

"I'm not a kid, ya know. Why I'm near fully growed," Millie replied.

"I'll say your fully growed. I've been in your dressing room."

Millie grinned.

"And you're beginning to sound like Peck."

Lunch was more laughs than it was lunch. Sasha was seated and had ordered off-menu cucumber sandwiches and a large fruit and cheese plate they would share.

"I'm impressed, Millie," Sasha said.

"Huh?"

"You are quite the dancer. Do you and Peck dance?"

"We will this summer. It wasn't easy going out when I'd come for a weekend."

They spoke of Charlie's Blue Note and of slow jazz and Dixieland, and whether Prada or Dior or a Christian Louboutin made a better shoe and how a thong needed some getting used to. Lily Cup told Sasha they had a talk about the Gabe episode and how Millie was good with it and would keep it under wraps. Millie asked if it was necessary that she get a waxed *coochie,* as she didn't want an itch like she was told it caused.

"Coochie?" Sasha asked. "I love it."

"You know what I mean. I heard it like itches after waxing."

"Ask them for a trim. They'll do a trim," Lily Cup said.

In the midst of the lunch Millie was impressed when Sasha asked them all to hold hands and they each said a prayer for Millie and Peck to find his mother and that their journey be rewarding, and they would return to New Orleans safe and soon. They said one for Gabe, as well.

The friendship the three of them had bonded in the past eighteen hours brought a tear to Millie's eye, and she suggested they treat themselves to sherbet and cookies if Coquette had them. Pecan or key lime pie if they didn't. Sasha and Lily Cup took turns expressing their views on why there were no spoons or dessert forks on the table and the nuances of differences between diets for women pushing forty and young college bitches who could eat anything and still not know what a tummy is.

The drive to Baton Rouge was uninterrupted by conversation or radio noise. It was a blending of silences between two new friends perhaps playing the evening together in their minds, the rooftop séance, the dancing. Talk of the week that lay before Peck and Millie would be a spoiler. Conjecture was not a good way to start anything of this nature. Millie couldn't take her eyes off the bridge to Baton Rouge as it carried them over the longest stretch of Acadian bayous and moss-dripping cypress trees Millie had ever seen. It looked as if she was imagining the gators and snappers Peck had talked of so many times before, with his arms around her as they lay on the bed, looking up through the window at a full moon.

Lily Cup pulled into a parking space on South Fourteenth Street just behind Peck's pickup. She lifted her cell and pressed a key and put the phone to her ear.

"We're here; come get your lady. I have to get back."

Lily Cup leaned over and kissed Millie on both cheeks. They squeezed hands.

"It's been fun, sweetie. We'll see you soon. You're on the payroll. Keep me posted by text once a day. Call me if you need help with something."

Millie stepped out of the car with her bag as Peck came through the front doors and with a wave Lily Cup made a wide U-turn and drove off.

CHAPTER 21

AS THOUGH SHE WERE SLEEPWALKING, Millie closed the medicine cabinet and switched off the bathroom light before pulling the door open. She could see Peck's leg sticking out from under the sheet. She stepped quietly into the hall and followed a glowing kitchen nightlight until she could see Elizabeth on the sofa, a summer quilt blanketing her. Millie knelt beside her.

"Elizabeth?"

"*Oui?*" Elizabeth asked, raising her head.

"I'm so sorry to wake you."

"Is there a problem?"

"Do you have any Tampax?"

"Look in the cabinet under the sink."

"In the bathroom?"

"*Oui.*"

"Thank you."

"No worries. Help yourself."

"The dinner was totally awesome. Did you cook all that?"

"Some, but no, I'm not the head chef."

Millie stood.

"G'night. Sorry to wake you."

Millie made her way back to the bathroom, did her business and crawled in behind Peck, putting her arm over his chest and kissing him on the back.

"You hokay, cher?"

"I had a visitor."

Peck raised his head. "Hanh?"

"Mother Nature."

Peck turned inquisitively.

"A girl thing. Go to sleep."

Peck rested his head as if he understood. They lay silently, Millie gathering her thoughts.

"Peck?"

"*Oui?*"

"Lily Cup told me about Gabe and that man. It's so sad for Gabe."

"*Oui.*"

"He had every right to hit a man who was like attacking him with a knife."

"*Oui.*"

"He hit him like the dog. Remember that dog, Peck?"

"*Oui.*"

"It'll be better coming from you. Will you tell him I still love him and nothing will ever change that?"

"I will."

"When are we leaving?"

"When we get up."

"Where're we going?"

"Millie, I t'ink I should tell you about some t'ings when I growed."

"I know some of it, like you ran away because your stepfather was mean."

"Do you know what he did to me?"

"How would I know?"

"I was t'inking maybe Lily Cup or Sasha tole you."

"Nobody told me anything."

Peck was silent.

"Well, that's not all true," Millie said.

Peck waited.

"Lily Cup let me hear the voicemail."

Peck bounced on his elbow and turned, facing Millie's silhouette shaded from a streetlamp leaking through the center of nearly closed bedroom drapes.

"You heard it?"

"I listened to it. It only made me love you more."

"I love you, cher—so much."

"I know you ran away from home when you were young. There must have been a good reason, and you didn't know she was your momma."

"I love you, Millie."

"We have all our lives for you to tell me about those things. Let's go try to find your momma in the morning. Do you know where to start?"

"Killian, to the bank there. A man at the bank knows maybe where mamma is."

The room was still. They heard a car driving by on the street below. Peck was nodding off.

"Elizabeth is nice," Millie said.

"Nice."

"Do you love her?"

Peck lifted a hand sleepily, touching Millie's cheek and he thought.

"Charlie?" Peck asked.

"My baby doll, Charlie, or the Blue Note Charlie?" Millie asked.

"Your baby doll Charlie."

"What about baby Charlie?"

"Peck loves Elizabeth like Millie loves her Charlie."

"That's so sweet. Would you say you and Elizabeth are like brother and sister?"

"Why you ask me, cher?"

"Because I drank too much last night and let a man get fresh with me dancing at Charlie's. I could have stopped it but he was holding me and I was thinking of you up here with Elizabeth."

"Cousins. Elizabeth and Peck like cousins."

"Did you make love?"

"Peck drank too much wine and, yes, I made goodbye love with Elizabeth, dass for true. I know'd her like ten years. She'll be our good friend always. I love you, Millie, and only you. Elizabeth knows this and she likes you very much."

Millie pouted.

"Will Millie forgive me?"

"Will Peck forgive me?"

"*Oui.*"

"*Oui oui,*" Millie said.

Peck lifted and kissed Millie's hand.

"We need to do something nice for her. You know, for her letting us stay here," Millie said.

"Okay. Millie tell me what we do and we can do that."

"When we go home, you know back to New Orleans after we find your momma will we be coming through Baton Rouge?"

"Yes, I'm t'inking."

"So, we tell Elizabeth we're taking her out to a nice dinner when we come through."

"Good, cher. You tell her that."

Millie kissed Peck on the back as he turned and began dozing off.

"Peck, have you and Lily Cup ever…?"

"Hanh?"

"Go to sleep."

Millie awakened with the brushing sounds of the early morning street washer. She rolled to the edge of the bed, got up and went into the bathroom. The aroma of percolating coffee was in the air, and she followed the scent to the kitchen only to find Elizabeth standing in her chef school pants and no top, scratching marmalade onto both halves of a toasted English muffin.

"Oh?" Millie asked.

"Would you like an English muffin?" Elisabeth asked.

"Sure."

Elizabeth took one from the package, split it in half with two forks and dropped it in the toaster.

"My uniform top is in the bedroom closet. It's on the left. White, heavy starch. Do you mind getting it for me?"

Millie walked down the small hall into the bedroom and brought the chef school coat back on the hanger.

They stood drinking coffee and munching on crisped English muffins and Millie inviting Elizabeth to be their guest for dinner when they came back through and Elizabeth admiring Millie's cinnamon hair and did they enjoy their meal last night? They spoke of how charming downtown Baton Rouge was and of Elizabeth's wish to live in Paris when she graduated and for Millie to take several tampons until she could get to a drugstore. In the bedroom they heard Peck moving about. He came into the kitchen dressed, packed, and ready to go.

"What time are you leaving for school, Elizabeth?" Peck asked.

"I'll go at nine."

"Hokay, we can leave when you do, so you can lock the door. We drive an hour and the bank will be open at ten, so all is good."

"You want coddled eggs, Peck?" Elizabeth asked.

Peck looked at Millie. "Oh, cher, you have to taste Elizabeth's coddled eggs. They are so good, dass for true."

"Sure," Millie said.

"I'll make four," Elizabeth said.

"I better get ready. I'll be right back," Millie said.

Millie went and closed the bathroom door behind her.

"She's nice. You're a lucky man," Elizabeth said.

"The first time I saw her I knew I wanted to be with her. I never thought Peck would ever have a chance, dass for true, but here we are. She loves me."

"She adores you, Peck."

Elizabeth leaned and kissed Peck on the cheek.

"*Tu es un homme tres chanceux,*" Elizabeth said. ("You are a very lucky man.")

After small talk over breakfast snacks, Peck and Millie bid adieu and tucked bags behind the seat of the truck. Peck drove first to a service center station and filled the tank. He went inside with Millie where she picked up a few things, and he bought water bottles and Fritos. When they got back to the truck he asked if they should maybe get the truck washed before they left. It was an hour drive to Killian where the bank was. Just as he was about to start the engine Millie took his wrist in her hand and pulled it to get his attention.

"Peck, do you remember when I first met Gabe, that time you came up for Thanksgiving…"

"I remember."

"Gabe would come down and sit with me on Daddy's fishing dock while I fed the ducks and he told me stories of the times he was at the hospice and how he couldn't wait for Thursdays to come because that was the day you came to mow the lawn and how excited he was that you were coming. He told me everything you did and how you would wave hello and walk right to the bayou without stopping and you would put your gear on the ground and you would stretch out your trotline and you'd put bait on those things…"

"Snoods."

"That's it, the snoods—and right after you had the bait on he told me how you would twirl it around and throw it out as far as you could into the bayou, and then how you would tie it on a tree root, and you'd stand and watch it for a minute and then go mow the lawns."

"Dass for true, cher."

"Peck, you got all that done quickly every Thursday morning before you mowed?"

"Yeah?"

"So why are you stalling about going to find your momma? Why are you coming up with excuses—these things you have to do?"

Peck smiled with clenched lips of defeat. He looked over at Millie. "I love you," he said.

He started the pickup.

"I have to find Interstate 12," Peck said.

Millie lifted her phone, tapped into her Maps app and typed Interstate 12 and pressed.

"See the second light up there?" Millie asked.

"*Oui.*"

"Go to that light and turn right."

Off they went.

"What's the name of the place we're going?"

"Killian National Bank."

Millie pressed some buttons.

"It's fifty-five minutes. Turn up here on Interstate 12 and stay on it until I tell you to get off."

Peck reached in the paper sack sitting between them. He pulled a small bag of Fritos corn chips and began to tear them open. Millie took them from his hand, reminding him they had just eaten and they would need them for a snack later, and he didn't want to make a mess in his new truck and what a pretty truck it was, if trucks were pretty.

THE HOODOO OF PECK FINCH

The last two days had been such a fun whirlwind for Millie, it hadn't dawned on her to charge her cellphone. Peck examined every home and farm and swamp they passed. Nothing from his childhood seemed to come to his memory. It was when Millie saw the painted wooden sign for a bait shop on the Livingston exit she figured they had gone too far.

"My phone is dead. Where's yours?"

"In my bag."

"Better get off here. We need to ask directions."

Peck slowed and exited while glancing about for a service station—anyplace where there would be someone they could ask.

"The arrow on that bait shop sign over there points this way. Let's go see if it's open," Millie said.

The exit was a paved road and the arrows pointed to the right. The road turned into a narrow dirt path. Not far into it, nestled back under low, hanging pine tree branches was a medium size, egg-shaped travel trailer from the 1960s. There were six Styrofoam ice chests on a long wooden harvest table in front. The visible tire was flat and the front trailer hitch was resting on two cinder blocks. It had an awning over a two-by-twelve counter on the ledge of an opening that appeared to have been hacksawed out of its side, framed with cedar.

A flat, painted board sign read, BAIT. Crushed shells lined the drive up to and around the bait shop trailer. Peck pulled in and turned the engine off. He got out while Millie moved the seat and pulled his bag from the floor behind and looked for Peck's phone and charge cord. There was no sign of life in the trailer until a voice from inside sounded.

"You fishing for catfish or bass, friend?" the voice asked.

"Nah, nah, not fishin' today, frien', just driving," Peck said.

"I got fresh bait case you do."

Peck felt French was a door opener in Acadiana, a signal he was friendly.

"*Je lance pas fois des trotlines dans Carencro bayou, mon ami*," Peck said. ("I throw trotlines in Carencro bayou at times, friend.")

"I don't speak z'ee French, friend. My wife speaks it. She's Creole. Oh, I know zee *oui* and zee *merci* if I have to and enough to let her z'ink I'm learning zee French, so I can be a good American."

"You're not American?"

"I'm from Russia. Been a citizen three years now. I come here to read my books and sell my bait to buy more books. What you fishing—catfish or bass?"

"Nah, nah…" Peck started.

"Catfish go for smells. I've got good frozen chicken livers. Z'ay love chicken livers. Have lots of cut-up shad too. Z'at smells too. Catfish go for smells."

The curiosity of the fisher in Peck peaked.

"Shicken livers?"

"Z'ay smell so good to catfish. Why, what you use?"

"Purdy much cut snake and maybe snapper innards," Peck said.

"Chicken livers work good for catfish around here. Just keep checking your hook, z'ay crumble off easy. You want to try my chicken livers? Frozen quick, z'ay'll keep 'til you get to where you're going."

"Nah, nah, not today, but t'anks," Peck said.

"Ahhh, I understood you said Carencro. I never been z'are—Carencro. Been to Lafayette, z'o," the voice said.

"Mister, I t'ink we lost, t'inking maybe you can help."

"What, you both driving z'at new truck to get lost?"

"No, I'm drivin' it. The name's Peck."

"Well z'en, seems Peck is the one z'at's lost, seems to me," the voice said.

The voice snorted chuckles as the trailer began to rock with motion inside. A large hand set a hardcover book on the counter and the end door pushed open.

He was a tall man, looking to be 275 pounds or more, like Sydney Greenstreet from a vintage Humphrey Bogart movie. He stepped down, causing the trailer to rock, squeaking on broken springs. Bright red suspenders held up his khaki pants. He had an apron tied around his waist with gloves in the pocket. His posture was proud, his head up with full, black, curly hair. It looked as though he was looking under his glasses to see Peck. Broad shoulders with chest out. As imposing as his body was on first impression, he had a gentle, warm smile with his large hand outstretched to officially welcome this lost traveler. It was as if Peck were a break in his morning. Someone to talk to.

"I'm Alex," he said.

"Good to meet you, Alex. How are you?"

"What you need, frien'?" Alex asked.

"Where'd you get all this oyster shell in your drive, frien'? No oysters hereabouts – maybe in New Or-lee-anh, though," Peck said.

"Z'ay aren't oysters."

"Hanh?"

"Z'ay're mussel shells."

"Mussel shells? Where from?"

"My wife's broodher, in Alabama. He fishes the Tennessee River. He gets z'em just for haulin z'em off."

This was when an exasperated Millie walked up.

"In Carencro, where did you get your snake, was it good bait?" Alex asked.

"I catched 'em mostly by hand. On a snood sometimes. Snakes are good for snappers. Turtle innards good for catfish."

"What did you find out, Peck?" Millie asked.

"Oh, we talkin' bait. Millie, meet Alex, here. He's from Russia."

Alex extended his hand, and measuring the look on her face, he'd felt he best leave oral cordialities to her.

"Ma'am?" Alex asked.

"We're looking for Killian," Peck said.

"Which way you been driving?" Alex asked.

"From Baton Rouge."

"Well, you missed it, I'll say."

Alex pointed. "Go get on 12 and head z'at way. Go one exit. Get off and go south on Satsuma Road. You can't miss it," Alex said.

"You know anything about Killian?" Peck asked.

"I know Killian. What you need to know, friend?"

"Killian National Bank," Millie said.

"Z'ay'res old man Aucoin and old man Hebert. Z'ay own z'ee bank," Alex said.

"You know them?" Peck asked.

"Z'ay don't loan money on bait, but z'ay love to fish—least'n Aucoin does. Gets his bait here," Alex said. "He brings me books in trade for chicken livers."

"I have to go meet them," Peck said.

"If you want to come back by, come try my chicken livers. We'll go fishing, Millie too," Alex said.

Peck and Millie walked to the truck. Millie crawled up and in. Peck turned to wave, then hesitated with second thoughts. He left his door open and walked back to Alex.

"Alex, you ever heared of gator man? You ever heared of him?"

"Important to you, friend?" Alex asked.

"Very important," Peck said.

"Lots of men call z'emselves gator man, but I don't know a, like you say, 'gator man,' but I can ask cousins." Alex said.

"You got a lot of cousins?" Peck asked.

"My wife does."

The tracker in Peck's eyes lighted up. "This is good."

"You got a phone, Peck?"

"I do."

"What's your number?"

Peck gave him his number. Alex pulled his phone from his apron and punched it into his phone and pressed send.

"I'll send you a text. If her cousins know of z'ees 'gator man,' Alex will text you, friend."

"T'anks, frien," Peck said.

Peck turned to walk to the truck. He paused, considering if he had more questions.

Millie sang out.

"Oh, Boudreaux Clemont Finch?"

Peck looked at her.

"You're stalling again. There's nothing to be afraid of in Killian. So climb in the truck and let's go."

Peck paced their ride to best give him advantage looking at every yard, house and barn. He recognized nothing on Satsuma Road, and nothing on his drive into Killian. He pulled up to the bank and parked.

"You goin' in with me, cher?" Peck asked.

"I think you need to go in alone," Millie said. "I'll wait here. I saw a drugstore down that street. I may walk over and see if they have a charger cord for me."

CHAPTER 22

MAY I HELP YOU, YOUNG MAN?" the bank teller woman asked.

"Dr. John Price called a man here to talk about Alayna Prudhomme. Can I see the man, please ma'am?" Peck asked.

"Do you know who your doctor spoke with?"

"Nah, nah. I forgot to ax, sorry."

"Let me check," the teller woman said. "What's your name?"

"Boudreaux Clemont Finch, ma'am."

She went to the end of the booth and pulled a door open, stepped through and closed it. Peck looked about the bank, at the pictures on the wall, the flags. He looked through the front window at his truck. Millie was not in it. Two boys rode by on bicycles, the taller one holding two fishing poles, the shorter one with a back bag.

The teller woman came through the door and held it for an elderly gentleman, using a cane. He had thin, neatly combed hair, wire-rimmed glasses. He peered out at Peck.

"Why don't you come in, son? Come in," the old man said.

Peck obliged and stepped into the office.

The old man extended his hand. "Walter Aucoin," he said.

Peck shook his hand. "Boudreaux Clemont Finch," Peck said. "Proud to meet you, sir."

They both sat.

"Mr. Finch, do you have any form of identification?" Mr. Aucoin asked.

"Oh, *oui*," Peck said.

Peck lifted his wallet from his back pocket. From it he pulled his driver's license, his social security card, and a copy of his birth certificate. He handed them to Mr. Aucoin, who in turn looked at each and set them on his desk before him.

"I'm not familiar with a Dr. Price, young man. Let me phone my partner and ask if he knows the man."

Mr. Aucoin dialed and waited.

"Harold, there's a young man here, a Boudreaux Clemont Finch."

"Finch?" Harold repeated.

"That's right, a Mr. Finch," Mr. Aucoin said.

"Can't say I know a Mr. Finch," Harold said.

"No, Harold, I don't think you have ever met Mr. Finch, but he mentions a Dr. John Price. Are you familiar with a Dr. Price?"

"Oh yes, Dr. Price. I recall the name. I spoke with him not long ago," Harold said.

"Well, the young man, Mr. Finch, is here to speak with you. Should I put him on the phone?"

"No, don't put him on. I'm leaving the house in ten minutes. Have to stop by the hardware store. Walter, tell the young man to get himself a cup of coffee at the café and when I get in I'll fetch him. Ask the young man if that will work."

Mr. Aucoin looked over at Peck.

"He knows Dr. Price, but it'll take him an hour or so to get here. Will that be okay with you, son?"

"Oh, *oui*, sir. That'd be good. I wait."

Mr. Aucoin spoke into the phone. "Harold, the young man will wait. Tell Constance hello."

"Who's there with you?" Harold asked.

"Flo and Norman. Why?"

"There are three boxes in the old vault. I'll need them in my office, and they'd be too heavy for Flo."

"I'll have Norman get them out."

"Good. Tell Norman there're three boxes marked 'Pontelban' on them. I need them in my office."

"Oh my," Mr. Aucoin said. "How long has it been since the doctor passed?"

"It'll be five years this October," Harold said.

"I'll have Norman move the boxes. See you when you get in, Harold."

Mr. Aucoin set the phone on its cradle.

"Mr. Finch, there's a café and grill just up the street. If you go have a coffee, Mr. Hebert will come get you after he runs a couple of errands. Will that be all right with you?"

"Yes, sir, Mr. Aucoin, sir. Alex tells me you're a fisher. What you fish for?"

"You know Alex?"

"He give'd me directions to come here," Peck said.

"I fish mostly bass. Did Alex tell you I wasn't much good at it?"

"Nah, nah." Peck smiled.

"He's a good man, Alex. He's a big reader. Russians love to read. I trade him old books for his bait, so neither of us lose out," Mr. Aucoin said.

"Nice man, Alex," Peck said.

Peck stood and started toward the door.

"The café is to the right, from the front door, son," Mr. Aucoin said.

Peck waved and walked out to find Millie sitting on a park bench near the street corner.

"I found a charger," Millie said. "How'd it go with you?"

Peck spoke of the Mr. Hebert who was coming in to see him and how they should go have a cup of coffee and wasn't it a nice town?

Millie observed that people in Louisiana were friendly, and it wasn't as dark and frightening a place as Gabe thought it might have been. They ordered coffee and one grilled bacon and cheese sandwich they would share. They spoke of where their farm might be and was Peck thinking more softshell crab or crawfish and had he ever eaten a snake? Peck told Millie her nail polish was pretty and did she have fun with Sasha and Lily Cup in N'Orleans?

An elderly gentleman edged up to their booth.

"Young man, are you Mr. Finch?"

"Yes sir, dat's me."

"I'm Harold Hebert. Would you like to step over to my office?"

"I'll just wait here," Millie said. "You all have things to talk about."

"You come too, cher," Peck said.

"You go on. You can tell me about it later."

Millie loved Peck too much to not let him paint his past from his own pallet, using his brushes. She would respect any story he told her, and she would respect the privacy he held to his chest.

Peck and Mr. Hebert walked over to the bank.

"Flo?" Mr. Hebert asked.

"Yes, sir, Mr. Hebert?"

"Can you see Mr. Finch and I aren't disturbed? We may be some time. We have things to go through."

"I'll see you aren't bothered, Mr. Hebert. How's Mrs. Hebert, sir?"

"It was a late bronchitis. Gave her a devil of a time. It's passed now. Thank you, Flo. She'll appreciate hearing you asked about her."

Mr. Hebert led Peck into his office and closed the door. He pointed to a chair for Peck. On top of his desk were three large cartons labeled with black marker, "Dr. Pontelbon." He walked around his desk and rolled his chair to a spot to best have Peck in sight and sat down. He picked up some papers clipped together.

"You left your papers, son."

He handed Peck his driver's license, social security card, and birth certificate. As Peck organized them in his wallet, Mr. Hebert studied Peck's face, just as if he were in a garden studying the new bloom on a wild flower.

"What do you go by, son?" Mr. Hebert asked.

"People mostly call me Peck, sir."

"Peck it is, then. Call me Harold, son. I'll be helping you today, best I'm able."

Mr. Hebert took a pocketknife from his desk drawer and cut the packing tape.

"Let's have a look," Mr. Hebert said.

He cut the tape on all three boxes and folded the flaps down.

"Mr. Hebert, sir – can I go get my Millie?"

Mr. Hebert looked at Peck as he folded his knife and returned it to his desk drawer.

"Go get your Millie, son."

Peck grinned and made his way through the lobby down the street and into the café and grill."

"Millie, I want you with me."

"Peck, it's personal. Won't you be more comfortable finding out what the man has to say first?"

Peck knelt on one knee, took her hand and looked Millie square in the eyes.

"Do you remember the day we met, Millie? In Tennessee?"

"On the bus. I remember. Why?"

"You remember first thing you told Peck, cher?"

Millie wrinkled her brow with a broken guess.

"That I needed to use the bathroom?"

Peck guffawed. "After that, the first was you told me you had water and then you told me about Charlie. Remember, cher?"

"I remember, and you held my Charlie and didn't laugh at me."

"*Oui.*"

"Today is different, Peck. Mr. Hebert is going to maybe tell you some very personal things."

"When I holded your Charlie I know'd I wanted to be with you for the rest of our whole lives, and dass for true."

"You're the sweetest man."

"Come with me, cher. We together forever. Please."

Millie dabbed a tear from her eye. She paid the check and hand-in-hand they walked the street in downtown Killian to the brass door of the vintage bank. Mr. Hebert stood and welcomed them in and reached for a picture of his wife, Constance, and handed it to Millie.

"I do understand these things, Miss Millie. When love is true, there are no walls."

Millie handed the picture frame back with a gentle smile.

"Romans 12:9 and 10 tell it, Mr. Hebert. I learned it in bible study. *Love must be sincere. Hate what is evil; cling to what is good. Be devoted to one another in love. Honor one another above yourselves.*"

"Such a lovely thought, young lady. I'd say whatever we unfold in these boxes that might pertain to your young man here, will be no match for the love you share."

"Thank you, sir," Millie said.

Mr. Hebert set the picture of his Constance on the side table and sat. He lifted a yellow legal pad and pen and handed it to Peck for notes. Peck handed it to Millie.

Mr. Hebert rummaged through the boxes that appeared to be filled with heavy manila envelopes with large rubber bands holding them secure. Dates were scrawled on each from a marker pen. Mr. Hebert lifted each envelope with the tips of his fingers, scratching at them from the side, like a squirrel digging for a buried nut. He came upon two white envelopes, one with "Finch" penned on it, one with "Dr. Pontelban" on its flap.

"Here we are," he said.

He set the two envelopes before him on the desk.

"You're on a great search for truths, son. I know a little about you. Not much, but least what I've been told. I do know about Dr. Pontelban though, son. I've known him since the early days when he moved nearby. We would fish together. Are either of you fishers?"

"I'm a fisher, sir. Trotlines mostly, though. Five snoods, what I can throw," Peck said.

"I didn't have the arm for a net cast or a trotline throw," Mr. Hebert said.

"Big sinker helped me, sir," Peck said.

"You being a fisher, son, I don't have to tell you that two bodies can spend years together in a boat waiting for that strike, and not talk too much more than the pleasantries. Fishing time is a restful meditation between you and nature…or God, as my Constance would say."

"Dass for true," Peck said.

"Best I start by telling you about Dr. Pontelban. Why don't I read his obituary? I think that would be best."

"Nah, nah," Peck said. "Did you fish wi'd this Dr. Pontelban a lot of times, Mr. Hebert?"

"I'd say twice a week for twenty-five years or so, son. We'd meet here at the bank or at the lake. He had a skiff we'd take off shore and anchor maybe a hundred yards or so out."

"What lake?"

"Lake Mourepas. We'd catch mainly bass or catfish. We'd throw the sunfish back. More luck with bass, I'd say."

"Peck think you can tell me more about this doctor man than a newspaper thing."

"You would have liked the man, Peck. He had a gentle kindness about him. I know he was dedicated to his work, and I know he was a generous man. Lived simply. Always helping others. He worked at the women's insane asylum since the sixties. They call it *mental health* now. He passed in his sleep."

"Did he leave anyone behind, Mr. Hebert? Any family?" Millie asked.

"Not that I was aware of. He never married. Oh, the funeral was a large one. More than a hundred at the gravesite, but no family."

"Happy and sad at the same time," Millie said.

Mr. Hebert opened his desk drawer and pulled an opened envelope from it.

"I received this letter a few weeks before he passed. It was from him, and it was postmarked Killian. He could have just dropped it by. He had to walk by the bank to get to the post office. It says on the outside, 'Open after I'm gone.' I waited."

"The doctor know'd he was goin'," Peck said.

"Was he sad?" Millie asked.

"Sad?"

"If you fished with him two times every week you could tell, did he look sad?" Millie asked.

"He looked tired," Mr. Hebert replied "Let me read the letter to you."

He pulled a single page from the envelope and unfolded it.

"'*Hal*'—he always called me Hal – my nickname for Harold.

'Hal, I've been on the mend, but I need you to do something for me, dear friend. Keep the Prudhomme checks going until she passes and then give any balance to your church and close the account. My safety deposit box key is in the envelope. When I go, can you empty it and put the contents—there's two envelopes and my granddaddy's pocket watch. Put them with my bank records and store them, if you will. If you ever hear from a gentleman by the name of Boudreaux Clemont Finch, there's an envelope marked with his name that you may read to him. Hold the other. You may give him the watch. Hal, we most never said

goodbye when we fished, we waved. You've been a good friend, good company. Here's a wave, my friend. My best to Constance.'"

Mr. Hebert held up the watch and chain as if it were his old friend, and he dabbed his eye with a handkerchief. He started to talk, choked a sob and waited.

"He signed it 'Doc,'" Mr. Hebert said.

"What a beautiful friendship," Millie said. "You were both so lucky to have your lives cross."

Mr. Hebert nodded, lips clenched.

"I need some air," Mr. Hebert said. "Would either of you like to join me for a stroll around the block?"

Peck and Millie stood.

"We'll read the envelope when we get back," Mr. Hebert said.

On the first street they walked without talking. On the second street Mr. Hebert pointed to the old church that was built by a Cajun French community in 1831. On the third street Peck asked Mr. Hebert what he used for bait and had he ever tried shicken livers. On the street back to the bank, they set a promise to get Alex the bait man one day and go fishing. Before entering the bank, Mr. Hebert stood looking up at the town clock on the corner. He lifted the watch and chain from his pocket and set the time to the clock and wound it. He lifted it to see under his bifocals before handing it to Peck.

"Wind it once a day, son, in one direction, forward, not too tight."

Chapter 23

MR. HEBERT ASKED PECK to lift the three cartons to the floor so he could best see over his desk as he read the contents in the envelope. Peck obliged and was about to sit when his phone rang. It was Lily Cup's phone calling.

"Hello?"

"My brother, I just had to call to see if you were okay," Gabe said.

Peck excused himself and stepped from the office, through the lobby and onto the sidewalk.

"Hey Gabe, how you are?"

"Lily Cup and I've been sitting here trying to get organized so you and I can throw an engagement party for Sasha and James. I'm just scribbling notes. She came by for coffee. How are you son? Are things going well up there?"

"It's all good, Captain. Nice people are helping Peck. This old man in Killian give'd me a, how you say, pocket watch that belonged to a doctor's granddaddy. The doctor know'd my mamma, he say."

"Sounds like it's an eventful trip. If you need anything, you know who to call."

"I know, Gabe. Millie and me, we doing so good. People are nice."

"I'll share that with Sasha and Lily Cup. They'll be happy to hear it's going well."

"Yes, sir. It's good."

Peck made his way back into the office where Mr. Hebert was lifting a stack of typed pages an inch or so deep. He read the title page: A Story for My Best Friend. He pondered it as if he were looking the doc in the eye. He clutched it to his chest with his left arm and with his right hand he cleared the top of his desk, setting things on the console table behind. He placed the stack of papers on the desk and sat down. He looked over at Peck.

"You ready, son?"

Peck nodded.

Mr. Hebert turned the title page and set it to the right of the pile. He picked up the first page and began reading.

"Dear Hal,

"I don't mind telling you that God and I have not always seen eye to eye, but in all the years I shared my skiff with you, Harold Hebert, my dear friend, for longer than I can remember at this writing, I could always trust the man in you to do the right and good thing.

"I have no way of knowing what time has passed since my own passing. Has it been weeks, months, or years? I was raised to believe in miracles, and I did pray that it would be you reading this letter, Hal, and if you are reading it, it would be a miracle at this time in your life because I'll assume there's a gentleman, alive and sitting across from your desk with the name Boudreaux Clemont Finch. I also prayed that the young man's mother, Alayna Prudhomme, would be alive if and when this time came. There is so much to say, it would only be fitting if Mr. Finch knew the story and then shared it with her, if that was his choice."

"Mr. Hebert, do you have any tissues?" Millie asked.

Mr. Hebert opened a console door and pulled three Puffs boxes, handing one to Peck, one to Millie, who was weeping, and he opened one for himself. He picked up another page and read aloud.

"Louisiana in 1963 and 1964 was not like the Louisiana you and I fished in all those years, Hal. They were darker times in a state fraught with levee breaks and lost lives, a time when New Orleans was a boiling caldron both with equal measure of celebration and sorrow over the shooting death of President John F. Kennedy. His killer, New Orleans own Lee Harvey Oswald from Magazine Street, was considered a hero in some non-Catholic circles. I was ashamed to hear there was cheering in some

schools. It was following that time, in January of 1964, that I was assigned to do my residency program riding with the Louisiana State Police, observing and serving what was to later become paramedics at scenes of accidents, fire, spousal abuse, suicide, and murders.

"My story begins on February 25th,1964. There was a blackened, moonless sky with a pouring of rain, and I was answering an emergency call about a pregnant woman disturbing the search and rescue craft on the north shore of Lake Pontchartrain in Mandeville. When we arrived, we found the woman standing among the floodlights at the water's edge, with no coat and her sweater soaked with rain. At the risk of losing her unborn baby she stood there like a cold marble statue, her hands to her face. She was staring out at a child's baby doll that was floating on its back about thirty feet out, bobbing up and down in the wakes of the search boats."

Mr. Hebert set the page down and picked another and studied it.

"I remember that airline crash like it was yesterday," he said. "It haunts me still. Fifty-one passengers and seven crew members went down that day when the jet exploded and fell into Lake Ponchartrain. They only found thirty-two bodies. The rest sank to the bottom of that cruel mean lake with the plane. It's still there. I can still remember the headlines – they found a doll floating near a little girl's red coat. It was awful son. Unimaginable."

Mr. Hebert started reading the paper.

"Here he's addressing you, son."

"Mr. Finch, in all my life, I've never forgotten this day. It was the day I first met your grandmother. That desperately dark, cold, raining, predawn morning. The woman standing there at water's edge was your grandmother. Another two feet and she would have been lost in the abyss. It happened she was standing in that very same spot the day before when an enormous DC8 jetliner, an Eastern Airlines Flight 304, taking off from New Orleans airport, lost altitude and exploded above her head and crashed into Lake Pontchartrain in front of her. Mr. Finch, fifty-eight men, women, children, babies, and dreams sank to hundred-foot depths under the nightmare of silt that hides sin and so many souls. That was the morning, Mr. Finch, and that was how I met your grandmother. She was pregnant with your mother. That was how I met the woman. She was standing in a long skirt and sweater, as though she had lost her belongings in a fire. She had no purse, no wallet or identification of any kind. She clenched a bible in her hand. She appeared to be in her late twenties, perhaps thirty. I remember the icy rain on my back when I removed my trench coat and wrapped it around her. She was reluctant to move from the shore. She kept pointing at the floating doll and whimpering, 'Mommy? Mommy? Mommy?' The floating doll wasn't hers, but it had fallen from the plane in front of her and I could only imagine her picturing in her mind a face of a little girl who seconds before had her arms around the doll. Signs and superstitions were a norm in the day. They were compounded by Kennedy's death and now this, just a few months later.

"The crash was as though New Orleans was being cursed for the death of a president–a Catholic president. Mr. Finch, your grandmother would cry in haunting voice that disturbed the crews volunteering to search for bodies. No one offered to retrieve the doll. They claimed there wasn't enough fuel to go out of their way. From that morning on your grandmother convinced her mind that her mother or her father, even perhaps her baby's father—we were never certain which—was aboard when that enormous plane she watched exploded into flames and was swallowed alive by Lake Pontchartrain.

"From that day forth your grandmother was in a continual shock, Mr. Finch. We took her to a Mandeville hospital emergency for sedatives and warmth, but as it turned out, she never came out of the shock and the nameless woman was taken to the women's insane asylum in Acadiana, built in the 1940s. I was so moved by the incident, the look on her face, I joined the asylum's staff and continued my education in psychiatry. It was as though she were in a constant state of an awakened coma. I was young and in the innocence of the times, and I would spend late evenings searching through newspapers and local police blotters looking for missing persons reports. No one ever came forward inquiring about your grandmother, Mr. Finch. For days on end, although it gradually turned into whispers, your grandmother would look at a spot on a wall and repeat, 'Mommy? Mommy? Mommy?'

"Mr. Finch, your mother was born in that mental hospital and in the day, we were required to register a name on birthing certificates. The delivering midwife lovingly gave the new baby girl that would grow up to be your mother the name, Alayna Prudhomme. It was the midwife's own grandmother's name. Those were times when medicine was experimenting with mental health issues, and when we witnessed a noticeable change in your grandmother's demeanor after your mother's birth, we observed her carefully around the clock for several days. There was a calm that came over her whenever she held her new baby. With the baby in her arms, her heart rate would drop to levels of a calm. We felt leaving the baby in her care under close supervision could bring her around. That was our choice.

"Whenever your mother was swaddled and in your grandmother's arms, she would hold her and rock and sing quietly. As your mother grew we arranged homeschool for her close to the hospital and she would come and go with the blessing of the staff. Throughout her high school years, I saw to it she was cared for at a girl's boarding school where she could receive a proper education and perhaps a perspective of who she was. Alayna, your mother, Mr. Finch, would visit your grandmother every weekend, sacrificing a high school private and social life of her own to be with her mother."

Mr. Hebert set that page down and looked over at Peck. Peck appeared to be squirming in his seat. Millie was in tears, her elbows on her knees, her head lowered, tissues in both eyes.

"Is this making you uncomfortable, son?" Mr. Hebert asked.

"Nah, nah."

Peck turned his head, staring at a wall.

"Perhaps this isn't a good time," Mr. Hebert said.

"It's just—well, I don't remember all dat, sir."

"You can't remember it, son. You weren't born while this was going on."

"Nah, nah. It's I don't remember my mamma nanna so nice like she is in dat letter, sir," Peck said.

Mr. Hebert pursed his lips with a knowing, gentle smile. He nodded his head as if he could see what was happening. He reached for his phone.

"I think we need a small break. Let's have some coffee."

"Coffee would be good," Peck said.

"Yes, Mr. Hebert?" Flo asked.

"Flo, can you be a dear and run over to the café and get three large coffees to go? With cinnamon and bring some sugar packets if you would be so kind."

"Yes, sir."

Mr. Hebert cradled the phone and leaned on his desk, facing Peck. "Let me tell you a story, young man."

Peck appreciated the break. His face looked tormented. He leaned in to listen.

"Peck, I'm an old man. Back when it was time for me to go to college, I wanted to go out of state, so I went away to Ole Miss. Jackson was only about a hundred-fifty miles, but it was out of state. It was a grand time, son. I sang in the men's choir, I was on the debate team. I was away from home for the first time in my life…and son, it seemed every year I was there at Ole Miss my childhood memories became suspect to my bad memory and good imagination. Why it could have gone on for all the years I was there until that one Christmas break when it came to an end."

"End?" Peck asked.

"It was the time I brought two of my best college-campus friends home. They couldn't afford plane fare to go home for the holidays—one lived in Seattle and one lived in Toronto."

Peck put his two stacked fists on the edge of Mr. Hebert's desk and rested his chin on them.

"We were at dinner on Christmas day. My dad had just carried in the silver platter with the large, crispy golden-brown turkey on it. I remember it was surrounded by baked apples and sweet-potato halves. It was just as my dad was slithering the carving knife to the sharpener rod when one of my friends opened his mouth and a door of conversation that changed my life."

"Hanh?" Peck asked.

"His name was Riley. He was a junior at Ole Miss. The lad, this Riley fellow, was mesmerized by the sounds of the long carving knife with deer-horn handle slithering against the steel sharpener rod. He looked at my dad and said, 'Mr. Hebert, you sure don't look all that mean.'

"With that I dropped my fork and my dad said, 'Excuse me, son, I don't think I caught that.' And of course, as the young tend to do, my friend Riley kept on digging the hole deeper. That's the time he said, 'Harold told us how you'd whipped him with a bullwhip until he learned to make his bed. That sure must have worked, Mr. Hebert. He makes a good and tidy bed.' Of course, it was about that time, I felt like I blacked out and came to, chagrinned to know I was still sitting at the same table that my dad was hearing all this. And that is when my daddy said, 'Bullwhip?' and Riley just went on and on like a Gomer Pyle and said, 'My father would threaten a belt, but a rolled-up newspaper was all we ever needed. Good thing he didn't have a bullwhip like you do, Mr. Hebert.' Peck, that was the exact moment, I remember it like it was yesterday when my daddy set the carving knife and sharpener rod on the table and he said something that changed my life."

"What'd your daddy say?" Peck asked.

"He said, 'Riley, I don't own a bullwhip. I have never owned a bullwhip, and I wouldn't even know what a bullwhip looked like.' I remember him finishing that sentence with a fire in his eyes looking at me, his college junior son who had gone off and made some mountains from memories and the more I told them the bigger the tales grew. Boys of the same ages would try to outdo each other about the stories from home and their tragic lives. We learned in English comp that novels without tragedy weren't near as good."

"It wasn't true about your daddy?" Peck asked.

"It was my imagination taking liberties with exaggeration, son. Like most young boys I took a proper scolding about keeping my room clean, but then I took it to the extreme. Those were days without television and we were fond of our books and comic novels—and exaggeration was a part of giving our young lives and the hot summers some spark."

"Mr. Hebert, gator man tied me and pulled me back of his boat for gators, dass for true. He belt-strapped me for dropping bait buckets, dass for true. He dog-collared me and chain me under the porch, dass for true. S'why I hided in the cypress tree holler for three days standing on buzzard eggs or Wood Duck eggs and ants and I runned away to Carencro."

Mr. Hebert let the moment rest. He watched Peck's eyes.

"Young man, I have known you for less than a morning and I already have a sense I can trust you at your word. An old man knows these things. I believe all of this, as you describe it, happened to you—just as you say it happened."

Peck sat up, settled in his face that someone was listening.

"But I ask a small consideration, young man," Mr. Hebert said.

"Hokay, what is it, sir?"

"Peck, did this gator man do these things to you at your house or at his house?"

"His house," Peck said.

"Was your momma ever there when he did these things to you?"

"Nah, nah. Mamma nanna not there."

"Peck, these papers are about your momma. They're not about that gator man. Why don't we give it some time and see where the story goes?"

"So maybe gator man is Peck's bullwhip, not my mamma nanna?"

"Yes, son, just maybe."

It made sense to Peck. He was learning about his mamma from the doctor's story and he was eager to learn new things. Mr. Hebert smiled as though his offering made a difference. He sat back and picked up the next page and read aloud.

"Mr. Finch, your grandmother had only one possession when we found her at Lake Pontchartrain—a bible. The pages were stuck together and when we were able to pull the covers back there was no name in it, so it was left by her bedside. It was when

your mother, Alayna, was of high school age, she wanted to take the bible as a keepsake and was trying to unstick the pages when she found a page with a name penned on it. It was written on a page under Proverbs 22:1 about names. That was the day we learned your grandmother's name was Abella Blanchard. There were no Blanchards on the plane that crashed. We were able to trace her family name to Bayou Chene, eighty-nine miles away. We could only assume she had walked that far."

"I know'd what happened," Peck said. "I know'd what happened, Mr. Hebert."

Mr. Hebert paused and looked up.

"Go on, son," Mr. Hebert said.

"Bayou Chene drowned, dass for true. Church and all the houses and lots of people drowned when the levee broke. It was same time like that. Flora told'd me."

"That's right, Peck, it was in the early sixties," Mr. Hebert said.

Mr. Hebert continued reading.

"The town sank under silt and many died. It's very probable that your grandmother's husband and parents died in that flood and she walked in shock to Lake Pontchartrain."

"You ran from your demons, Peck. Gabe told me you ran ninety miles," Millie said. "Your gramma ran from hers and she got stopped at the edge of Lake Pontchartrain. She could have fallen in and drowned. Dr. Pontelbon may have saved her life."

Mr. Hebert continued reading.

"Mr. Finch, when your mother graduated from high school, I let her live on a houseboat I owned but seldom used. I eventually gave her title to it. It was on a short inlet by the Diversion Canal and Amite River."

"The willer," Peck said. "Tied to a willer."

"Your mother had a fondness for the flora and she'd read many seed catalogues and books on the subject and she took jobs and made a proper living minding gardens for some and plants for homes and buildings for others within distance of a bicycle ride. I offered to get her a used car or a Toyota pickup, but she insisted on her bicycle and its oversized basket on the front and wire saddle baskets on the back fender. Every Saturday morning and every Wednesday morning, like clockwork, your mother would catch a ride to the clinic to visit and spend the day with her momma, and she would read to her and they would speak a Cajun French and she would bring flowers and arrange them in a green vase on her momma's bedside.

"Mr. Finch, I'm about to tell something I've always kept from everyone. I'm sorry, Hal—even you, my friend. I'm not proud of it. Only one man has ever known about it. It's important that you know it from me, Mr. Finch. I would have told you in person had I known your whereabouts. In late 1990, the mental health hospital hired a handyman in their maintenance department. His name was Guillaume Devine, a Creole who worked shrimp boats in the gulf most of his life. He was maybe thirty when he started working at the hospital. Hal, three women were raped at the hospital, one staff, one patient. The third was Alayna. He attacked her in the lady's restroom. This Devine fellow threatened the women's lives if they ever talked to anyone. A patient by the name of Ellen McDowell and your mother, Alayna, were impregnated. Ellen McDowell and her child died that same year in childbirth. Alayna, with the help of a midwife and myself, gave birth to a healthy baby boy. That was in a day a single woman could explain an adoption, so I took the birthing papers and named the new baby boy Boudreaux Clemont Finch. Mr. Finch, if you're still in the room, please take a look at your new pocket watch."

Peck pulled the watch and chain from his pocket.

"You'll see, Mr. Finch, the engraving on the watch is BCF—for my granddaddy—and it's now etched there for you, friend. My granddaddy was a good man and he would have been proud for you to have the watch, Mr. Finch.'"

Millie stood and stepped over to Peck and knelt on the floor, her arms around him.

"Mr. Hebert, I love this man so much. We are so blessed and fortunate to have this strong name from such a wonderful man."

Millie looked in Peck's teary eyes.

"Peck, I will be proud to be your Mrs. Finch. So proud and I will be so proud to know your mamma and to call her Mamma."

Millie kissed his cheek.

"Peck," Mr. Hebert said. "I know when the doc set up the account to have checks sent to your mother every month, the word was you were dead."

Millie and Peck started, heads up.

"Hanh?" Peck asked.

"Everyone assumed an alligator had taken you under, son," Mr. Hebert said. "Things would have been different had the doc known you were alive, Peck. I know the man. He would have put out searches."

Peck was stunned to learn they thought he was dead. As an experienced fisher and tracker, it was beginning to make sense to him.

"They find d'is man?" Peck asked.

"Which man, son?"

"The man what raped…"

"Keep reading, Mr. Hebert," Millie said.

Peck sat back and Millie returned to her seat and her tissues.

"Peck, may I continue?" Mr. Hebert asked.

"Oui," Peck said.

Mr. Hebert lifted another page.

"Since the rapes weren't reported, no suspicions were hovering. I knew the two pregnancies were illegitimate, and I chose not to make uncomfortable inquiries, but to help as I could. Alayna would always bring you, her young Boudreaux, to the hospital for her regular visits and you would spend the day with your grandmother. The grandmother would rock you and bottle feed you in daylight feedings and Alayna would stand by the window and breastfeed you under the moonlight."

Peck leaned his face down into his hands. He was in tears.

"Two things you need to know, Mr. Finch. The first, my friend, Hal, is about to read to you. The other is something special for you in the second envelope.

"The first happened two years after you were born, Mr. Finch. Mr. Devine and I planned a day of fishing. Before he got to the lake, I packed my end of the boat with a thermos of lemonade, my small iced cooler with sandwiches, and a paper sack with two bags of potato chips. I rolled my yellow slicker around my shotgun in case I saw a low-flying duck. It wasn't legal, but the thought of duck for dinner crossed most fishers' minds and most law would turn a blind eye on a single duck. Devine eventually showed. He packed his end of the boat with a small cooler, some beer, and a hoagie sandwich. I backed the boat into the lake and then parked my car and trailer before we headed out on the Mourepas. We went to the middle of the lake for the bigger bass.

"Mr. Finch, it was after his fourth beer when the man asked me whatever happened to that gal that used to come by. When I asked him who he was referring to, he described your mother. When I told him she still came by to visit her mother he made a comment...he said he sure would like to get with her. Mr. Finch, I'm not the sort of a man who blurts out without thinking, but for some reason all that came to my mind was to say, 'You're the one, aren't you?' I remember him looking at me, first in surprise, then with a low sneer. 'So, what if I am?' All I remember, Mr. Finch is that I wasn't afraid. I even repeated 'You did it.' Two women—or was it more? He tossed his sandwich in the lake and began unsnapping his hunting knife. 'You'll never know, old man—and you'll never tell, neither. You're about to get out and swim with the gators.' I remember every word he said. I reached in my slicker and took my shotgun and just that fast I shot him in the face, pumped quickly and shot him again in the chest. He fell overboard and floated face down. I motored back to shore where, off in the distance, I could see him floating. I went directly to the Sherriff's office and told him the story. He sent me home and that was more than twenty years ago and he hasn't said a word about it.

"I'm sorry, Mr. Finch. I don't know what came over me that day. I hope you have a good life. Please say hello to your mother. She's a very nice lady."

Mr. Hebert turned the last page and set it on the stack.
"That's his story, Peck. I don't know what more there is to say."
"He's a good man, that doc, dass for true. A good man."
"So you're all right with the...?"
"Him shootin' that man? I'm good wit' that. I see it haunted the doc, though. The man would have killed him sure."
"I believe he would have," Mr. Hebert said. "Here's the other letter, Peck. Do you want some privacy so you can read it?"
"Nah, nah," Peck said while taking the envelope and removing a blue envelope and letter inside. The envelope inside was addressed to the doc. The letter was handwritten and it was from Peck's mamma. It was in script and Peck couldn't read script. He looked at Millie to help. He handed the letter to her. She read it to herself, her tears turning to sobs.
"Read aloud, cher," Peck said.
Millie read it aloud the second time. In it Peck's mother was telling the doc that on a few occasions a man she knew from church, a man known as gator man, would offer to watch Peck for her while she had to go garden hoe or reseed a place or pull weeds somewhere. The letter went on that she heard Peck talking in his sleep about dying and of alligators and of his tossing and turning while having nightmares, and she was scared for what it meant, and could the doc talk to the boy to see if the gator man was maybe causing the nightmares and tell her what she should do about the boy's dreams. Millie held the letter in her hand and Peck was in a daze, looking off into nowhere.
"I didn't know your momma had written this letter, son. I remember we all thought you were dead. I remember the talk. A gator grabbed you, was the thinking. We had no evidence of foul play," Mr. Hebert said. "I know your momma stopped seeing that man at the church."

Peck reached and took Millie's hand. He took the letter and envelope and held it.

"Are you all right, young man?" Mr. Hebert asked.

"Nah, nah, I'm good, Mr. Hebert. Peck is good."

"Is there anything I can do?"

"Can you tell me how I find my mamma, sir?"

CHAPTER 24

MILLIE EXCUSED HERSELF to go to the ladies' room; Peck stood and paced, stirring around Mr. Hebert's office pensively looking on tabletops cluttered with civic awards and photographs framed and hanging on the walls. He studied one that caught his attention. It was a dated eight-by-ten black and white photograph of a younger Mr. Hebert standing with someone in front of a trailered skiff with a string of bass and with smiles on their faces.

"That's the doc and me," Mr. Hebert said as he lifted his phone and pressed a button.

"Flo, can you make copies of something please?"

"How many copies, Mr. Hebert?"

"One copy, but it's many pages."

"Yes, sir, I'll be right in."

"Peck if you don't mind, I'd like to make a copy of my old friend's words here as a keepsake and I'll give the original to you," Mr. Hebert said.

"That'd be good, Mr. Hebert."

"How are you feeling about today, son? I know it's been a long day for you and your lady."

"I feel so good, Mr. Hebert—sorry though, I didn't know all d'is and just runned off like I did. I was plenty scared bag then, I'll say. Plenty scared. Gator man tape my mouth and pulled me back of his pirogue for gator bait."

"You did what you felt was right. You protected yourself, son. I would have run off too."

"Dass for true, Mr. Hebert?"

"That's the truth, son. In the same situation I would have probably run off."

Peck stared out the window.

"Peck, I know you want directions to see your momma. I have good maps at home. Let me suggest you and your Millie join my Constance and me for a home-cooked meal. You need a break. We're having grilled chicken and bratwurst and cob corn. You both have to eat. You can rest up at our place and we'll look at maps."

"That'd be hokay with us," Peck said. "T'ank you, Mr. Hebert."

"It's settled, then. May I ask you to step out of my office for a bit? Perhaps you and Millie can take a walk? I have one call I have to make."

"Yes, sir," Peck said.

"I promised I would call your Dr. Price and tell him about our day. Will that be all right with you, son?"

"Nah, nah, it's all good. Tell John—dass his name—tell him Peck is doing so good."

Mr. Hebert smiled.

"We'll leave for home after I'm finished the call. I'll find you. The old church has some historic photos hanging in the vestibule, if you're interested in that sort of thing."

Peck left the room, and he and Millie walked a city block and then another, with Millie letting the love of her life ramble on as if he had seen Santa Claus under the tree. Peck talked about the frightening airliner crash in Lake Pontchartrain and what it must have been like for his grandmother. He talked of what his mamma must have thought when she thought he was gator-grabbed and dead. He talked about whether she would forgive him for running off as he had or not speak to him.

"A momma will always forgive," Millie said. Millie was measured with her words. This was Peck's time...his reawakening.

Mr. Hebert was able to get through to Dr. Price and the feedback was positive, and Dr. Price offered his best to Peck and his word that his door was always open to him if he ever wanted to talk. Dr. Price added that he had talked to the mental health hospital and the grandmother was still alive, passed eighty, but not in good health. The fear was she could develop pneumonia, or lung blockage of some kind. Flo rested his copy and the original manuscript on the desk in front of Mr. Hebert.

While talking, he rustled through his stack and found the page he was hoping to find.

"Dr. Price, tomorrow is Wednesday. Alayna always visits her momma, the young man's grandmother on Wednesday and Saturday. Do you think it might be wise that Peck reconnect with them both at the same time?" Mr. Hebert asked.

There was a pause.

"Mr. Hebert, I think that could be a blessing, both for the grandmother who rocked that young man in her arms and for the momma who nursed him and unwittingly trusted a churchgoing man from the devil's own. I think it would be a wonderful idea. I would even have Millie join him. Let them both, grandmother and mother, witness a sense that they had a hand in raising such a good and caring young man."

"Any suggestions I can share with the young man?" Mr. Hebert asked.

"Just tell Peck to be himself. Tell him it would be a blessing if he could forget the past—to put it behind him. Suggest to him that that past has been a nightmare for the mother and sleepless nights for her all these years thinking an alligator ate her only son. Tell him I suggested that closing that book and opening a new book with Millie at his side would be the greatest gift he could bestow on his mother and grandmother."

"Anything else, Doctor Price?"

"You say his mother likes flora?"

"She earns a living at it."

"Suggest he and Millie take them each a bouquet of flowers. That would be nice."

Dr. Price and Mr. Hebert spoke of other pleasantries and what a marvelous day it had been for the lad, his lady and for Mr. Hebert himself. He didn't share Dr. Pontelbon's darker secrets, but he did say how comforting it was to hear from his dear old friend nearly five years after his death. Mr. Hebert put Peck's original copy of the manuscript into a manila envelope, left the office and found Peck and Millie holding hands and walking with strawberry ice-cream cones. They followed behind Mr. Hebert's car to his home and parked in front.

"This place has been in my family since 1888," Mr. Hebert said.

"It's beautiful," Millie said.

"How many acres do you farm?" Peck asked.

"It once was a section, so that's 640 acres. Sold much of it off, a little at a time over the years. It got to be too much for me. We have the three acres fenced here. No farming now, but in the day, we planted soybeans or sugar cane, depending on prices. Now we mostly enjoy counting our sunsets. I have a woodshop in the barn for making birdhouses for friends. It keeps me out of trouble with Constance."

Constance was a pleasant, grandmotherly looking woman, a gracious hostess, and she suggested they consider staying over so they could be properly rested for the day ahead. Peck asked Millie if they should, or should they go to Baton Rouge and stay with Elizabeth and come back in the morning to find his mamma? It was just as Constance was finishing mixing her homemade potato salad that Millie's phone rang. It was Lily Cup calling. Millie excused herself and stepped into another room.

"Hello?"

"Millie, are you two okay?"

"We're good. We're with Mr. and Mrs. Hebert and about to have dinner. They're so nice."

"You'd tell me if anything was wrong, right?"

"Of course, I would. Peck would too. Mr. Hebert is the man from the bank. Everything is just fine. Today was a beautiful day, but I think Peck should be the one to tell you about it. We learned a lot. All I can say is everyone here has been so nice," Millie said.

"Where are you?"

"Just outside of Killian. We're at their house. It used to be a farm."

"I'll tell Gabe and Sasha that you're okay. Where are you staying tonight?"

"We don't know yet. Peck suggested maybe we drive to Baton Rouge and come back tomorrow. I'm not sure. Mrs. Hebert invited us to stay here. I'll know more after dinner."

"Text me when you know, so I can tell Gabe."

"I will. Love you."

"Love you back."

Millie offered the blessing before Mr. Hebert began passing platters of chicken, bratwurst, and boiled cob corn. Peck particularly liked the barbeque sauce. He held the bottle and wrote the name of it on a paper napkin for later reference. Constance asked Millie if, while at Baylor in Waco, she got to enjoy the wonderful Texas grapefruit as much as she did and how with his heart medicine poor Harold couldn't eat grapefruit. Peck recounted his recipe for turtle soup and Millie spoke of the farm they wished to have one day and was it safe to free range chickens in Acadiana with the predators about?

Mr. Hebert kept his eyes on Peck's expressions as a father might watch a maturing son at one of life's crossings. It was as if he could sense what depth the boy went through that day emotionally and what must be going through his mind now—or later, as it replayed in his memory. Mr. Hebert would glance over at the coffee table with the envelope holding his copy of the doc's letter to him and Peck, and there would be a small bubble of glassy tear in his eye. It was as if his old friend, the doc, was sitting there on the sofa, waiting for an after-dinner coffee and chat.

"Peck, I had a nice talk with your friend, Dr. Price." Mr. Hebert said.

"John?" Peck asked.

"John," Mr. Hebert said. "Care to talk about it now, son?"

"It'd be good. Sure," Peck said.

"Peck, if you can remember in that letter we read today..."

"I remember."

"It spoke of your mother visiting your grandmother at the clinic every Wednesday and every Saturday. Do you remember that?"

Peck set his fork down and looked over at Mr. Hebert.

"I remember."

"Tomorrow is Wednesday, son. I was thinking tomorrow would be good. Dr. Price thought it could be a blessed time if you and Millie would meet them both at the clinic."

Mr. Hebert set his fork down and waited. He kept his eyes on Peck's eyes, giving him the courtesy of silence as he waited for a reaction. Peck took his eyes from Mr. Hebert, turned them to Millie's eyes, her brow raised in anticipation, and then he too glanced over at the envelope sitting on the coffee table.

"I t'ink dat'd be good, Mr. Hebert. Peck and Millie will go and see my mamma and gramma tomorrow. John know'd these t'ings best, I say," Peck said.

Millie grasped her hands in joy. The nightmares that had been predicted of the giant evil cypress, the desperate swamps and forbidden bayous, were leveling themselves over a linen tablecloth on a dinner table and being replaced with an excitement of angst and anticipation born adventurers loved to feel. Peck and Millie were as one soul in this world of wonder. They were ready.

"Miss Hebert," Peck said. "Maybe can my Millie and me stay here tonight, please?"

CHAPTER 25

UNBEKNOWN TO PECK AND MILLIE and even Mr. Hebert, Dr. Price had called ahead to the clinic, telling them the visit was happening on Wednesday. The call virtually eliminated red tape. A caring ward attendant went out of her way to brush his grandmother's hair and put her in a flowered dressing robe before visits started that day. Although she was able to walk, the grandmother was in a wheelchair next to the bed at the time Alayna, Peck's mamma, came in and soon after, the wheelchair was over by the window.

Alayna was sitting in a rocker next to the wheel chair, reading aloud in French when the door first pushed open. Peck held the door with his right hand and Millie's hand with the other. His eyes were wide, inquisitive, wary.

Alayna glanced up and then back at the book she was reading, as if Peck was a service attendant of some kind. The door closed behind them both, and Peck let go of Millie's hand. He stood and watched his mamma's eyes as she read. Her eyes looked up at him and away...and then up again. Peck froze in fright.

Millie was standing behind Peck with her hands clasped as if in prayer, a tear rolling down her cheek. Alayna set the book in grandmother's lap and stood slowly. She moved tentatively toward Peck, her eyes riveted to his. Two fingers buttoned her collar and she ran both hands and fingers back through the sides of her graying hair, as if to look as presentable as a moment's notice might allow for this haunting stranger.

Standing before him, she studied his eyes, his mouth, his chin, his ears. She leaned to the left to see a profile. She looked over at Millie, standing behind him with a wrenched smile on her face, in tears.

With a mother's instinct, she stepped closer to Peck and put her hands on both sides of his temple and gently lowered his head, running her thumbs through his scalp.

"*C'est toujours là, Mamma,*" Peck said. ("It's still there, Mamma.")

Peck let his mamma know he still had the birthmark on his scalp.

Alayna's eyes squinted nearly to tears as she raised her son's head and studied his eyes as if they were the last thing she would remember every night as she had knelt in prayer from that day he went missing.

She pulled him to her, her head on his cheek, and she hugged her baby boy as closely as she promised God she would if He ever graced her with her son just one more time before she died.

Peck wept with his eyes closed, his arms around his mamma. They didn't have to say a word. Not a single word.

His mamma was a seasoned gardener with strong legs and heart from bicycling. She knew what God could do. She witnessed it every day in gardens.

Peck was a seasoned tracker and fisher. He knew patience. He knew that everything good could come true with time. His life was rich now, rich with his Millie, rich with his being able to read. He was even richer today. Having his mamma in his arms, it was as though he knew it was time to put the nightmares that hung over his life like sawblades in a sharpening shanty into a drawer and to push it closed and locked.

He took his mamma by one hand, his Millie's hand with the other and stepped over to his grandmother, who looked off at the rocker her baby girl would sit in every Wednesday and Saturday and read to her.

Peck turned to his mamma.

"*En Anglais, Mamma?* ("English, Mamma?")

"Yes," his mamma said.

"Mamma, this is my Millie. We getting married after Peck finishes school. I'm going to university, Mamma."

Peck smiled, letting his mamma take it all in. She looked over at Millie, placed a gentle hand under Millie's chin and smiled approval with her eyes.

"Millie," his mamma said.

"She loves me, Mamma. She loves your Peck and I love her so much."

Mamma turned her eyes to Peck, reached her hand to his face and grasped his chin in a smiling scold.

"Boudreaux!" Mamma said. "No Peck."

"But Mamma…"

"No Peck…*non, non, non.*"

"I love Boudreaux too, Mamma," Millie said.

Mamma looked at Millie, who had just called her Mamma. A tear appeared.

"Watch this, Mamma," her Boudreaux said.

He sat on the rocker, took the book from his grandmother's lap and held it up to read. He glanced at the book in puzzlement and looked up at his mamma.

"*Anglais, Mamma?*"

Mamma took the book from him and got another from the bed table and handed it to her Boudreaux. His eyes gleamed as he proudly opened it, read the title page and turned to chapter one. His grandmother gazed at his hands as he read slowly, his mamma standing at his side, running her fingers through his hair, as though she was braiding closed the void that had consumed nearly two empty decades of her life. His words were measured, careful; his annunciation was with an effort, but warm.

"Wait, I have an idea," Millie said.

Peck started, looked up at the interruption, but there was a look in Millie's eyes that only he could know would be a good interruption.

"Hanh?" he asked.

"Peck—I mean Boudreaux—let me have the keys," Millie said.

"Keys?"

"The truck keys. I have an idea."

Boudreaux handed Millie the keys and picked up the book again.

"I'll be right back," Millie said.

She scooted from the room. It was just as the door closed behind her when Mamma knelt beside Boudreaux.

"I like your Millie, Boudreaux. You must marry the girl."

"I will, Mamma. I promise I will."

It was on the eighth page of chapter one when the room door opened with Millie pushing it with her back. Her smile was a Christmas morning smile, and her arms cradled her baby doll, Charlie, swaddled in his baby blanket. Without speaking a word, she walked over to the wheelchair and leaned down.

"Gramma, this is your grandbaby. Isn't he such a sweet baby boy, Gramma?"

Millie handed the baby doll to the grandmother, who turned her eyes from beyond to the baby's face and blue eyes looking up at her. She smiled a tear and took the baby in her arms and cradled him, rocking her shoulders back and forth. It was her baby girl's Boudreaux Clemont Finch. Baby came home to grandmamma.

"He's such a pretty baby," Mamma said.

"He's her Charlie, Mamma," Boudreaux said.

"No, he isn't, P—I mean, Boudreaux. That's little Boudreaux Clemont Finch now, and he's Gramma's little baby to take care of, always.

Boudreaux looked into Millie's eyes with a love only true love knows. He looked at his gramma, rocking with the baby doll in her arms. She was humming as if she was trying to remember the words. As he opened the book to page nine of the first chapter he looked over at his mamma.

"I'm going to marry her, Mamma, dass for true."

CHAPTER 26

MAMMA WASN'T COMFORTABLE letting her son and his Millie see the houseboat until after she straightened it up, maybe had it painted for company, but she did accept an invitation for dinner with them at the Hebert's. This was a blessed time for her, she wanted to spruce it up for her son's first visit home.

Alex, the Russian bait man was also invited for the cookout of fresh chicken livers and dove breasts stuffed with jalapeno, wrapped with bacon. Mamma said Labor Day weekend would be a good time for them to come visit her on the houseboat.

Peck pulled his wallet from his back pocket, assuring his mamma with his debit card and driver's license he was a real Boudreaux Clemont Finch, and Peck was only a friendly nickname. He and Mamma were smiling and chatting almost as if he had been off to war and had finally come home. Mamma relented to his using Peck, but only with Millie's vow that her babies aren't named Peck. Peck said Labor Day was a perfect time, as university would be out and could they bring their friends and he explained about Gabe and Sasha and Lily Cup and was there a place to dance nearby?

Mamma was good with all that and Mrs. Hebert said Gabe and Sasha and Lily Cup could stay at their house and Millie and Peck on the houseboat and Alex spoke of taking everyone fishing and the bait and the use of his wife's cousin's boat would be his gift.

When back in New Orleans, Millie was immersed in research projects for the summer at Lily Cup's office, while learning to cook at home when she and Peck were not making love.

Peck got his GED and Gabe had it framed to make it two pictures on the mantle, and everyone celebrated at Dooky

Chase's, filling a table with laughter and love. Sasha and James decided they liked the arrangement as it was, and why spoil it with marriage, as that would require he go to Charlie's Blue Note on occasion, but Gabe and Peck threw them a party anyway, an un-engagement party.

On the Thursday before Labor Day the plan was for everyone to make an early morning drive to Killian in Sasha's Caddy SUV. Lily Cup asked if she and Peck could ride alone together in his pickup. Having the pickup there he and Millie could stay on a day or so if Mamma was good with that. She wanted to ride alone with Peck just so she could take him to Angola for an early morning visit. Gabe and Sasha knew what she had in mind, and they suggested it would be a good learning experience for him, and they'd meet at the Heberts' for a late breakfast. Lily Cup said they wouldn't be more than two hours behind them.

Early morning visitation at Angola was celebrated on holidays. Lily Cup's client, André, was permitted to meet visitors in the sitting room as his was a nonviolent crime—illegal gun sales. The guards couldn't let her take a thermos of coffee in and apologized to her. He was due to be released by Thanksgiving.

Peck and Lily Cup sat in adjoining chairs.

"Peck, you can't shake hands with him and you have to keep your voice down, but say hello to André," Lily Cup said.

"How you are?" Peck asked.

"This is that boy, Lily Cup, the one you maybe told André about?"

"Yes."

"The tracker?"

"This is him, André. Ain't he a looker?"

André laughed, his head back. "I'll say. Cher, what you doing with someone so young and so handsome?"

"It's not like that, André. Peck here is engaged to a wonderful girl," Lily Cup said.

"Engaged? So when you getting married, young man? André wants to get you a wedding present. Any friend of Lily Cup here."

"They're waiting until they're out of school, André."

THE HOODOO OF PECK FINCH

"So why does André have this honor? What's on your mind?" André asked. "Something always on that pretty mind of yours."

"André, I'm really proud of you. You've been a good boy and they're cutting you loose in November. That's a whole year early."

"You're the best. I'll see you get paid proper."

"You've already paid me, André. Just promise me no more guns."

André held up his hand as a promise.

"So why you bring this boy all the way out here, Lily Cup—just to congratulate me?"

Lily Cup leaned in, motioned her head, asking Peck to lean in as well.

"It's time you know," Lily Cup whispered.

"Me, cher?" Peck asked.

"Keep your voice down, just listen, Peck."

"Time I know what, cher?"

"Last year I was telling André here about how a gator man had treated you when you were a helpless little kid. You don't mind I told him that, do you? André is my friend."

"Nah, nah, cher. Gator man was a bad man, dass for true."

"André, tell Peck what you 'heard' about that gator man—you know, the Christmas Story you told me."

André caught Lily Cup's wink. He looked at Peck, thought for a moment, as if he were reflecting a best approach.

"It was just something I heard about this rich man from England or France or somewhere—André doesn't remember. You know those rich men who travel all over trying to spend money? Well this one rich man, see, he hired a gator man to find him a big ole gator. He wanted a prize gator, maybe twenty feet, and story is I guess the rich man's money was good, so that gator man sure enough found him a twenty-foot alligator and, *oops*, wouldn't you know—the pirogue tipped and don't you know that gator man standing in that pirogue fell in that bayou and *chomp*, that was all it wrote for gator man?"

"Dey both fall in?" Peck asked.

"Oh, no—that's just it—you see that rich man, he was in his own, what you'd call a party boat. He was following behind gator man's pirogue and watching, like a tourist. Lucky for him too, my friend. Gator man's boat up and jerked and over the side he went and *chomp*. Yum yum, for that big ole gator, I'll say."

André stopped talking and looked Peck in the eye.

"Least that's what I heard," Andre said.

Millie watched Peck. Peck was in a blank stare.

"Are you okay, Peck?"

"Nah, nah, I'm good, cher," Peck said.

In the parking lot Peck pulled his door and sat holding the steering wheel, looking through the windshield in thought.

"You sure you're okay, Peck?" Lily Cup asked.

She waited a time for him to gather his thoughts.

"How'd they do it, cher?" Peck asked.

"Do what?"

"How'd they do it?"

"I don't know what you're talking about, Peck."

Peck turned his head and looked into Lily Cup's eyes and stared. It was just less than a full minute when Lily Cup broke the stare, reached in her bag and pulled the empty spool of 200-pound black test fishing line out and handed it to Peck.

"Is that mine?" Peck asked.

"No."

"I got one like that in Memphis and lost it, cher," Peck said. "Where'd you find this one?"

"This isn't the same one."

"Hanh?"

"This isn't your spool, Peck. I took your spool from your bag one night when you were cleaning our offices. I emptied it and showed it to André. I told him how gator man would tie gator's snouts with it. The guards wouldn't let me bring one in with fishing line on it. Your empty spool is back at my office in my drawer."

"Whose is this one—this spool, cher?"

"Andre wrapped this one with a bow on it and gave it to me as a present last Christmas."

"Last Christmas?"

"It was empty when he gave it to me. That's when he first told me the story he just told you."

Peck started the truck, backed around and pulled onto the highway. He drove without talking for twenty minutes. It was another twenty miles when he raised his fist slowly with a smile for an approving fist pump.

"You know somet'ing, cher?"

"What?"

"They ain't no such t'ing as a twenty-foot gator."

"And now there's no such thing as gator man," Lily Cup said.

Lily Cup obliged his fist pump with a smile of satisfaction, knowing this Angola visit wouldn't be spoken of again.

Peck's nightmares were over.

"Look at the morning moon, Peck. It's huge."

"Ah *oui* – it's a crepe, cher."

Peck had found his mamma.

Lest I forget...

Thank you, New Orleans.

Thanks to your Orleans Criminal District Court especially to Counselor Lindsay Jay Jeffrey for patience in putting order in my court.

A heartfelt thank you to the esteemed Leah Chase, matriarch of the historic Dooky Chase Restaurant and the iconic leading lady of New Orleans for the best part of a century. I'm humbled and flattered by the hours given myself and my researcher by Leah Chase. What you taught me about life, the hope you always saw for America, the roads you have traveled inspired my painting an accurate mural of my Acadian heritage and of New Orleans in my story.

Thanks Marty and Corneilius, my research assistants; Eddie (Ned) Reid for my Gabe—and the Big Easy and its legendary Pontchartrain Hotel and The Columns Hotel.

Special thanks to the one who made it possible - Judge Laurie A. White for encouraging members of the courts of New Orleans to help the arts, and this storyteller in attempting to present an accurate picture of events in the city of flavors she loves so much...and thank you Judge Laurie A. White for turning a blind eye on a bit of my 'misspelling' the letter of the law here and there for my spin of a tale.

...and thank you Pamela.

JMA